Atheist Tales

Edited by
David M. Fitzpatrick

Epic Saga Publishing
www.EpicSagaPub.com

ATHEIST TALES

Contents

Introduction

What is mythology? If you're a member of the target audience of this anthology, you might agree, at least in part, with this general sort of answer: "Mythology is the collection of stories of various cultures that are fantastically fun, wildly entertaining, impressively imaginative, and vital as representations of the cultural progression of human civilization over thousands of years."

If you're not one of the target audience of this anthology—that is, you believe in a Higher Power or Supreme Being or God or Devil or whatever—then you probably also agree, at least in part, with that statement as it applies to every single religion in the world... except for yours.

That's one of the many fun things disbelievers get to enjoy about religion. It doesn't matter how outlandish the stories from the mythology of a believer's religion are, because he knows for certain that it's the true word of his followed deity of choice. In the same breath where he laughs at the stories of Zeus throwing thunderbolts down from Olympus, he'll believe Jesus walked on water. While shaking his head in holier-than-thou fashion at the tales of Sigyn catching the snake's venom as it drips onto Loki's face, he'll believe he'll have seventy-two virgins waiting for him in paradise. Although scoffing at the idea that Ganesha had four arms, an elephant head, and rode around on a rat, he'll believe that Joseph Smith used seer stones to translate golden plates provided to him by Moroni. As he slaps his knee over the absurdity of the Aztec mother goddess Coatlicue, the serpent-skirted deity who gave birth to the moon, the stars, and the god of the sun and war, he'll not give a thought about Yahweh creating the heavens and the Earth in six days, just a mere six thousand years ago.

It would all be amusing if it weren't for the power these ardent believers have over global society and all our lives. Overzealous religious types seem to have two basic tenets: They don't want anything they've always known to change, and they want everyone to believe everything they do. And when things change, or when people tell them they don't want to believe, they don't seem to take it very well. Despite so easily identifying the silliness of other religions and being astounded that anyone could believe such silliness, they don't see such silliness in their own beliefs.

Those of us who embrace common sense, intellect, and reason are able to identify the silliness in all belief systems, and it's only logical that we don't have atheist mythology of our own. But there's no reason we can't have fiction! And fiction, after all, is what all that religious mythology is about. The difference is that we understand that stories are just stories; even if they have themes or morals or points to be made, the characters aren't real, the situations aren't real, and the events aren't real. We understand that.

That doesn't change the enjoyment of good stories, and this anthology offers several of them. Moreover, this anthology is about giving a forum to talented, imaginative writers who have something to say about the perils of religion, and within the framework of speculative fiction. Having been blacklisted by more than one offended editor for submitting irreligious tales, it was clear we needed a place to show off *our* mythology — clearly labeled as the fiction that it is.

I've worked to find a balance to the types of stories contained herein so that there's something to appeal to everyone. The only main requirement was that there was some sort of speculative element to the story that sets it apart from mainstream fiction. That means a story could be a near-future dystopia where religion has overrun society (even more than it actually has), or one set in a fantasy world with theocracy is the norm, or a tale simply imagining what might have happened — or what could happen.

We have a great mix here, and I think that there really is something for everyone. I hope there are a few somethings for everyone.

David M. Fitzpatrick
Brewer, Maine
January 2011

Dedication
Bill R. Moore and
Jade Woods Moore

"They locked up a man
Who wanted to rule the world
The fools
They locked up the wrong man."

That bit appeared on the back cover of Leonard Cohen's 1971 album *Songs of Love and Hate*. By all reports, Cohen, who spouted this and other thoughts during a live performance in 1970 at the Isle of Wight, was just messing with his audience by trying to sound deep and insightful. Whatever it meant to Cohen, and whatever it means to other people, it meant something to Bill Moore, a contributor to this anthology.

It never occurred to me to ask Bill just *what* it meant to him, which is odd since it was the tagline at the end of every email he sent me for nearly a year. I have no doubt it meant something deep indeed, because being deep was the essence of Bill Moore.

"I love the idea of your anthology," he told me. "It is indeed about time atheists got one. It is one of my main personal goals to spread atheism and agnosticism through literature, and I am glad to see a kindred spirit. There are far too few of us, as you are, of course, painfully aware."

Like me, Bill had had what he called "startlingly little success" getting his atheist-centric fiction and poetry published. His revelation was old hat to me; being sixteen years older than Bill, I'd had ample time to alienate myself from many religious editors who were offended that I had dared to send stories featuring themes about the drawbacks of religion.

Bill and I talked at length about the lack of markets for such fiction—and, especially, for such poetry. Poetry was a love of Bill's, and he submitted many poems to me for potential inclusion here. I'm not a poet, so I'm a hard sell there, and rejected them all. Now I wish I hadn't.

But Bill took it all in stride, and we discussed at length the lack of good markets for atheist-centric poetry and for speculative poetry in general. Before I knew it, we'd decided to co-edit a book of atheist poetry. We had found a great thread together; he was eager to work on any projects, and he appreciated an editor who truly cared and actually edited. He was never one to let his ego stand in the way, and approached constructive feedback in the spirit it was intended.

"I truly appreciate your comments and commend your efforts," he once said. "I hope we can find some common ground, publication-wise, because it certainly isn't every day that one comes across a kindred spirit in this arena … Thanks again for all you do—for me and the noble cause of atheism."

A lot was happening in Bill's life through 2010. Most notably, he was relocating from Oklahoma to New York state, as his wife, Jade, had received a scholarship to attend Cornell University for her graduate studies. Jade Woods Moore, named Susan at birth and changing her name at age 19, was from Colorado. Born premature and with a heart problem, she dropped out of high school in the ninth grade and schooled herself. She and Bill met online and visited back and forth for a while before she moved to Oklahoma, earned her GED, and started college with Bill. Both of them graduated summa cum laude from Southeastern Oklahoma State University, Jade with a degree in political science, and Bill with a degree in English.

Jade's dream was to go to law school, and eventually to be a lobbyist for the March of Dimes in Washington. Her goal was to help disadvantaged people, and going to Cornell had been her dream. The scholarship was for the Cornell Institute of Public Affairs, a two-year program through which Jade would earn a Master of Public Affairs.

"At CIPA, Jade was concentrating her studies in public and nonprofit management," said a write-up on the CIPA site. "She felt that her experiences in life had allowed her to see firsthand the importance of equality in education, housing, and health care, and her goal was to pursue a career in public policy that would engender social change."

Jade was excited about Bill's writing. She was interested in whether I had landed any female contributors to the anthology; she was concerned about the apparent dearth of non-religious women in any arena, but particularly as writers. I referred her to a few titles, such as *Women Without Superstition,* a collection of women's writings edited by Anne Nicol Gaylor.

Having run into many brick walls trying to publish his atheist-centric work, Bill was extremely avid about *Atheist Tales.* "We are such a minority, after all, though the speculative genre is certainly less religious than most," he once said. "I've often suspected that I've been rejected out of hand for being anti-religious. That's why I was so excited when I saw *Atheist Tales;* it seemed a gold mine!"

When I ran into trouble getting enough quality submissions, he eagerly offered to write another story. "I wish I could send you something else for it," he said. "I've been trying to think of something but haven't done so yet. Hopefully I still will, at least in time for the second installment, which I hope comes out."

He enjoyed the amusing antics religious people often displayed, like when he'd get immediately booted out of Christian chat rooms because of his nickname, VoodooLord7, which he'd used since the eighth grade. He prided himself on being more knowledgeable about the Bible than most of the Christians who opposed him—like one time in high school, when he was reading *And the Ass Saw the Angel* by Nick Cave. A Christian student began lambasting him for reading something with such a vulgar, immoral title, only to be become utterly perplexed when Bill pointed out that it was a verbatim Bible quote (Numbers 22:23, for those of you keeping score).

In a college creative-writing class, students were to rewrite an original English poem, and a classmate chose the Song of Solomon (despite the fact that that wasn't originally in English, which Bill pointed out to no avail). During discussion, Bill noted that his favorite part was when the narrator talks about bowels moving. This led to a frantic debate about what that actually meant, and Bill just sat back and enjoyed everyone panicking over whether Biblical characters ever defecated.

The last time I traded emails with Bill was in June 2010, when he and Jade were preparing for the big move to New York. "It'll be nice to leave the Bible Belt!" he said—exclamation point included, for he was very excited.

We didn't talk for the next three months. On October 16, I finally finished editing all the *Atheist Tales* manuscripts that I had accepted and sent them out to their respective authors for approval. I didn't hear from Bill right away, which should have seemed odd, because he was usually very quick to respond. I didn't think much of it, but I had no way of knowing what had happened just eleven days before.

On Tuesday, October 5, 2010, at about 3:15 p.m., Bill and Jade were traveling along Mineah Road, Route 13, in Dryden, New York. Jade was driving their 2005 Honda, and there was a terrible accident at an intersection. A tractor trailer smashed into the driver's side of the car. Both vehicles ended up in the ditch. Jade was pronounced dead at Cayuga Medical Center a short time later. Bill suffered massive head trauma; he was transported to Robert Packer Medical Center in Sayre, Pennsylvania, where he died the next day. She was 24; he was 25.

I only knew because Bill's mother had gotten his computer and was going through the difficult task of cleaning up all the loose ends of her son's life. His contribution to *Atheist Tales* was one of those loose ends, and she really wanted to make sure his story could still get published.

Bill said he grew up in "the buckle of the Bible Belt." The irony of him leaving that buckle and quickly losing his life is not lost on me. I can already hear the cries of some heartless and insensitive types as they claim it was God's retribution for Bill's atheism. But of course it wasn't anything related to mythology; it was just something that happened, one of those terrible things that is, unfortunately, the stuff of life. No gods. No meaning to their deaths. No reason for it all. Just an absolutely horrible thing that happened, out of anyone's control.

I'm honoring the memory of Bill R. Moore and Jade Woods Moore by dedicating this anthology *to* them, but it isn't *for* them, because they're gone forever. This dedication is for you. It won't bring either of them back, and I know Bill won't be smiling at us from some far-beyond afterlife. But he would be if it were possible. Even for atheists, it can feel better if we imagine, for a moment, that there is something after, and that our lives aren't just blinks of eternity's eye.

But that's what they are. Bill Moore made the most of his life, however brief it was. He knew what mattered to him. He wrote about those things. He spoke of atheism as a noble cause, and he was right. He knew that life was fleeting, and that only what we do with our time here matters. It's the worst tragedy that he didn't live a lot longer than he did. If there were any better example of making the most of the time we have, I can't imagine it.

*I*n this brief science-fiction tale, Bill Moore postulates what might have happened if an advanced race of beings, perhaps of pure thought or energy – dare we say "souls"? – arrived on Earth and implanted their consciousnesses into lower life forms. What if such a race could exist for eons like this, always conscious, constantly directing their evolution, little by little? With Bill's untimely passing in October 2010, perhaps this imaginative story might make us hope that, somehow, our consciousnesses will last for eternity – or at least wish that they could.

A New Beginning

Bill R. Moore

They had traveled throughout many universes and seen many suns on Their search to find the race that met Their singular needs. They had seen many possible subjects and passed on them as if they were nothing. Occasionally, They even tried them but always without success.

And then They found Earth.

The moment They saw the planet, They knew it was perfect, for it was a planet with the ideal atmosphere, climate, and water content to supply Them with the very thing They needed: intelligent life. And on it were any number of species on which They could experiment. But not just any race would do. No, He was very selective in choosing a species He and His kind were to overtake.

After endless tests, speculation, and arguing amongst themselves, They found a sufficient life form to meet their needs. After exhausting the land, They settled, inevitably, on the creatures of the sea. Then, slowly at first, but at increasingly faster intervals, They began to overtake these creatures.

They were not parasites; They had reason enough to do what They were doing. In Their own universe, Their sun was going nova, and They had to exile and regroup. But, since Their peculiar bodily apparatus let Them function comfortably only on Their own planet (and, for a limited time, in Their spaceships), They had no choice but to insert Their consciousnesses into the bodies of another species. They had searched many centuries for a suitable race and planet—but now, at long last, the wait was over.

Many years hence, Their consciousnesses had been transposed. Now they had to begin the far more difficult task of making the beings civilized. Earth was an extremely primitive planet compared to Theirs. Indeed, its inhabitants may not have even been seen as intelligent, were They not in such a dire situation. But the inhabitants were by far the best example that had been found to fit Their needs and would have to do.

It would take time, and most importantly, patience—but it could be done in the end. They would have to take these beings, newly equipped with Their own consciousnesses, of course, and make them civilized. Soon they would become sentient, and, in time, intelligent. They set to work on this particularly difficult job, one that would give Them job security for a long time to come.

As centuries turned into millennia, and millennia into eons, Their job was at last done. The creatures whose bodies They inhabited were newly sentient. They could hunt and survive, and were, to a limited extent, capable of intelligent thought. Not only did Their mind evolve, but Their outward appearance changed also. The creatures had grown hair, orifices, and sense organs. He rejoiced. But for all Their success, there was a problem.

They had always intended, of course, to extract themselves from these beings if the need arose. It was possible, They knew from past experiences, however unlikely, for Them to fail. They did not believe it likely, but it could happen again. And, though They did not know it, it had. For, though They did not consider themselves parasites, in essence, they were. Not only that, but They had reached the final stage of parasitism; They could no longer survive without Their hosts. They had not realized it, but as Their eons-long stay in the creatures wore on, They evolved. Not only did They evolve, They evolved to an extent where They depended on Their hosts for survival. After all, it was "survival of the fittest," and They had never before experienced an ocean world first-hand. It was only natural that They would evolve to fit it and to depend on the creatures whose bodies They now inhabited, the ones that were there in the first place. And so, ironically, They were trapped in the bodies of the very beings that They had hoped to enslave.

They knew, of course, that They must face reality and accept the situation. Make the best of it that They could. If They were to forever live in these bodies (after all, they *were* immortal), then They would do so. Indeed, They had no choice. And it was in this fashion that decades, and eventually, centuries passed.

Given time, even the most extraordinary surroundings can be made to seem commonplace. Such was their situation. Year after year, They had swum Earth's oceans, surviving and evolving. They had defeated all challengers, a surprisingly unexciting accomplishment for immortals, and were now kings of the sea. He decided, and the Council unanimously agreed, that the next generation would no longer reside in the sea. They could now afford such luxuries of thought since They had taught the creatures to reproduce.

It was in this way that They spent their last days in Earth's oceans. The time had come for Them to set foot on land. All inhabitants They passed over in the early days of contact were long since extinct. With no intelligent race to guide other species along, they perished away into nothingness as they were bound to do. They, of course, were a different story, and it was inevitable that an intelligent race bound to the sea would one day dream of sitting foot on land.

The day came, just a few short centuries down the road, a mere nothing in the eyes of a race that had already lived for eons upon eons. He experienced a feeling of deep, driving emotion when he witnessed His young century-old son crawl out of the water and become the first to reach land. He even did the thing that so many of their fellow races frowned on — shed a tear. A new chapter was written in Their evolution; They had conquered the sea and now were set to conquer the land. One by one, They followed His son. It was a new beginning, a new time, the beginning of a new era in the history of the universes.

And He, watching peacefully as the last set foot on the ground, got a strange feeling. He felt something different when he looked on His people, something new and dignified — something not there before. Despite the incredulity of the thought, He felt almost as if He were viewing another race. But He swept the thought aside and began on the task of conquering the land, as He and His kind had conquered the sea.

This was the first step in a long, long process, each lasting again as long as this had. In course of time, They changed more from this point even than they had before. Thus, though each step was nearly imperceptible in itself to Them, an outsider would hardly have recognized one stage from the next, much less first from last. And so They continued to grow...

And, thus, Man was born.

*W*hat if atheists are wrong? What if there really is an after-life — or afterlives? With all those competing religions, maybe we have to wonder. And if there is something that comes later, who's to say which of the world's many religions has it right? Jane Gallagher offers a story that begins as a near-future social-SF tale set in a theocratic Hell on Earth, but segues into a mythic fantasy that just might give us something to think about. But no matter how outlandish his religious beliefs are, a believer won't likely see any potential for Jane's absurd fantasy. After all, only his particular mythology is correct. Right?

It's All About Soul

Jane Gallagher

The fact that the United Earth Convention of 2244 had declared human cloning illegal didn't sway John Benning's decision in the least. He wasn't even concerned about the scores of undercover Acolytic Police he knew were out there, dispatched by the Church and constantly hunting for those breaking the morals. Anyone off the street stopping by Benning's genetics shop in search of something as mundane as a new pair of eyes, even though appearing as an average Congregationalist, could easily be an officer of the Church. Breaking any number of morals could cause a business to be shut down, or worse.

For genetic alterations outside moral allowance—a very rigid set of rules outlined by the Church—the punishment depended on which moral was broken. Extreme tithing, public ridicule in the stocks, or Net-broadcast whippings were not uncommon for small violations. Deviances of greater extreme commanded more serious judgments, and cloning a human was, by far, the worst. Certainly, only violations of the Ten Commandments and a few other select Words of God were grounds for death by crucifixion, but cloning could command amputation and organ removal.

In all other respects, Benning was a completely moral Congregationalist in society. At his genetics shop, he sold completely moral things such as age-reduction procedures, genetic repairs, stimulated regrowth of limbs and organs removed by the Church as punishment (provided the ordered suffering period was over), and certain vanity replacements approved by the Church. But Benning knew he could do it and could hardly resist himself.

He had several factors in his favor. First, he was a geneticist by vocation and an extremely good one, and had a lot of morally allowed equipment used in animal cloning. Second, he was respected by local Church authorities and was friends with several street-police Acolytes who trusted him. Third, he had a sub-basement hidden beneath his shop in which to perform the lengthy cloning process, a suitable hideaway that was impervious even to the periodic full-premises search-and-seizures that the Acolytic Police routinely conducted.

But the most important factor of all was that John Benning had once had a twin brother. Jacob had died three days after birth and John's mother hadn't reported it to the Holy Authority. His birth, however, had been reported, so as far as the Church was concerned, there were two humans with the same DNA walking around on the Earth. A clone could easily be explained as a long-lost brother come back to his sibling.

So, in the secrecy of his shielded sub-basement, John Benning used his years of experience and chemical concoctions not legally available since before the Great Crusade a hundred years before to clone himself. Intensive, controlled accelerants and constant nutrient baths brought quickly to life a full-size genetic duplicate of him in under a month's time. There were a few things to take care of; even identical twins had different fingerprints and retinal patterns, for example, but it was a mere hour's work in his upstairs lab to work up a new set of eyes for the clone. Reworking the DNA was a minor task early on in the procedure; while twins' DNA was identical to most tests, a good geneticist with the right equipment could determine if it were a perfect duplicate—and that wouldn't do. Even with identical twins, there were minor micromutations that began as soon as the fertilized egg started dividing; so Benning had to artificially introduce such anomalies.

The final step was to imprint the clone's brain. If he activated the clone's bioelectrical impulses now, it would be little more than a newborn baby in adult form. In preparation for this event, John had downloaded his own brain about a year before, so the clone would not be an up-to-the-minute copy of himself.

Thus Jacob was brought to consciousness, and it didn't take long for him to understand the situation. Having all of John's skills and capabilities, they went into business together as the Benning Brothers. The Church investigated them top to bottom, of course, suspicions of cloning in their minds, but in the end there was no way they could determine Jacob was a clone instead of the twin brother both claimed he was. There were questions about Jacob's whereabouts the past forty years, but that story was easy enough. He had been stolen at birth by Atheists, taken far north to the frozen Unholy Lands, raised in the shocking denouncement of God. Jacob had always known there was a God, however, and eventually escaped the terrible tyranny of the Unbelievers. He finally arrived in the Free World of the Christian States of Americanada and had sought out his brother. This was enough for the Church to end their examination, since there was no way they could investigate the savages to the north. Jacob was made a member of the Church, given absolution for his sins, and finally allowed to live among them, free at last from the atrocities of the Atheists.

The only person who could possibly have been up for moral punishment would have been John's mother for not reporting her baby's kidnapping in the first place, but she had gone to God six years before. His father had been gone twenty, killed in an anti-Atheist rally where he was accidentally trampled by overzealous fellow activists supporting the Church. That left John and Jacob free and clear to live as brothers without fear of further scrutiny by the Church.

Business prospered for the Benning Brothers as they worked side by side for twelve years. As time went on, Jacob and John found their minds growing different ways; Jacob ceased to be a carbon copy of John and became his own person. John had been divorced ten years before the cloning and had no interest in women, but Jacob, logicking that what had happened to John had not really happened to him, took an interest in the opposite sex and began dating. All the while, they were a prize genetics team and they made more than enough money to support themselves, pay heavy tithes to the Church, and live comfortably.

They worshiped, as was their moral obligation, but in the privacy of their home they would muse on the nature of God and the afterlife. Jacob would wonder whether a clone had a soul; John would reassure him that anything alive and aware of its existence indeed had an everlasting soul, so long as proper worship of God was observed. Their separate personalities allowed for different perspectives on what began as the same insights and perceptions. It allowed for intriguing conversations and explorations into the realm of religion.

Their bodies were like their minds: vastly different despite their innate similarities. While Jacob was a genetic duplicate of John, his body was a fresh, new version of the old, untroubled by the years of physical maladies John had endured. It didn't suffer the ravages of time John's body had — the broken pelvis from falling during choir practice when he was nine, the mandatory brain surgery he'd undergone to enhance his moral values when he'd been caught masturbating at age fourteen, the ulcerative colitis that had left him with a stapled stomach and missing parts of his small intestine at age twenty-six. The most important factor, though, had been the years of eating foods that had built up cholesterol in John's bloodstream. Like a plumber who always had a leaky sink, John was a geneticist who worried about his own body last.

So one day while Jacob was downtown picking up their weekly required Volunteer Assignments at the Sanctuary, John suffered a monstrous heart attack. The medics said the wall of his left ventricle had been so weakened over years of unnoticed need of genetic repair that it had finally given out. It burst, they said, like an overinflated balloon. The resulting trauma killed him where he stood. John had gone to God literally before his face had slapped against the cold, hard floor.

Jacob had been terribly upset for a month following. Everyone perceived the grief of a brother who spent forty years trying to escape the Atheists and finally found his only surviving family member only to lose him; but Jacob had a bond beyond brotherhood with John. It was something like a father-son relationship, in a way, as well as that of best friends. There were never any secrets to keep, since all those for the first forty years they shared anyway. Now, Jacob was without the closest friend he had in the world—the only family member, the only *anyone*, he knew. Eventually, he went on with his life despite the great void. One day, he knew, he would be reunited with his brother in Heaven.

John had died at 52, and while Jacob's actual age was only 12, he appeared to be 52 as well. He ran the genetics shop for thirty-three more years until, one day, the new church that had been built in his neighborhood collapsed. Poor architecture and even worse engineering, one investigator had said, was why twenty-seven people had lost their lives, and it seemed to have had nothing at all to do with God's will. The investigator, a suspected opponent of the Church, had gone so far as to say that uncaring oversights by the Church were why those people were dead. He had been crucified as a result of his public lies, although he argued until he died there on his cross that they were not *lies*, they were *opinions* and, more importantly, *truths.*

Jacob Benning had been in that church helping set up the new Net camera system. Only those in the direst straits were excused from services, of course, and those excused were required to cyber-attend as long as they were at least conscious. He was standing on a ladder, a workerbot floating next to him helping with bolting a camera to an upper beam, when he heard the ominous splitting sound — the sound of a synthetic support beam, improperly jointed, letting go at its master coupling at the zenith of the massive hall. It was the main support on the left side of the church, and when it went, they all followed suit like dominoes. Jacob fell from his ladder, chased to the floor below by countless tons of synthetic stone. He lived a few minutes deep beneath the rubble, gasping for air, the debris above settling, crushing the life out of him, and his last living thought was, *Well, managed to fool them for forty-five years...*

Jacob wasn't terribly surprised when he found himself at some pretty elaborate gates. They seemed to stand fifty stories high, wrought in silver and gilded with gold, bejeweled with a rainbow of gemstones. A choir of angelic voices emanated from all around. Cherubim and seraphim frolicked about the puffy clouds overhead. It was just what he'd always thought Heaven was supposed to be like. It was certainly better than suffering beneath the rubble where he'd been only moments before.

There was a man at an elegant, massive podium. He wore white robes, and a shimmering circlet of light glowed over his head. He was hunched over and appeared to be energetically writing, with an enormous feathered pen, in an immense book. The plume of feathers on the pen flourished two feet up and over and were of a dozen vibrant colors. He appeared oblivious to Jacob's presence.

Jacob figured he knew what came next: go to the man, identify himself, and be judged. He either got in or was kept out. He took a deep breath and approached the towering podium.

The angelic man looked down at him from his book. "Yes?"

"Ummm..." Jacob began, and didn't know what else to say. He figured the man would have known him.

"I do not have all day, you," the man said, clearly perturbed. "What are you and what do you want here?"

"Ummm..." Jacob tried again. "Isn't this... Heaven?"

"Well, of course it is," the man said haughtily. "But you, I can see, have no soul. So you have no business being here."

"No... soul?" Jacob staggered back. "How can that be?"

"Let me see..." The man flipped through hundreds of pages in his book, periodically looking up at Jacob. "Well, although you bear a spiritual resemblance to a John Benning, you are not him. John Benning died some time ago and his soul was allowed entry into Heaven." The man looked at him quizzically. "Are you another one of those androids?"

"No," Jacob said, wishing for a place to sit down but knowing there was nothing but happy clouds. "I'm John's clone. He cloned me."

"Aha!" the man said triumphantly. "That's it! Well, personally, I don't think they should have let John Benning in here in the first place, seeing as how he cloned himself, but I don't make those decisions. Cloning is playing with God's work, you know."

"How is it that I'm here when my body is dead on Earth, if I have no soul?" Jacob asked.

"Don't confuse 'soul' with 'spirit,'" the man chastised him with a waving, pointed feather pen. "Anything with life force, you see, has a spirit, an essence that survives after death. But God hands out the souls. You didn't get one. You lose."

"But I worshiped God," Jacob argued. "I went to church and dedicated my life to him and—"

"—and if you had died first, that soul you shared with

your human creator would probably have been yours," the man finished. "Then he would be having this conversation with me when *he* died."

"But... I thought... God would let all who believed in his son and worshiped him... into Heaven."

"You thought wrong," the man said bluntly and with what Jacob thought was a contemptuous sneer. "You humans — and their clones — have a bizarre interpretation of how we work, but this is the basic idea: this is a private club. Only those of you with invitations get in. Your soul is your invitation. You don't have one. You don't get in."

"An... an invitation?" Jacob said incredulously.

"That's right. Come on, now, you don't think we let just *anybody* in here, do you? You won't find Muslims here, or Jews, or Hindus... this is a *Christian* Heaven, Mr. Clone, and of a few specific denominations at that. And you won't find dogs and cats and other animals here either; there are afterlives for them, but this isn't it."

"But... what do I do now?" Jacob's mind was reeling. This couldn't be. It just *couldn't*.

"Not my problem," the man said. "And for the record, I'm not aware of any clone-specific afterlives. You're what we call a detached spirit, Mr. Clone; nobody ever had dibs on your spirit, so you don't have an afterlife to go to. Before there were afterlives, that's how everybody did it — if you can imagine!"

"Isn't there... anywhere I can go?"

The glowing man sighed. "It's not my job to ship you else-where, but there are a few non-specific afterlives you might check out. I'll send you on to the nearest one we normally dis-patch our rejects to. Have a good death."

The feather pen whirled and the happy clouds swirled around Jacob. When they cleared, he was standing in an alien forest, trees of strange shapes and colors sprouting every-where. He was in a clearing of sorts, and sitting on and by a fallen tree was a curious arrangement of individuals. There was a human-like being who appeared to be made entirely of metal, sitting closest to Jacob on the log, metal elbows on gleaming knees, metal head in shiny hands, looking almost distressed. Sitting next to him were what appeared to be two normal human beings: a man drawing designs in the dirt with a stick and a woman biting a fingernail. Next to her, off the log, sat a German shepherd.

The metal being took note of Jacob's magical arrival and sat up. "Welcome, human. Another detached spirit, I see."

"Evidently so," Jacob said.

"What is your story, human?" the metal man said. "Have you just come from the gates of Heaven, the pits of Hell, or the side entrance to Purgatory?"

"Heaven," Jacob said. "I'm a clone... a genetic duplicate created from another human. He died many years ago, rest his soul... and it appears that soul was his and his alone. I don't have one. I shared it with him and he died first. Heaven told me there are other afterlives and this was one of them. I don't know where to begin."

"Welcome to the club," the nail-biting woman said.

"Who are you all," Jacob said, "and what are your stories?"

"I am RCV-9801," the metal man said with a metallic timbre to his voice. "I was constructed by a scientist against the morals of the Church. He brought life to me. I think, therefore I am, yet once I was damaged and ceased to function, I ended up at the gates of Hell. Heaven didn't even wish to consider me, and Hell simply laughed. So here I am, with no afterlife to go to, and no synthetic skin to hide my metal form."

"My name is George," said the man drawing in the dirt with the stick. "I'm an atheist. Apparently, I was born with a soul, according to the man at the gates to Heaven, but my decision to not worship God disallows me entrance. Hell won't have me since I didn't believe in them, either."

"And I am just a sinner," the woman said. "I'm Janice. I

believed and I worshiped, but I questioned God in many ways. Heaven sent me to Purgatory where I had to change my ways of thinking. I couldn't, because I still couldn't understand why things are the way they are, why God is so selective. I was also deemed unworthy of any Godly afterlife, good or bad. So here I am."

"All three of you were turned away as I was," Jacob said.

"How about all four of us?" said the dog, and Jacob gave a start. The dog smiled, lolling its tongue the way dogs do. "Yep, that's right, buddy, I'm a talking dog. Bowser's my name. My master did a little upgrading to my brain and gave me human-level intelligence. As such, none of the dog afterlives are interested in having me, and none of the human versions, either. So I'm stuck here in this nowhere afterlife with the rest of you."

"But… what are we all to do?" Jacob said. "I've lived with the idea that there is an afterlife and I'd be able to go there."

"I've lived with the thought that I would die and that would be it," George said, "so I'm just as perplexed as you are."

"It isn't right!" Jacob exclaimed. "I did all that was asked in the Bible. I honored God and followed the Church. Why am I being treated this way?"

"Get used to it," Janice said with a sweet smile. "We don't have a choice. That afterlife is invitation only, like the man told me. And mine was revoked."

"I was sharing mine," Jacob said.

"I never had one," the android said.

"Me either," said Bowser.

"Mine was revoked, too," George said matter-of-factly. "But I say enough of sitting here feeling sorry for ourselves. We obviously don't need God for everlasting life. Clearly, he was just one of many 'supreme beings' playing with us for his own personal amusement. Screw him."

"But what is this place?" Jacob said, looking around.

"The Afterlife of Alien Trees," Bowser proclaimed wryly,

and the others tittered in laughter. Even Jacob smiled. "Hey, I'm kinda tired of sitting around here trying to decide what to do," Bowser continued. "There're five of us. That's a party. I say we explore this afterlife, and if we don't like it… well, we'll find another."

Everyone was in agreement. Together, they headed off through the alien trees, looking for their own truths.

*I*n John Lance's entertaining and intriguing tale of the beginning of the end of the world, what starts out as Ragnarok becomes a religious free-for-all. Earthlings are faced with the coming apoca-lypse — at the hands of whatever faith ends up dominant — wondering whether they'd backed the wrong theological horses. But there are other players involved, using the religions of the world to their own ends. It's a game with the strategy of chess, the bluffing of poker, and a bit of the silliness of Twister. Such is the nature of "true believers."

All Hail Splork

John Lance

"So, this is awkward," said the President of the United States as he adjusted his red-and-blue striped tie.

"What do you mean, mortal?" asked the giant Viking sitting astride an eight-legged horse on the White House lawn. The Viking wore an eye patch over his left eye and glowered at the President with his right. Several ravens were perched on the Viking's shoulders and helmet, and they watched the President with the same unblinking stare as their master. The President decided not to mention the bird poop.

"Well, you see, no one really believes..." the President's voice cracked. Taking a moment to compose himself, he tried a second explanation, using his best 'I-need-to-raise-taxes-please -don't-vote-me-out-of-office' voice. "You see, times have been hard. Very hard, since last you were, ummm, here. And I'm afraid that the situation is not what it once was."

The Viking's eye narrowed. The President tried not to notice. He hated giving speeches in person. It was so much easier to lie directly to a camera. The President also had the nagging suspicion that he had met the Viking previously, but couldn't remember where or when, which always annoyed him since he was usually excellent with names and faces.

The President continued. "In the last couple thousand years, humanity has grown fond of a few other folks. Personally, I'm a fan of Jesus, but plenty of other people follow Mohammad or Yahweh or Buddha, or—" Suddenly the President knew why the Viking looked so familiar. "I just need to pause here and ask: By any chance are you aware of how closely you resemble the mascot for the Minnesota Vikings? It's really remarkable."

The one-eyed giant adjusted his horned helmet but did not reply.

"No, you're probably not. I shouldn't have even mentioned it. Anyway, what I'm trying to get at here, Odie..."

"Odin," said the giant.

"Right, Odin, sorry, Odie is the dog from the comic strip. What I'm trying to say is that, well, we were expecting someone different for the whole 'end of the world' thing. What did you call it again?"

"Ragnarok, the twilight of the gods," replied the giant.

"Right, that. Anyway, we all thought there'd be four horsemen who ride on horses that have, you know, four legs, and an angel that was going to blow a trumpet and, well, the truth is, and I'm being honest with you here, Odie, this is going to be a very hard sell to the American people."

"Speak clearly, knave."

The President sighed. He hated speaking clearly. Unfortunately, there were times when it had to be done. "The truth is we just don't believe in you anymore."

"You don't believe in the gods? You are atheists?"

"No, no, we believe in *a* god—just not you."

"You are pagans?"

The President hesitated. "Are you sure there isn't someone else I could speak to, Hera or Hercules perhaps?"

*   *   *

The grim anchorman on the television announced, "We are now getting confirmation that Norse gods have appeared throughout the world, declaring the end of days." Then, brightening slightly, he added, "We'll have more on this story after the break." The announcer was replaced by a commercial extolling the virtues of a new cell phone that was guaranteed to improve the life of its owner.

"Well, isn't this a fine pickle," Sally said to her husband, Herb, who was sitting next to her.

"Uh huh," said Herb.

"Forty-six years of Sundays wasted. I suppose we should get rid of this before some Viking god spots it." Sally plucked the cross off the wall over the TV and quickly tossed it into the trash bin. After a moment's consideration she moved the trash bin so that it was behind the curtains.

Unfortunately, the blank spot on the wall now made the room feel tight and unbalanced. Sally regarded it for a moment. "I wonder what we should hang in its place. Maybe a picture of one of them crows the big gentleman had on his shoulder?"

"Uh huh," said Herb.

Sally pursed her lips, annoyed at her husband's autopilot tone. "Are you even listening to me?"

Before Herb could reply the television image jumped, cut in and out, and then devolved into snow.

Sally frowned. "Now what's wrong with this thing?" she asked, slapping the side of the box. "I told you we needed a new television, and not one of those cheap ones either. We need one of the expensive ones that hang on the wall."

Herb continued staring out the window at the blond women in iron brassieres riding flying horses. To his wife, he said, "Uh huh."

In the mountains of Tibet, a young acolyte ran through the

halls of a temple shouting, "Master, master!"

The master was in the lotus position surrounded by candles in the middle of the temple floor. Though meditating deeply, he could not block out the youth's nasal voice. He frowned but did not open his eyes.

"Master, you must come! Strange beings have descended upon the Earth. Some say they are gods!"

The master slowly opened one eye. It was the new boy. The monk sighed deeply. It was his own fault, he supposed. The boy's father had made it clear that he felt the boy to be a bit "slow" which, given the father's intellectual prowess, was saying something.

Still, the master had thought that the boy could be trained to be quiet and deferential. Unfortunately, even that was proving to be a challenge, and was only further highlighted by the annoying manner in which the novice was currently tugging on the master's sleeve. The master would have liked to sternly rebuke the acolyte, but he was in the fourth year of a decade-long self-imposed silence, and really didn't feel like starting over.

With a profound sense of regret for his lost meditation, the master rose and followed the boy outside.

On the next mountaintop over stood a huge, red-bearded man armed with a war hammer. The giant whirled the hammer over his head and sent lightning bolts flashing across the sky.

Suddenly a great fire-breathing serpent rose up out of the snow. Bellowing a challenge, the giant leapt at the beast. They clashed in midair and tumbled down the mountainside, punching and biting and kicking the entire way.

The master was knowledgeable in the ways of the world and familiar with other religions and myths. He recognized Thor and the Midgard serpent when he saw them.

Turning to the acolyte, the master said, "Well, this sucks."

* * *

Nasir and Jamal sat in the back of a van. Jamal was tightening the straps of the vest Nasir was wearing. He was careful not to jar the explosives.

"I so admire you, Nasir," Jamal said. "You are soon to be a martyr and enter the kingdom of heaven to receive your just reward. You are so fortunate to be chosen." The van's CD player was playing a recording of one of Jamal's favorite sermons.

"Thank you Jamal, but I wonder if all those funny-looking men and women who have recently appeared do not mean we should rethink our plan," said Nasir as he wiped a bead of sweat from his brow. For some reason he did not feel half as lucky as he thought he should.

"Those are lies and propaganda to shake the faith of the weak. Now remember, my brother, try to get as close to the playground as possible before you achieve salvation."

"Still, I think we should consider postponing, if only for a little while. There will be plenty of children on the playground tomorrow."

"You cannot postpone destiny. When God calls, you must answer the summons."

"I understand and I know you have helped Akmed and Yusef and Amal and Fadi achieve martyrdom. Yet I wonder if this time God is calling you instead?" Nasir asked as he tried to loosen the harness so it didn't cut into his shoulders quite so much.

Jamal tightened the harness further. "Sadly, God has not yet summoned me to his embrace. I am to remain a humble servant whose role is to assist those that have been chosen. It is my greatest desire to achieve martyrdom but that honor lies with you, my brother."

"But how can you be so sure?" wondered Nasir.

Jamal's reply was interrupted by a burst of static from the CD player. Jamal growled, "Now what is wrong? I've had trouble with the radio in this van since I bought it. If I ever see that pig of a car dealer again — "

Jamal was interrupted by a soft 'beep' from the control box strapped to Nasir's chest. Before Jamal could mention that the suspect car dealer had also supplied him with the detonator, Jamal's greatest desire was granted and he received his just rewards.

High in the Earth's upper atmosphere, a spherical ship spun on its axis. Cubes of gelatin manned the ship's command bridge.

Through a complex series of quivers, quakes, and shifting color patterns, a green cube communicated, "Captain, the projecto-matic is malfunctioning. It is interfering with radio waves and other communication channels the humans commonly use."

"Is it serious?" asked the purple cube resting in the middle of the bridge. "We do not want to alert the humans to our presence."

"There should be no risk of that, captain. We will have it repaired momentarily."

The captain calmed. The first officer was quite capable and could be trusted to perform to the highest standards. "Excellent. Move to phase two when the projecto-matic is fixed."

"Yes, captain." The green cube oozed back to its station.

The captain quivered as a warm wave of satisfaction flowed through it. The operation was going quite smoothly. The emperor would be pleased.

There was a knock on the Oval Office door. An aide popped his head in without waiting for a reply.

"Mr. President, there's someone to — um, sir, why are you wearing that helmet?"

"What? Oh, this? I always wear this on, errr, religious holidays. I'm one-sixteenth Norse on my mother's side, you know."

"I did not know that, sir," the aide replied in a neutral tone.

"I always honor the old country and its traditions. Say, Bob, I've been trying to get onto that Web site, wikitedious, wikimedia, wiki-something or other just to be sure I, umm, remembered everything there was to know about, you know, being Norse. But I keep getting an error."

"I'm afraid the site crashed, sir. Everyone is doing exactly the same thing."

"Hmm, can't we just boot them off?"

"Boot them off what, sir?"

"The Internet. I am the President after all."

"I'm not sure it works like that, sir." Before the President could reply, the aide hurried on. "Sir, about this visitor. He says his name is Jesus and he's here to see you."

"Hey-zeus."

"Sir?"

"It's pronounced hey-zeus. He's from the Pentagon."

"No sir, this is a different Jesus." The door opened wider. A man who was the spitting image of the picture on the President's bedroom wall strolled in.

"Jesus Christ," whispered the President.

"Exactly," said Jesus. Then, after a moment, he asked, "Why are you wearing that hat?"

"Where the hell is the cross, Herb?!" yelled Sally as she shook the empty trash bin at her husband. "After twenty-four years of my having to nag you to take out the garbage, now is the one time you get off your ass and do it on your own? If I'm going to Hell because that cross got thrown out, you can be damn sure I'm not going alone!"

Sally charged out the house and ran to the shed where the trash barrels were kept. From the window, Herb watched as Sally scattered the contents of the barrels across the front lawn and began tossing great fistfuls of trash in the air as she conducted a frantic search.

Herb wondered whether Sally would remember that she had thrown the cross in the other trashcan before or after she noticed the three bat-winged Furies fluttering around her head.

Grabbing a beer from the fridge, he pulled a chair up to the window and decided to see.

Usually the President enjoyed press conferences. They were like little games of peek-a-boo and the journalists, like his six-month-old granddaughter, never got tired of them.

But today the President felt uncomfortable and off-balance as he stood in the Rose Garden surrounded by deities, some of whom he recognized and some that were completely new to him. Obviously he recognized Odin and Jesus, and he was pretty sure the naked chick was Aphrodite (he wasn't even going to try to imagine the conniption the FCC chair was throwing right now). But there were others whose identities he couldn't even guess at, like the cat-headed woman and the feather-covered snake that kept hissing in his ear.

The President stepped up to the microphone. There was some jostling behind him as the each deity tried to get a premier spot in front of the cameras.

The President resisted the urge to mop his sweaty brow with a handkerchief. He just hoped that the glare didn't show on camera. "Good afternoon. I would like to begin with a plea for calm. The sudden appearance of every deity that has been worshipped by humanity throughout the ages will undoubtedly cause friction. However, we should view this as an opportunity to, um—"

The President was interrupted by some shoving and shouting behind him. One of the toga-clad Greek gods pushed a multi-armed Hindu deity. The Hindu deity stumbled back and bumped Odin's arm, causing him to spill his mead on

Mars. There was the flash of a sword.

The Secret Service grabbed the President and dragged him away as a full-scale celestial rumble broke out behind them.

In a military bunker buried deep under the Nevada desert, two men in white lab coats stared at a floating blue speck. The speck was kept suspended in mid-air by a complicated arrangement of electromagnets set in a ring around it.

"I can't believe we did it, Ralph: antimatter genesis." Jerry patted his friend on the back.

Ralph smiled. "It's amazing, Jerry. With just this particle, we can power the electric grid for the next thousand years. And there's no limit to how much of it we can make or what we can do with it. We can use it to power cars, airplanes, trains, even spacecraft. We can share it with other nations. It's the answer to the world's energy problems."

"Sounds like Nobel Prize material," said Jerry.

Ralph's smile grew larger. "I should think so."

"You know what this is like? This is like when the Vikings beat the Packers in overtime to go to the Super Bowl, only better. Remember that?"

"Yes, I remember it, Jerry," said Ralph, his smile shrinking just a fraction.

"Of course, it probably wasn't as much fun for you, you being a Packers fan and all," added Jerry.

Ralph wasn't smiling anymore. "It was a bad call, Jerry, and you know it. The Vikings won because a referee screwed up. That receiver was out of bounds on that last touchdown drive."

"The replay was inconclusive. Anyway, it doesn't really matter now. Particularly since the gods are on the Vikes' side."

"What are you talking about?"

"You just know all those Norse gods are Minnesota Viking fans. The playoffs have to be a lock, don't you think?"

"For crying out loud Jerry, you're Jewish, just like me."

"I converted."

"What?"

"Well, why not? If Odin and the others are real, why not worship them?" asked Jerry.

"Now you're just being ridiculous. Is this why you've been wearing that stupid helmet?"

"Yes. And I would ask that you not be disrespectful of my religion."

"Football is not a religion!" shouted Jerry, flicking Ralph's helmet with his finger.

"Leave my helmet alone. And you're just sore because no god or goddess would want to be associated with a bunch of losers like the Packers."

"You're an idiot," said Ralph swatting the helmet from Jerry's head. The helmet sailed across the room and into the electromagnetic field. There were sparks and a terrible clanging sound as the helmet rebounded like a pinball off one magnet and into another. The magnets toppled over.

The piece of antimatter dropped toward the floor.

"Oh crap," said Ralph.

In the blink of an eye, Nevada was vaporized.

In orbit, the green gelatinous square quivered with barely contained excitement. "We've received great news, captain. The latest reports indicate that holy wars have broken out across the Earth and the humans' antimatter research has suffered a significant, if not irreversible, catastrophe. Our current computer models project that the combination of events reduces the likelihood of humans achieving faster-than-light speed drives in the next thousand years to be a statistical impossibility. Indeed, based on past ideological conflicts and the advances humanity has made in weaponry, there is a distinct probability that humanity will wipe itself out within the next century."

"Without faster-than-light drives, there is no risk the

humans will invade our territory," quivered the captain. "The emperor will be quite pleased."

The first mate pulsed with confusion. "I still don't understand why the emperor considered the humans so dangerous to begin with. They obviously aren't very bright considering they could be fooled into destroying themselves by some elaborate holograms."

The captain shook angrily. "That is none of your concern. You are but a round-edged blob next to our sharp-cornered lord. How dare you presume to comprehend the emperor's thoughts? Your lot is to obey orders, not to question."

The first mate trembled with remorse. "I apologize, captain. You are correct, of course."

The captain's anger faded as quickly as it had come. The first officer—indeed, the entire crew—had been recruited from the best in the fleet. Undoubtedly they were all wondering about the reason for their mysterious mission. Yet the emperor and the high council had decided that only the captain would be privy to the disturbing images that had been broadcast through space from this troublesome planet.

It was a decision that the captain had agreed with. The terrifying pictures of humans ruthlessly devouring little gelatinous cubes with delight, all in the name of some terrible god called JELL-O, had left even the captain quaking with horror.

Had the emperor revealed the reason for the mission to his subjects, mass panic would have ensued. Better to deal with the matter quietly.

The first mate quivered, "Well, thank Splork the humans were easily manipulated."

"Yes, we should give thanks to Splork," replied the captain.

They faced the cubic idol that was in the center of the bridge and shivered in unison. "All hail Splork, the one true god. All-knowing, all-encompassing Splork, we gel only for you."

Satisfied and feeling quite chipper, the first officer oozed back to his station.

The captain considered the idol. The captain thought about the humans and their strange false gods. Why had Splork not touched them? Why was the demon JELL-O permitted to exist and innocents allowed to suffer?

For the first time, the captain began to wonder about Splork.

And somewhere, deep in his gel, the captain began to doubt.

*I*s there something beyond death? That's the question that has probably occupied the minds of humanity since we first understood death and first began inventing supernatural answers to things we couldn't comprehend. Of all the theological debates, this one probably strikes a chord in most of us. While those who think beyond the mythology generally believe that our lives are one-shot deals, I suspect many of us would prefer there were something beyond our mortal existences. In this story, James Hickey explores the repercussions following the death of one man who returned to life — and had a unique point of view to relate.

Resuscitation

James Hickey

ANNUNCIATION

These days, half the headlines make me feel like what's his name, in the Bhagavad-Gita. Watching, over the shoulder, as I write this, her laugh tickles my ear as she whispers, "Arjuna!" I look up from the Jimbo Resuscitation Blog that she created for me. "His name..." She gestures as I smile.

"Right. I always forget that." Acknowledgement, nodding: "You are the best, baby."

"Beautiful friends," she says, smiling now, "you know, like you said."

Ah, yes. So I did. Anyhow, like Arjuna, getting ready to raise his arm and drop his sword to commence the slaughter for that greedy bastard Krishna. On any given day, all the cousins are ready to lock and load and rock and roll. The Gulf Wars, 9/11, and the systemic economic meltdown a generation past—everybody feels it. Every city crowd, every gathering of people who are the least bit strange to each other, even if the

Dalai Lama himself has keynote responsibilities. Feels like the end of a cattle drive, when the steers smell the finish and fear is a fist around the heart.

No wonder, as it stands, that everyone also seems obsessed with "the afterlife." This is where my story comes in. I have personal, first-hand, I'm-betting-my-resuscitated-life definitive data about all of those currently irresistible issues of Heaven and Hell. I could offer all kinds of 'po-mo' details about setting and psyche here, but what are they compared to this magnificent material, the very stuffing of nirvana versus nothingness? No matter how the shit hits the fan, I have to honor this.

I've died, I've come back to life, I've written a book—moderate-to-nothing sales, until that idiot Robertson, "Pat Jr.," bless his heart, declared jihad against me—and lately I've been doing the book-tour deal. The media hipsters have been filing their nails before their stories, and now here I am back in Atlanta. I'll just say up front that hometown turf has never felt so foreign.

Anyhow, that's the setup. Ms. Free Speech Radio News, my marvelous *compañera*, is still here, taking advantage of her exclusive access, assured of the continuation of our wonderful "friendship," and keeping watch over me, another miracle in the chain of serendipitous circumstances that this whole scene suggests. The lucky accident of life beckons us to accept it all, whether we have the stomach for it or not. Part of acceptance is memory, which is what I'm doing right now.

I knew that the midweek-afternoon crowd—over a hundred and fifty at the Peachtree Road Borders Cafe, not including security, media, various gawkers more or less clueless—represented success, at least from the business perspective of booksellers. Still, given the extremely sharp stick in fundamentalists' eyes that my story represented, I knew that the hazards of success were significant. More than this, I knew that Borders, for all of its trendiness and upscale pretension, needed courage, along with a profit motive, to host this gig under the circumstances that prevailed.

I knew furthermore, ironically if one leans in that direction, that the thousand Peachtree Road Baptist Church protesters boosted my sales with their frothing rants and wild-eyed threats, railing at my blasphemy beyond police cordons across the frosted six lanes of Peachtree. I knew that they needed their ardor, given the shivery conditions in which their anguished outcries occurred, although my tale suggested that the beliefs underlying their passion tied them to a doom even more frigid than this Appalachian winter storm. And finally, I knew that I was neither dismissive nor nervous, nor even particularly interested, about whatever risk I entailed from baiting the human loathing for the inevitable mortal freeze that ultimately cradles each of us, pointing out that each hot hour that we exist is potentially the prelude to an eternity on ice.

All this knowledge percolated through my brain as I looked at the sleet descending in dark sheets outside the second-floor plate glass, thirty feet above the sidewalk, less than a hundred short yards from my Christian detractors. To the day, this was all taking place eighteen months after Doris and I had flown to Reykjavik to begin the Arctic cruise we had always dreamed of taking, "before the ice all melts." I smiled, to think of the similar immersion in frigid fluid that my opponents were now enduring in order to discount the implications of my emersion from equally frosty polar waters.

Parallel to my multi-tracked pondering of this, my reading approached its end, from the last chapter of my just-released tell-all exposé of death and revival—"Jim Lewis' gauntlet to Creationism," the *Times* had called the book. And now, thanks to the hypertextual marvels that are part of the basis for what I call, in my work, "our quantum consciousness jump," readers everywhere can read my remarks, and at the same time know my thoughts about them at this later moment. From the edge of awareness, barely audible to my observant self, the words tripped off my tongue, from page 169 and the final few paragraphs of the fifth-printing's afterword.

Just hours before, my wife and I had been laughing at the passing icebergs, swilling Scotch, and slurring Robert Frost:
Some say the world will in end in fire,
Some say in ice.
From what I've tasted of desire,
I hold with those who favor fire.
But if I had to perish twice, well
Ice is nice,
And would suffice.
And then we drowned, in cold, dark water. Yet here I am, a writer with a book, pleading for attention, for just a modicum of thoughtful consideration. If ever a tale of love and redemption pointed out a future for our kind, this one does. Not because I've written this guide do I beg my readers' indulgence, but because, by the terrible grace of whatever guides the cosmos, I was the first to experience such an awakening from the long cold sleep of dreamless night that is death.

As always the applause was modest, albeit I sensed a deep psychic hush in a few listeners, which I found so gratifying. More often each time I read a growing gallery of folks attended who obviously were about to succumb to the reaper: There the palsied old fellow with the respirator, there the young woman with the chemo-glow, maybe eight or so others here in Atlanta, all of them with brimming eyes and a paradoxical patina of hope. It looked like hope in any case, as I paused prior to speaking again. To me, just the notion that people might choose something other than religious pap represented a powerfully positive sign for our kind.

"Hey all! I hope that some of you will stay for my broadcast remarks. Since that shooter in Chicago tried to kill me, I'm on all the stations. You know you've arrived, in terms of intellectual credibility, when even C-SPAN sees fit to give you the time of day. There's even a lonely stringer for Free Speech Radio News, bless her heart. I understand they pay really poorly, for hard, hard labor.

"Anyhow, I just wanted to say that my speech for the cameras is a little didactic, almost stentorian, unfortunately. I'm not trying to be a know-it-all; it was just my luck to be in that place, to know. So here goes."

One of the amazing things about the electronic visual media that predominate now is the manner in which they, among all the ways of recording we humans have devised, cut out all reality in the moment, except for the reality that they intend to project. On that dim, fluorescent afternoon, the arc lights caught fire, the cameras and microphones thrust their demands in my face, and the dreary winter's chill, the icy wet, the protesters' shrill noise, all disappeared as the spotlights crackled, hummed, and fixed me in their blinding beams to assist in recording the following words.

"Hello, and salutations. Folks are here to get books signed — except the TV crews, of course. The controversy, the sense of an historical moment — proof of the non-existence of God, whatever — it's all pretty interesting. Authors who babble incessantly are not the norm, but that is what I'm going to do. It's the main reason I wrote *Resuscitation,* to be able to reach out to real people and make some real connections that might make some real difference. As the song says, 'I was blind and now I see.'

"My name is Jim Lewis, and I'd ask everyone to take a close look at me. A 'typical, fifty-something, freaky-fitness-nerd' is what a lot of people think, given the frame, the glasses, the pocketful of pens; 'Maybe a teacher or a lawyer.'

Given my emotional state, my outlook now, such a view really unsettles me, because nothing inside of me is routine anymore, or anything like it used to be. I've had difficulty conveying this transformation, as if I'd had a really nice nap, then awoken to inhabit a different universe. Compared to every second I lived prior to what I wrote about in my book, not one second presently resembles anything before. So I've begun starting these 'chats' with a question. To wit, after appropriate dramatic hesitation:

"Do you know how rare it is for anyone to fundamentally change?

"It's not as unlikely as catching a tau neutrino, or a listening to a cat that reads Shakespeare. But none of us is likely to meet, in an entire lifetime, more than a handful of people who have utterly transformed themselves.

"The categories of people who are relatively likely to undergo basic change include those who have died, or nearly so, and then returned. I am one of these folks, a revenant if you will, and that is why I'm here today, to sign a few books and deliver this talk. Appearances notwithstanding, I have undergone a complete metamorphosis from the man who looked just like me last year.

"The facts of the story are straightforward. All the details occupy only one hundred and fifty pages of *Resuscitation: The Story of a Revenant Who Lost His Soul and Found a Life.* I and twelve other hardy people ventured forth July first, two summers ago, on the ultimate Arctic cruise. We consisted of downsized over-fifty sorts such as me, with lots of time and good retirement benefits, along with a smattering of trust-fund kids and Internet wizards with way too much money, and precisely two scientists on sabbatical. The four crew members quipped that we were on the 'iceberg-and-borealis circuit.'

"A week into our fortnight run, at nine-thirty in the evening on a day of endless light, something took a huge chunk out of our ultra-safe double-hulled ship. We sank so quickly that we barely had a proper chance to panic before we submerged, when, at least for me, the water numbed so fast that even my terror froze, into one long, dreamy scream. I expired without pain. Just like they say, drowning doesn't really hurt. Eventually, I just let go and breathed in the brine.

"When I first revived, almost two full days after I 'passed away,' I sat up with such a start and screamed with such force that I threw completely out of whack my third and fourth cervical vertebrae. I thought about the joy I get from visiting Dr. Bob, my chiropractor right here in Atlanta's Virginia Highlands 'hood, for just an instant, before realizing I was no longer fighting the pressure of ice-cold water, simultaneously resigned and terrified that I was on the verge of inhaling freezing liquid into my lungs a hundred feet below the surface of the Arctic Ocean.

"Instead, I found myself attached to a variety of sensors and tubes, with IV devices and monitors all around my bed. All over my torso, and covering most of my arms and legs, was a form-fitting rubber suit, through which I felt warm fluid pulsing rhythmically. The entire experience was like some science-fiction vision, and it may well be the final image which comes to mind when I exit this world a second time.

"Here I stand now, brimming with vitality, speaking to you, and eager to sign my modest tome, despite nearly two days as a dead man. This miracle resulted from work the Department of Defense has been conducting in resuscitating victims of accidental death in freezing or near-freezing conditions. My friend Jack Danley—I hope he's still my friend anyway; he and everybody else on his team tried to persuade me not to write this book, and they've just about freaked out about the speaking tour—advised me that, for reasons of national security, I shouldn't be specific about the methods and protocols that led to my presence before you.

"For the most part, however, you'll find the answers in the book. The science is really nothing new, and the fact of my revenance blows the cover off their network and endeavors. Along with my hypothetically complete recovery, two of our seventeen adventurers made their ways to comatose states that never advanced beyond vegetative function. Truly, humans are on the cusp of a new age, but we haven't developed new attitudes to support this transformation.

"I have not forgotten to mention, though discussing it is unbelievably difficult, that my wife of thirty-three years was with me on this trek. Ours was not a storybook marriage. We both did some wild things, and we brought each other plenty of pain to balance our joy. But we were lovers from beginning to end; we had a connection I can never explain, that lives in me still like the sun lives in tropical sands throughout the night. She was below and I was on deck when we sank. My return makes this separation at the end, after we had lived through so much together, especially excruciating.

"I know indisputably that everyone here now, and every reader of my text, can feel the nausea and fury of my loss. When I looked one final time at my beautiful woman's lifeless flesh, following my miraculous revival, I saw that neither drowning nor attempts at resuscitation had marred the form of what I had adored. But she was—simply and completely—gone, as lost to me as dinosaurs and dodo birds, except inside my head.

"Weeping before the remains of my wife, I made a commitment. It parallels the searing necessity of producing this book, and of speaking about it relentlessly. 'Not only will I love again,' I swore, 'but I will seek the fullest measure of passion and relationship each day, every second that life allots me.' Even as I watched my mate interred, I renewed this vow.

"This is the core reason I have written *Resuscitation,* and it's why I embarked on a speaking tour. I don't need money, and neither adulation nor ego-stroking intrigue me in the least. It's why I so blithely accepted DoD censorship of the manuscript. It's also why the hateful opposition and brutal threats from fundamentalists around the world bother me not at all.

"The reason is this: The life we now lead—our breath, our sight, our hunger, our lust, our coursing blood, the unimaginable marvel of our brains and the imaginative capacity that they have—is the sum total of what we have. I was dead forty-four hours, twelve minutes, and thirteen seconds. While a corpse, I saw no 'light.' No power came to transport a 'higher' part of me away. No God intervened to salvage the soul that I had hoped lived within me, somewhere, somehow.

"Like most Americans, my wife and I were people of faith, even as we reveled in the life of the flesh. Our faith endowed the Doris and James Lewis Scholarship Fund. Ironically, it will continue to help some woebegone Methodist freshman each year, indefinitely. But my faith, the yearning for spirit—separate from gore—vanished as I awoke with that shriek of terror.

"Most people have trouble accepting such a view, and of course some reject it out of hand. I understand. Not only do I sympathize, but in the true sense of the word, I empathize. The views I have no choice but to accept are harsh, but their reality is the factual foundation for the miracle of our actual lives.

"Those who would enforce an opposite view want their eternity in Heaven, and pray that I spend mine in endless hellish pain instead of having an endless nothingness await. Since consciousness has arisen in our species, the stark face of this truth about our final fate has fed life-after-death fantasies that are impossible to sustain in the face of what happened to me. More importantly, though, these fantasies absolutely prohibit dealing with the actual potential that exists in the life that we do have, now and not hereafter.

"Realizing that, truly, I had returned from the dead, I came to comprehend that I only began an honest existence when I recognized the finality of death. As seven billion people face today's multiple intersecting crises, overwhelmingly we look to soul sources for salvation. My experience, however, suggests that a generalized acknowledgment of a radically carnal creed would better serve us—that the capacity to feel a measure of ecstasy in miserable moments, the sense of some heat at the core of that which is coldest, the ability to love and nurture the children who are our only organic link to anything akin to everlasting existence necessitate a frank admission of the facts of life and death—instead of clinging to the notion, and insisting on the primacy of the chimera, that a 'soul' inside of us will continue to live after us.

"To those whose hearts I wound with these words, I apologize. These ideas contradict the way that I lived before I died for the first time. But as much as I hoped and prayed for the face of God to appear to me then, nothing came; nothing except nothing. The mystery of death will always be with us. And people's faiths are their own, to nurture and develop as they see fit. I just ask anyone willing to listen to consider: Perhaps the time has come for a change. Perhaps, in fashioning some sort of meaning out of living in the omnipresence of death, we need to seek our magic in blood and our power in science.

"I'll leave you with these ideas for the moment. I've got a surprise announcement, a real doozy, but it can wait until I've dispensed signatures, answered questions, and we've sucked down some coffee and wolfed a few cookies and such. Thanks very much!"

Only the ten members of the audience who seemed hospice-ready remained to listen till the end of my ramblings, along with three of the media reps who, with the exception of the wan Goth FSRN stringer, showed no interest in follow-up inquiry. I promised Ms. Free Speech as extensive an interview as she desired, after I gulped down some tidbits and my caffeine limit and signed a hundred-odd copies of my book.

Before I imbibed anything, though, or escaped to provide autographs, the young chemotherapy waif approached, a stitched indentation that marked her skull a sign of the cancer that would likely consume her. Her benighted companions stayed back, around whom paced my security consultants, between the two of them seeming to look every direction at once. Since the shooting in Chicago, inasmuch as I wouldn't deliver many messages as an unrevivable corpse, I had hired a pair of bodyguards who were among the odd assortment of ex-Rangers who somehow find a way to a secular and progressive perspective on life.

The girl whose malignancy appeared imminently lethal asked what she could do to prepare herself for eternity. I looked her in the eyes, our gazes unwavering. Though the words seemed pitifully weak to convey what I felt, I sought to communicate that such courage as she evinced, though hard beyond belief to manifest, is perhaps the primary precursor of wisdom. Thus, I held her hands to speak, and told her that her life and courage were so important "to vocalize, to emote, to demonstrate to everyone the potential for living this moment, even while staring death in the face," I said. "That choice would add up to something worth dying for. To stand like that," I started to suggest, was tantamount to a life of such fierce intensity that her own chilly end would not matter—even to her it would not matter—could she but hold on to her fiery present passion.

I hesitated. *She's dying,* I thought. I wanted to say that her fierce intensity now would obviate her own chilly end, that her present passion would outlast her headstone, but I never got the chance. Before I could fairly begin to articulate all of this, the massive windows above Peachtree Road exploded from a rattling burst of ordnance, the clatter of high-velocity assault rifles a counterpoint to the cascade of tinkling glass. The lights went out. And the snowy wind flew into Borders, its cruel bite as bracing as the thought of tumbling bullets, its howling mixed with the screams of the small throng nearby who had been awaiting my signature, which had become slightly famous since I had become the quarry of these other sorts of hunters.

One bodyguard went down, blossoms of blood on his polo shirt, his powerful pectorals heaving. The other, ducked low and not paying any attention to me, looked about, wide-eyed, for the source of the incoming fire. He must have found it, because he squeezed off one short burst after another in the direction of the customer-service desk. The wails and screams and panic-stricken scrambling of customers and crowd should have drowned out the sound of gunfire but, somehow, the pings and pops continued to form a staccato undertone to the pandemonium.

Having learned something from my experience in Chicago, and having studied duck-and-cover, elude-and-evade protocols in the aftermath, within a second of the first rounds, none of which seemed to have done more than minor damage—I was seeping fluid down my forearm from flesh on fire, but I was fully alive, senses honed—I was skulking along the floor to hide and survey the damage from the hot-food and coffee bar adjacent to the podium I'd been using.

The odd, dark girl from Free Speech Radio News, head tucked into her shoulders, reached out to pull me behind the cover of the counter. Her already-dark complexion having assumed the purple hue of a mad merlot, sweat dripping from her face, she was a little intimidating. I didn't know what to expect.

"Good!" she exclaimed simply, pulling out her little digital jewel of a recorder. "Are you getting used to this?" she asked, a smile struggling to light her visage as she continued breathing heavily.

"Welcome to the new America," I muttered, grinning and figuring, 'Why miss out on what might be my last interview?'

"I'm thinking, like, you know, *Casablanca?*" She was breathing a wee bit easier, still smiling.

"I see," I mused, at once laughing, listening, and raising

my head to look around. "A beautiful friendship, huh?"

CORONATION

The presence of this text in front of an audience — all praise the power of the 'innernet' — is indicia that, for now, I have continued to elude eternity's cool repose, our only certainty beyond this throbbing instant. I've found a love for life; she's minding and making the books now, so I can try to keep us both a step ahead of the reaper for a time, to continue to insist that people pay attention and 'seize the day,' so to speak.

Of course, the surprise announcement that I promised in my talk, corrosively interrupted by the Army of God's repeating rifles, remains to tell. It's devilishly delectable, full of bizarre conspiracy, worthy of a new testament of life.

As luck would have it, I can convey it briefly now: my life's first end, the sinking of the *Arctic Queen*, was no accident; in fact, its purposive destruction ironically has conceived the sort of devolution toward dystopia that it was meant to preclude. However, a fuller telling of all of that is a tale for another time.

*T*he Rapture is supposed to be a major event, since it would be the prologue to the Biblical Armageddon. Although supported by religious folks using various justifications, its concept seems to be a recent addition to Christian mythology. That doesn't make the idea any less entertaining. But before Sarah Trachtenberg even begins to touch on that subject, she crafts a deeply thought-provoking story that postulates what could happen to society if science discovered how to "turn off" that part of the brain that enables people to build their lives around fairy tales. With the feel of the Left Behind books from an atheist's point of view, Sarah brilliantly intertwines these two ideas into one story that will keep you thinking long after you've read it.

Rise Up, Rise Up!

Sarah Trachtenberg

I know it sounds too coincidental to be true, but I really was on an airplane when it happened, flying home from Stockholm.

Let me explain. It's hard to sound humble when I say this, but I was collecting the Nobel Prize in Medicine. My wife took the time from her research to join me and we received as many congratulations as we had at our wedding twenty-seven years ago. I was on top of the world, but my wife later told me that I hadn't smiled much during the award ceremony.

"It was just such a serious moment," Sally said afterwards over one last glass of champagne in our honeymoon suite. Maybe she was right. Olympic athletes didn't smile when they received their medals, even if they said they were the happiest moments of their lives. On the other hand, hadn't Sally and I both smiled ear-to-ear when our two children were born?

Part of me felt silly about the whole Nobel thing. Sure, I was proud of my achievements. I was proud of what I had done to deserve such recognition. Why not? I had worked hard and I earned it. Still... well, my finding wasn't exactly what I had been looking for. Earth-shattering though it may have been, it was, like Fleming's penicillin, something into which I had fallen ass-backwards.

I'm a neuroscientist. Not a brain surgeon, mind you, at least not exactly, and I do joke, "It's not brain surgery." When I share the nature of my research at cocktail parties, people make a lot of mad-scientist jokes as if my work were implanting ideas into people's brains. Really, it's not. When examining the physiology of depression, in the interest of drug development, my data revealed the exact area of the brain, which the press quickly dubbed "god-shaped hole," that enabled religion. The geography of the brain contained the exact spot—so amazing, the brain! It never fails to fascinate—that was the cause of so much pain and guilt. And now, it would be possible to shut it off like a light switch.

It was a perfect time for that perfect windfall. New Atheism was in full swing: advocates, mostly biologists and physicists, organized and came forward to speak out against the existence of god and for the idea that religion was doing more harm than good. More and more atheists stood up to be heard, either having come out of the closet or recently "converted." For the first time, mainstream movies and TV shows had atheist themes and characters. Books about religion, and specifically whether religion was extremely good or extremely bad, sold almost as well as Harry Potter books. The news media, with an almost bloodthirsty delight, were reporting what I was tempted to describe as catfights between the pro- and anti-religion camps. As for myself, I paid little attention to such matters and hadn't even read all the popular books until my discovery thrust me onto the stage. I didn't expect to be in the limelight and didn't know quite what to do with it at first.

When the pharmaceutical team was about to release Nogerinoil, the gravity of the matter hit me. This may sound childish, but unlike the way the researchers on the Manhattan

Project couldn't seem to surmise, despite all their brains, that their creation was going to be used to kill people, my realization wasn't one of dread; really morbid curiosity. I had encouraged Nogerinoil. I knew, of course, what it would do: cure depression. Many people were depressed due to religion. Patients knew this, or at least their psychiatrists knew, and wanted to get rid of the factor of religion. Simply inhibit the god-shaped hole and patients would be spared the misery that plagued them.

Nogerinoil could save lives, since many depressed people killed themselves, to say nothing of the rest of the damage: depression caused car accidents, industrial accidents, child abuse, and so forth. Economically, the media pointed out that Nogerinoil would alleviate the problem of depression-related absence and lack of productivity at work, which cost corporations tens of billions a year. What a boon!

I hadn't given serious thought to what Nogerinoil would do for religion itself. For the religious. For those who weren't depressed and wouldn't "need" the psychopharm. Would the non-depressed world even notice yet another prescription drug on the market?

Finally, when TIME magazine interviewed Ronald Barlofski, the top pharm guy, and me, and buzz had it that TIME was thinking "men of the year," what I hath wrought hit me. The journalist was one of those aging hippie types who had a Pulitzer under his belt. When things got more comfortable and chatty between him, Ron and me, the journalist asked me point blank:

"Dr. Ray, do you think that the world would be better without religion?"

So simple, and yet... I knew from previous interviews about my god-shaped-hole discovery that journalists rarely asked yes/no questions, but at times, nothing else would do.

Ever since the media reported my findings and especially after Ron spearheaded Nogerinoil, I had fielded much more loaded questions. How would you describe your religion? None, I'm an atheist. How are you involved in New Atheism? I'm not. What would you say about people who sacrifice religion to get rid of their depression? If it works for them, I'm all for it. How would you describe your feelings towards religion? And so forth.

With TIME, though, the point was naked. Would the world be a better place?

I hemmed and hawed and told the aging hippie, "There are a lot of depressed people, many of whom can attribute their symptoms to religion, so yes, curing their depression by removing religion will make the world a better place." What about besides depression? The journalist pointed out to me what I already knew in the back of my mind: that non-depressed people would take the drug, for what might be called recreational purposes. If everyone took it, would religion cease to exist? Hypothetically, what if we put Nogerinoil in the drinking water?

I added to the journalist, "Yes, it would be a better place, because religion is what makes good people do evil. It doesn't make evil people do good."

The smartass in me couldn't resist asking a journalist in a later interview, "If God is omnipotent and doesn't want this drug, why did he allow its development and release on the market in the first place?" The press figured that this put me squarely in the pantheon of the top anti-religion crusaders and reported me as such. "Ray challenged God," one news site said.

It goes without saying how the public responded to the release of Nogerinoil. First, it was credited, for good or bad, directly to me. That was wrong. I merely provided the means and, therefore, the impetus. In a world in which atheists no longer wanted to stay silent and tip-toe around religion, and believers were on the defense, the drug wasn't just adding fuel to the fire: it was like adding an entire oil well. Despite the fact that the drug was voluntary, believers feared that the end of faith was near. Their faith, they said, was in danger of being brainwashed right out of them. Conspiracy theorists who were religious were scared that atheists would drug them, and maybe they were right.

In one of the debates about the drug's societal effects, a neuropsychologist who happened to be an atheist pointed out that Nogerinoil wouldn't stop patients from being "themselves." Her opponent, a religious pharmaceutical attorney, hammered home that, for a believer, religion was inseparable from the self. There was serious talk of forcing, though advocates preferred the word "treating," the drug on Islamic terrorists and other "religion criminals" as part of their sentences, much as radical feminists had, without success, advocated for rapists to be chemically castrated.

Ron and I denied accusations that we had set out to destroy religion deliberately and fielded hate mail from religious people all over the world. Protesters camped outside our labs holding signs that said things like "No Religion, No Peace" and "God-killing drugs—Go to Hell!" In any case, it was necessary to take on extra security and I didn't know for how long. Perhaps forever?

I knew that the protesters were just baiting me and it would be wise to not respond, but one day a protester, a young woman who looked a little like my daughter, standing inches away from the security boundary, shouted at me that I was smashing civilization's moral compass. I said the first thing that came to mind: "If religion is your moral compass, I'm not impressed." When the media reported it, they made me sound a lot harsher than I'd been.

Sally spoke for me when she told a reporter that the media seemed to be missing the point entirely in that Nogerinoil was a voluntary drug. Patients who took it wanted to free themselves from religion; no one was "drugging" anyone. It was for people who wanted to "quit" religion and couldn't; even if they acknowledged the harm religion did to them, they couldn't just forget a lifetime of guilt and indoctrination. They couldn't "forget" on their own. Nogerinoil did that for them.

In the weeks following the drug's release, intelligentsia in cities like New York, London, and Tel Aviv were having "God-Shaped Plug" parties, drinking Curacao cocktails, mimicking the blue capsule. One science educational fund in Los Angeles took the theme and ran with it, hosting an eight-hundred-dollar-a-plate charity dinner in which not only were the decorations and dress theme blue, but all the food was blue, as well. Newsweek called it "Blue Plate Special" when they reviewed it, lamenting that I hadn't been there to speak in front of the Who's Who of atheist scientists. I'd wanted to go, it wasn't that I was against the idea, but I didn't want to take the time to fly out to L.A.

In reaction, religious leaders all over the world mobilized their followers to pray that God would help His children resist this scourge. At least one Christian leader, a well-known evangelist, took a slightly different angle.

"This is surely The Rapture," he had breathed, in a speech that was widely repeated on news clips and was the most-viewed on YouTube. "God sent us this test, this great, final test, to cull the finest from His herd."

It was easy to scoff at the time, but what about now?

Here I was, on a plane, beside Sally, both of us napping on and off, and the crew and passengers fell into a panic when some of the passengers went just, well, missing. The crew roused us and the pilot went on the PA, telling us what was happening. One thing, though: their clothes and jewelry weren't left in their seats. It was as if those people had quietly, unseen, just left the plane mid-air. We prepared for an emergency landing in Halifax, the crew doing their best to keep everyone calm and in their seats. Sally and I, whimpering, did our best to maintain our sanity as we embraced.

I thanked goodness that the pilot himself had not been

chosen. I doubted I was the only one. Sally and I held each other close, fighting denial, trying to assess this "miracle."

That really was how it happened.

Count the number of Christians in the world and you'll get about two billion. Count the number of Muslims and you'll get over a billion and a half. Jews are negligible compared to Judaism's two Goliathesque daughters. All three had about half of their members gone; vanished; beamed up. Most, but not all, children from those faiths were gone. The believers who had predicted that children would automatically ascend were wrong, assuming that this really was a rapture.

There didn't appear to be a science as to who was "beamed up" and who wasn't. No one had seen anyone literally ascend, or at least no one with evidence, but these "raptured" people weren't dead or on vacation. In the face of half the world's adherents to Western religion just plain gone, atheists called it The Rapture just like everyone else did, all while knowing it had to have a different explanation. There was simply no way to explain it and the skeptic's usual last resort, "We don't know yet. Maybe someday we will," was still a lot easier to swallow than... well, than The Rapture. I knew that, after the dust settled, scientists would get right to work as best they could on solving the mystery: "Okay, what really happened back there?" It was perhaps one of the most important events in human history and, at least for now, we were stuck.

You'd think, had it been an actual Rapture, there would have been some kind of flourish, right? Thunder and lightning, maybe, or a chorus of angels singing, or the voice of God — something. There were none of these.

Those of us left got hurt in the wake. Sally lost her mother, a sweet little octogenarian; we'd never have another Christmas at her house in Pennsylvania. I'd liked Marcia, maybe even loved her, and Sally and I mourned as we arranged a memorial service, not knowing what else to do. I was so grateful that both of our kids were alive and well and we talked on the phone every day, doing what we could for each other.

Cars crashed because the drivers suddenly vanished; planes crashed because pilots suddenly vanished, or air-traffic control suddenly vanished. Doctors or patients gone mid-surgery. Houses on fire because people were cooking when they got ascended. Kids sent to live with relatives because their parents were gone. There was looting, but unless it was violent, the police hadn't paid much attention since they had more important matters, except for when a group of Christians looted an Arizona religious-supplies store. That was newsworthy. "We wanted to break as many rules as possible," one of them said. "I mean, we believed, and we're still here. Why not show God we're angry?"

In at least a few cases, left-behind religious people were angry enough at their god to vandalize their houses of worship. They believed in God, but in a god who hated them and in turn they hated him back. I was relieved not to have that point of view, but found vandalism of any kind distasteful, especially since so many houses of worship had such beautiful architecture.

Naturally, many people killed themselves, but these were a minority. Some adherents of Western religion who survived The Rapture couldn't help but gloat that at least they got the right religion and were vindicated there, but that was a small comfort since they didn't get to be with God and their more "chosen" loved ones. People blamed themselves and each other. Fingers pointed and heads rolled, but there was no greater scapegoat than Nogerinoil.

"If only I hadn't taken that awful drug," some teary survivors said when talking about their raptured loved ones in round-the-clock news coverage. "My husband was a good man. Maybe I'd be with him still if I stayed on the right path." Still, they kept taking the "awful drug."

For better or for worse, Sally and I were still a married

couple on Earth, and like everyone, adapting to this strange new world we inherited. Those left would be wise to count their blessings, and we had many. Everyone talked about where they were when the vanishing took place. As our left-behind politicians urged us to return to normalcy, we did, happy to get on with our lives and over with what history would no doubt call an extreme case of post-traumatic stress syndrome.

It was amusing to see who didn't get chosen. Which politicians? Which talk show hosts? Oprah wasn't good enough? Oh, dear! I mean, she's so beloved! What about priests and nuns? Not all of them, either? Those people must have made some terrible mistakes! God didn't elect to rapture all of His own salespeople? Celebrity rags, once they were running again after the first couple of weeks of shock, were jam-packed with pop stars weeping about what they had done to deserve not getting ascended. While a few did blame Nogerinoil, more of them blamed other things entirely. "It's because I didn't make it to the playoffs," moped one baseball player. "I should've known that that error would cost me my eternal happiness."

After the worst was over, one of the world's most vocal atheists, Rick, a friendly and very charismatic biologist who had lauded me as some kind of saint for Nogerinoil, told me that he felt "absolutely fucking great."

"I'm so tired of people asking me if this 'Rapture' proves me wrong," he said. He had called me; he would have arranged to fly in from London to celebrate my Nobel in person, but air travel was still a little difficult to come by during this 'adjustment.' "It could be anything—there's no such thing as a Rapture. You know what's funny, though, Gus? I have yet to hear about anyone—any atheist, that is—finding religion and repenting because of this."

"That *is* funny," I said. "Wouldn't you have thought they'd admit that they were wrong? Try to make amends?"

"But they don't," Rick said. "Know what I think?"

"What?" I was having trouble conceiving of a reason.

"It's too late anyway! Why bother sucking up to the invisible man in the sky at this point?"

"Yeah, I wouldn't have predicted that," I said.

"Not only that, but lots of former believers are becoming atheists! I bet you wouldn't have predicted that, either!"

"They're using Nogerinoil," I said. Believers were desperate for something to make them forget this entire smack in the face. They wanted to forget the god who didn't think they were good enough. They looked at the atheists, who seemed to have it pretty good. We didn't feel snubbed. In fact, some of us were feeling "absolutely fucking great."

"I'm so glad I bought stock in that," Rick said. The moment begged for us to clink our brandy snifters while patting each other on the back.

"Look," Rick continued, "once we get to work on what really happened back there, everyone will just heave a sigh of relief and we can move on. Things'll be great. Trust me."

While it was true that The Rapture strengthened many of those believers who God apparently snubbed, Rick was right in saying that many more figured that to be good for God now would be too little, too late. That is the epitaph of every civilization, every religion that fails: "Too late."

For the first time in a long time, I watched the TV ad for Nogerinoil. It featured a beautiful woman, about forty, in soft-focus, smiling while she went about the banalities of her day: picking up her kids from an ostensibly secular school, loading her car with groceries from the farmers' market, cuddling with her husband in bed after making love. The voiceover described how religion had contributed to her depression, making her life painful. "But now, Nogerinoil can help," she said. "With Nogerinoil, I can live the life I want—not what I was programmed to want."

The guilt that came from sex, food, life itself — the time religion consumed — you could make those go away. You would look back at your old self and wonder why you were so afraid.

When air travel finally became normal, Rick called an emergency meeting of the atheist think-tank equivalent of the Pentagon (the Pentagon itself was, by the way, still standing and running). He invited me, but I figured it was more out of courtesy than what I could actually contribute, and I declined since I didn't want to make the trek all the way out to London. Besides, after winning the Nobel and waiting out the worst of The Rapture, I wanted to take Sally to the country for a relaxing stay at a bed and breakfast and do some hiking.

It had been only weeks ago when the streets were filled with wrecks; now they were all removed. Many cars left behind by their chosen owners were simply available for the taking, the keys right there in the ignition, and atheists enjoyed driving free Lexuses while buying lots of cheap, newly-available real estate. Almost half the U.S. population had, you might say, gotten out of our way.

As Sally drove to the bed and breakfast, she exclaimed, "This is wonderful — there's so much space!" It was true. It was almost as if God were rewarding us.

We kept reiterating: The worst is over. The worst is over.

Finally, though, there was a trek I simply couldn't pass up: Rick and the other atheist brass organized a party at what was once Vatican City. The pope himself had ascended, but there were many rumors that he was just in hiding. All over the world, houses of worship were being turned into museums and libraries, and some were even divided into apartments, with their architectural splendor intact. And now that they were no longer houses of God, their new owners paid taxes like everyone else.

Roman hotels were booked solid and clogged with atheists

who'd come from near and far to celebrate. You might expect the party to have taken place in St. Peter's Basilica, but it was mostly in the adjacent buildings. Even though it was still too cold to celebrate outside, people gathered in the Piazza anyway after they had drunk enough. Organizations provided fine food and wine; one room in the Sistine Chapel even featured a small fountain of champagne. I drank a flute of that. Classical musicians entertained us as we celebrated in front of the most priceless pieces of art in the world.

I was hailed as the person who made it all possible.

"Not since Darwin," said Rick in his speech, broadcast live all over the world, "has a man done so much to make atheism thrive." Later, I told the audience of millions that Rick was being much too generous. He had mobilized a critical mass of New Atheism long before I'd gotten involved.

"This is our equivalent of NASA after the moon landing," Rick continued. "We have so much for which to be grateful. For many of us, it's the smaller things: more room on the bus. More spaces for students in our schools and universities. More resources to invest in our children. Surplus real estate. We are relieved from the masses who thump the Bible and try to convert us and persecute us. And as for those who are left, thanks to the relative scarcity of humans, we are more valuable. In many parts of the world, there is no longer such thing as an unwanted pregnancy.

"In the bigger picture, we are free. We are finally free. Freedom and democracy will progress unfettered. Religious terrorism won't threaten our safety and values. Science research and education will continue free of obstacles which religion created all these years. We'll enjoy exponential rewards of an enlightened, educated world.

"I know many of you are sad about the loss of your loved ones, but the human story has turned a new leaf. We are making the world a better place."

We toasted our victory again and again that weekend. At

one point, Rick took me aside.

"Wish you'd made it to the meeting in London," he said. "Since then, we've all been working on this Rapture thing. Let me give you a rundown. We think we know what it is."

I was dying to know — I mean, who wouldn't be, except for people who were so sure it really had been The Rapture?

"I've been talking to the astronomers, and they think..."

"Aliens?" I was impatient.

"Let me finish, Gus. Listen, we're talking about some heavy stuff here. You know how Sagan pioneered the idea of a multiverse? We think that it was wormholes."

Wormholes. I wasn't an astronomer myself, but even I knew that this was messing with the space/time continuum. My brain itched more and more as Rick explained what the astronomers were getting at: Here on Earth, those individuals whose god-shaped holes were in use, in other words, religious people, were more susceptible for some reason. Nogerinoil — atheism — well, they made one immune. Immune to what? To renegade wormholes? There were many questions left, but Rick's idea sure looked right.

"This is a force from another universe?" I said.

"That's what we're answering," Rick said. "Look, Gus, we need you. You and the pharmaceutical team need to get the astronomers in the labs and let's figure out what astronomical events have to do with the geography of the human brain."

All my years of research hadn't prepared me for astronomical events that humans could scarcely imagine, let alone what they would have to do with the human brain.

"Why just the monotheists then, Rick? What about the other religions? How come no one disappeared in, I don't know, Hinduism?"

"Gus, is it possible that Hinduism uses a different part of the brain? Does it have different side effects?"

"We need to meet up about this. And soon," I said.

"Next year in Jerusalem?" said Rick, referring to the party.

"You bet!"

After the accolades and speeches and celebrations, we got on our chartered planes and returned to the world that awaited us. On the plane, many people, Sally and I included, watched Rick's speech again. The second time she saw it, Sally actually shed a few tears. I thought she was weeping again for the loss of her mother. "I'm crying from relief," she corrected me. Her mourning was over.

I bought two Bloody Marys for us from the stewardess. I was anxious to return to my lab; I had a lot of work to do.

W hich religion is right? For the most part, the unanimous response from the adherents of any religion is "Mine!"; from the atheists' camp, our answer would be "None!" But what if they're all right? What if there's some grain of truth in each of them? What if humans have made them real simply by believing? Gary J. Beharry's tale of many theological figures is certainly one to provoke discussion — never mind the amusing idea of God and Satan vacationing in an apartment together. Lest that lead you to believe that the story is a comedy, rest assured it's a thinker, and a pointed commentary on the human condition.

Fried Eggs

Gary J. Beharry

"I'm trying to meditate here!" God yelled over un-tempoed bongo-drum beats from the other bedroom. When the pounding didn't stop, he poked his head out of his bedroom to see Satan in the room across the hall, naked, flouncing around two huge human-skinned bongo drums—somehow managing to stand out amidst crumpled candy wrappers, Popeyes Chicken boxes, empty ketchup packets, *Playboys, Swanks,* and ashes strewn about the floor.

"Satan!" God boomed at his first-time roommate.

Immediately, Satan stilled and smirked at his landlord. "What's up, doc?" he asked coquettishly.

God sighed, counting to ten while stroking his beard. "It's my meditation time. Can you keep it down for another half an hour?"

Satan spread his hands out in a placating gesture and said, "I don't get a chance to express myself down there. This is the only vacation I get. Remember, this was your idea."

God sighed again and grimaced. "All right. All right." He

looked away suddenly and, before retreating, said, "At least put some clothes on. I should have never exaggerated you."

He heard one drum beat, followed by two more. "I take after my father," Satan said, followed by more drumbeats.

God gritted his teeth. Why did he agree to this stupid arrangement? Of course, he knew why: It was part of his self-therapy. After all, how could he be an omniscient power who said that man should forgive, yet at the same time have his most beloved angel damned to Hell? So he recently decided that, for two weeks out of every year from now on, he would give his most disappointing one-time servant a supervised vacation.

"How ya feelin'? Hot! Hot! Hot!" Satan sang from his bedroom, banging on the drums with each word.

Freedom. It was such a taken-for-granted thing. God retreated to his room and continued his meditation, scowling when Guns N' Roses' *Appetite for Destruction* started blasting from Satan's room. Rhythmic bangs in tune with the guitar strums of "Sweet Child of Mine" brought to God's mind Satan jumping up and down, strumming on his air guitar.

After Axl Rose sang his entire album for two encores, God finally thought that Satan had tired himself out, but his face quickly reddened when he realized what Satan was actually doing: squishy rubbing and moaning sounds oozing through the bottom of the door and finding their way to God's ear, ending minutes later in a drawn-out moan.

God slammed his pillow over his head. Eventually, the great wail of ecstasy died away but was quickly replaced by heavy footsteps plodding down the hall. Water splashed in the bathroom, then the heavy footsteps returned, this time combined with a long, wailing yawn. Minutes later, God began to count the heavy snores, and gradually felt himself drifting to sleep.

God scratched his crotch through his striped boxer shorts, stretched his arms, and yawned.

"Yo, G, you ain't got no Pop Tarts or nothing?" Satan asked. At least he was wearing a robe—God's silk robe, already laden with food stains.

"Why are you trying to annoy me so?"

"Because I have carte blanche for the next two weeks, and I'm gonna take advantage of every fuckin' minute."

God frowned and tapped his foot. Satan grinned and said, "My bad. I know, no cursing. My bad."

Satan took another swig of God's favorite drink, Yoo-hoo, wiped his chocolate-milk moustache with God's silk robe, and let out a watery burp. He dumped the bottle in the regular trash, not the recyclables, and retreated to his room, but not before dropping a silent-but-deadly one while he passed by his Lord and Master.

God prayed to himself, realizing the futility of that particular gesture. He resisted the urge to contact Gabriel, for he had promised his second in command a chance to look over things for two weeks; ironically, this was also supposed to be a vacation for God as well. However, his thought of Gabriel forced an arched eyebrow, followed by a strong tugging of his beard as he marched to Satan's bedroom.

He found himself raising his hand to knock, then hesitated, and then, when realizing the millions of inappropriate incidents he could intrude on, decided to knock.

"Enter," Satan sang.

God entered into thick, foul-smelling smoke. "You're not allowed to sm— wait, is that marijuana?"

"A joint, a doobie, a fatty, a blunt, Mary Jane, the chronic, *the shit!*" Satan said with a dopey smile. The marijuana cigarette was profoundly long and thick, mimicking Satan's member. He took a long drag, held it for a moment, and then let the smoke slowly dribble out of his flaring nostrils. His eyes drooped, his movements became very sluggish and his head turned toward God "You want a piece of this?" he asked, unaware of God's building ire.

Luckily for Satan, God had a question which quickly shoved aside his ire. "Satan, who's in charge while you're up here?"

"Ah, now you ask me that. How come you didn't think of that before? I thought you were all-knowing."

"I know many things. Like the fact that you betrayed me." The words seemed to sting his former Number One so harshly that the joint went limp between Satan's finger and thumb. But Satan seemed to quickly recover himself.

"Good one. Still, you didn't answer my question."

Patience, God said to himself. He had to do this. He had been losing himself recently over the last fifty to one hundred years, losing himself to—

"Chaos," Satan whispered, with a dead look in his eyes.

"What?" God asked.

"Chaos. I am the Lord of Chaos. You, Order. You need someone. I don't. Isn't that right? Isn't that the way you wanted it?"

"I..." God paused, stroking his beard once again. "I wanted to punish you for going against me."

"Kudos," Satan said. "For over two thousand years, I have been punished. Curious. Man rapes, kills, builds weapons to annihilate each other by the billions, breaks every Commandment you set forth—and with a few prayers and a confession, they are forgiven, welcomed with open arms."

"Yes, well, finish your cigarette, and make this your last one." God turned, fisted his hands, and used his pinky to close the door. He stared at the white hallway wall which mirrored how he felt about his life right now—though perhaps a few dots of red for what part Satan had to play with his current emotional state would have been more apropos—and then retreated to his room, feeling defeated.

Now used to the wild sounds emanating from Satan's room, God allowed his mind-thoughts to drift away, for he had to partially be here, both physically and spiritually, in order to anchor Satan to the New York City apartment where they currently resided. He slowly began to separate himself from the sounds bouncing off the buildings from ambulances rushing to Lennox Hill Hospital, the conversation of college-bar bouncers, and the local comedy club releasing its hungry and inebriated patrons. He allowed those sounds to come and go, but brought himself back when a poor rendition of "Old Man River" crooned from next door. He harrumphed and forced himself to not get irritated.

He reached out his thoughts again, leaving behind the eighteenth floor of 214 East 82nd Street in Manhattan, where he had sublet an apartment for several months—only telling Satan for two weeks—wishing to get away from everything.

He reached out towards realms unknown to man. Yet he hesitated upon entering the nothingness, for to know everything about anything except for one thing would cause any man or deity to pause for a moment, but when he realized he had no other choice, because his emotional state and want of satisfaction and peace made him so desperate, he pushed onward, feeling a strange sense of coolness and unfamiliarity as he crossed the border.

"Hello," a soothing, familiar voice said.

"Hi, Sid," God responded, already feeling better. The voice was quiet and even; it was just one of the things he envied about his equal. And he hated himself for that feeling.

"You are troubled," his friend said. God was taken aback. He always could put up a front, yet he let his guard down only with two people: Gabriel, for he had to reveal everything to him if he planned to do what he eventually wanted to do; and Satan, for it had all begun with him.

"I feel lost, Sid," God said. "I'm not sure what I'm doing any more and it scares me." Again, there were the soft eyes—not penetrating, not in empathy, just there, observant. And the half-smile—not mocking, just a smile.

"So, why don't you sit with me? Let us meditate on this problem."

God pulled his robe up slightly and squatted to face Siddhartha, then closed his eyes. "Tell me what you see," Siddhartha said.

"I see nothing." He could feel Siddhartha nodding. "Not the nothing I can sometimes get from meditating—the feeling of oneness with the world—rather, it is the nothing of a total lack of feeling." God felt himself losing control, wanting to... what? Cry? Jump? Scream? Kill? Just like he had felt before, anything to purge this feeling, the reason for him being there.

He opened his eyes, not being able to stand the silence from Siddhartha. For years, his mind was filled with the voices of his children: living, loving, sinning, asking for forgiveness. He welcomed those thoughts because he felt needed, complete; it was what he had created and was responsible for. But over the past century, the voices in his head had become louder. At one time he could control the volume, could focus on one or another person, but over the past century he felt himself losing that control.

"I feel you are deeply troubled, my friend," Siddhartha finally said with a deep smile.

God sighed. "I confess I have not been getting better."

"The meditation has not helped?" Sid asked, with deep frown lines forming ridges in the middle of his forehead.

"Yes," God sighed, "and no. It has opened up more problems, more inquiries, more roads I have been afraid to travel. But there is one thing I have come to realize—rather, question."

Siddhartha, in all his wisdom and tolerance—that God wished he had—waited patiently, staring at God with a love that he would probably show Satan if Satan were sitting in this spot, farting and cursing and smoking his doobie. "Why did I make man?"

Siddhartha remained still. They never really questioned

each other's religion, just talked about enlightening one another; in turn, trying to bring these skills and habits to their brethren. God did not wait for a too-awkward silence to pass and tried to answer his own question. "I thought it was because I wanted to give something back for my existence, to see where I came from, to see if perhaps I could be duplicated. Do you understand what I mean?"

"Of course I do, my friend. Are you the chicken or the egg?"

God smiled, but continued quickly after Sid's last word, for he felt he needed to purge this. "But through my meditation I have come to realize something different. I have come to realize that they will never become like me because I will not let them."

Siddhartha remained pensive, nodding thoughtfully, the smile gone, the ridges on his forehead returning, even deeper. "How can you control what they do? I thought we agreed that man is responsible for his actions. A righteous life will lead to a righteous afterlife; you believe in the same. We take different paths to reach a similar destination."

"But when I look at what is happening down there, how can it be so?"

"What does that have to do with you?"

God reddened, became flustered. "I created it!" he yelled.

Still, Siddhartha remained calm. "A ton of bricks."

"Eh?" God asked.

"The guilt you have. You are holding on to it like a ton of bricks."

God shuffled uneasily on his behind; he tugged hard on his beard, curling the freed strands of hair around his index finger. "Don't you ever feel it?" he asked quietly.

"Yes."

"How can you just sit there, calmly, while all of this is going on? They are killing themselves down there! What have we done?" He rose up, towering over Siddhartha, who did not even move his head to look at him; instead, his friend was staring straight forward, between God's legs. His attention seemed so focused that God turned to make sure there was nothing behind him.

"Who told you to look behind you?" Siddhartha asked.

"I thought that perhaps there was someone behind me, because, well, I know you are the calm one, the enlightened one, but I thought my outburst would have made you flinch, even a little."

"But who told you to look behind you?"

"I just told you."

"No, you told me that I did not react to you standing up, bent over me, raising your voice, so you looked behind you. Who told you to *look* behind you?"

God stroked his beard, calmer this time. "No one. I just reacted to the stimuli I perceived."

"And suppose behind you there was the one who created you, raising his weaponed arm, ready to strike you down."

"I would defend myself."

"Would you kill this person, this person who created *you*?"

"I... I don't know."

"My friend. You are not the cause of their suffering, just as your Creator is not the cause of your suffering and so on. Just as you reacted to my un-reaction, so do they react to stimuli around them. It is not one thing, but rather a mixture of how we react, why we react, and what those reactions bring about that matters."

"And what if they destroy themselves?"

"Ah, now there is the conundrum again: Which came first, the chicken or the egg?"

"Can we exist without them?" God asked quietly. He had pondered this question since he became *aware*, because there was an emptiness that attached itself to his awareness, constantly following him no matter where he traveled in the cosmos, like a ball and chain; yet, once he made the Earth with abundant life and man came along to worship him, he found that the emptiness dissipated. Like an empty glass filling with clear water, the emptiness was forced out.

It was all so simple in the beginning: man, woman, and their children, all living together; then, as expected, communities which shared similar interests and goals; then, as expected, independent thinkers, great thinkers, and great, yet evil, thinkers; and, as expected, skirmishes leading to wars. But, unexpectedly, just as he had found himself, so did man have to find himself. Should it not have happened by now?

God winced when they cut down the jungles, but his underlings convinced him in the end it was to clear the path to truth, and along the way the raw materials would be used to build their houses and keep them warm during the cold nights. And when they created such wonderful machines he smiled with pride, but those machines came with a price, and they were now in debt trying desperately to pay that price. And when they began to look inward, rather than outward, he thought they would find their true purpose and this would satiate him, but instead they concentrated on how they could manipulate that knowledge to their desire. And the first time he saw that mushroom cloud, he knew the world would change forever, for never had their been such an invention that could destroy so much in so little time, rendering the natural order of things obsolete.

"You have discovered something about yourself!" Siddhartha said proudly and God opened his eyes, his hands resting on the sides of his knees, his breathing deep and steady, and his senses more acute. For the first time he saw something unfamiliar in the nothingness: the space between him and Siddhartha was actually filled with microscopic living things, a chaotic conglomeration of what he could only describe as spermatozoa with their dog-wagging tails, eager to unite but finding no ovum.

"What—" Unexpectedly, the spermatozoa spiraled away, north, south, east, and west, and he was once again left with just Siddhartha, and his friend looked worried, more worried than he had ever seen him. A tree appeared adjacent to Siddhartha. His friend's eyes watered. God was about to ask what was happening, but suddenly Siddhartha and the tree were yanked away, as if a great invisible hand had penetrated the nothingness, swiped them away, the owner of the hand jealous of having to share Siddhartha with someone, even someone as almighty as God, for any time.

Through the hole they were ripped from, God saw what he realized was the first instance of his great depression, the first time he had realized he may have made a mistake, only this one was new: a great billowing cloud of smoke reaching outward in concentric destructive circles and annihilating everything in its sight, not distinguishing between animal, vegetable, or mineral, between nature and non-nature. God reached out but when he placed his hand in the hole separating his space from the other place, it stung. His hand burned and he pulled it toward his body, grimacing at the painful pustules forming on the back.

Orange-red holes pierced through the nothingness, starting like tiny pinpoints and quickly expanding into flames, burning away at the nothingness and leaving a sulphurous smell in the air. God backed away from the flames; not scared from the heat that now filtered from the other side, and, like an osmotic skin, began to circulate on this side; not frightened at the sudden extraction of The Buddha; he was terrified at the fact that he did not exactly know what was happening, because *here* he was always cut off from the 'world.' He felt that the same hole which began to destroy the nothingness had somehow invaded his brain and was now eating away at his memory.

"Yo, G!" he heard Satan scream from the other side. "Wake the fuck up! It's war! It's war!" God jumped up and felt light-headed at the sudden body shift. His forehead dripped with sweat. He looked up to see a gaping hole with an orange-red flaming edge. Muffled human screams started strong but quickly died away. The other side of the opened circle was blurry, but he recognized the chaos.

"C'mon, before it's too late!" Satan screamed.

Remembering where he had entered, God looked to his left, and the nothingness remained untouched. He ran toward it, stumbling, feeling dizzy. Popping sounds and searing heat chased him. Flames lapped at his robe bottom and quickly jumped up, and up, engulfing the silk covering his chest and upper arms. God ripped his robe open, threw it aside and felt his adrenaline rise at the sound of fire eating the robe, yet still popping and thundering for more food.

He ran naked, feeling freer and lighter but still dizzy and confused, and when he thought he couldn't take the searing heat any longer he jumped toward the haze of nothingness.

Huge hands shook his body and great heated waves of foul-smelling air brushed against his face. He awoke to scary, wide, black eyes piercing into him. "Finally," Satan said, breathing heavily.

God tried to push him away and was shocked at how weak his own body felt. Where was he now? Why was he with his enemy? Satan scrutinized him, seeming to try to assess him, test him. "You're forgetting too, huh?" Satan asked.

Instinctively, God knew not to answer yes, yet he did by nodding.

"Listen, something is happening. I can't get in touch with my people down there. Can you?" Satan asked.

People? God shook his head.

"Shit," Satan said. "Listen, someone pushed the button. I think it was somewhere in Asia. There was live feed on CNN and then everything went black. India, China, gone."

"I have a friend in India," God said, suddenly remembering the great loss he had just experienced.

"Whoop-de-do. I got friends in India too. Lots of people wanting to take advantage of the poor. They're dead. And it's affecting us. Do you know why?"

The holes that had been slowly eating away inside God's brain seemed to be toying with him now. The synapses between neurons wanted to fire, to spark those memories, but he felt their microscopic strands slowly disintegrating.

"We are losing," God said.

"What do you mean 'we,' white man?" Satan said but with no mock smile. Suddenly, the TV snapped on, followed by the long, droning beep that sparked a memory. God used to hear that beep many times. That was when the voices began getting louder in his head, when he couldn't turn the volume down, couldn't control them. The beep was usually followed by:

" — carefully and in an orderly fashion, walk down to your building's basement if you live in an apartment; if there is food and water in your home, take it down with you along with batteries, radios, and flashlights. Take only canned food, non-perishables. Toilet paper, extra clothes. Please leave pets where they are; law enforcement has specific instructions to not accept any pets unless you are disabled. Also, take your medication. All pharmacies will be instructed to only dole out a thirty-day supply of medications until further notice." Yes, the newscasters' current instructions seemed oddly familiar.

Cars screeched around corners, vroomed loudly along 82nd street. Horn blasts bounced off the closely situated buildings and made their way up to the eighteenth floor. Shouts, curses, screams, windows breaking, people shuffling up and down the hall. Their doorbell rang.

God looked at Satan. Satan looked at God. Neither of them got up. They just stared at each other, because they realized how dire the situation had become.

"We are trapped," God said, rushed but quiet.

"They shouldn't be able to know we're here, right?" Satan asked.

The TV died again. Someone in the apartment next door started screaming. "The line went dead. They hit California!" More screams from outside, more horns, different languages, gunshots.

"What have we done with our existence?" Something in the way Satan sat forced a spark in one of God's dying synapses; he scrunched his eyebrows close together and tried hard, harder to think. Was it what Satan said? Yes and no.

God sat down across from Satan. Satan was thinking pensively, with his chin in the palms of his hands. He seemed about to cry. "What did it all mean?" he asked himself.

Again, somewhere in the recesses of God's brain, sparks ignited and stranded thoughts found a home, made connections, and for a moment God detached himself from the increasingly louder screams emanating from the mayhem outside.

He closed his eyes, breathing in and out. At first, his short-term memory attached itself to his fear of the nothingness he had escaped from, his friend and mentor, Sie — Sid, Siddhartha. Why did he disappear? He felt this was crucial in understanding his current situation. God's breathing became shallow again and he concentrated on the breath, on elongating the time between each breath.

Yes. That was why. The first strike killed many of Siddhartha's followers, of those who believed in him. But he was human, wasn't he? So why did he go away?

And what was Siddhartha? He was first, God was Creator and Master, was he not? That is what they believed?

"We're doomed," Satan cried. He began to whimper and God remained with his eyes closed but reached out his hand, stroked Satan's hands until they stopped trembling.

As Satan calmed, more of God's synapses began to fire. He opened his eyes. "I forgive you, Lucifer."

Lucifer collapsed before him, bowing deeply and wetting God's naked leg flesh with his tears.

Which came first, the chicken or the egg?

The building shook and then everything went black.

* * *

God caressed the smoothness of his cheeks and smiled. He cracked his knuckles when the elevator door opened on the eighteenth floor. The stair exit door opened and Lucifer popped through, panting but smiling. Through heavy breaths he said, "Hey G, you look pretty sharp without the beard. It took years off your appearance."

God smiled again and shook his friend's hand "Afraid to take the elevator with me?" God asked.

Lucifer mockingly backed away and then punched God in the shoulder. He patted his belly. "Tryin' to lose a few pounds. I always come in the same body and realized it's because it's how I really see myself. Thought I'd try the long way this time."

God smiled appraisingly and said out of the side of his mouth, "Try shaving a foot-long beard for the first time."

They stared in each other's eyes and then began walking to apartment 18E. "I kinda understand why you picked this place for the Summit, but is it the safest place? I mean, the humans are still trying to rebuild."

God walked a little slower and said, "That's why I picked it. I didn't want anyone to feel they had the upper hand. This is unprecedented, all of us meeting in one place like this, and it took the almost total annihilation of the human species to make it happen."

"You would think the humans control us, and not the other way around."

"Which came first, the chicken or the egg?"

Lucifer scrunched his nose. "Don't gimme that philosophical crap. I always knew we needed them. Why do you think there are no rules down there? Keep 'em happy. Keep 'em sad. Keep 'em scared. Whatever they want!"

"How are you managing with the influx of new arrivals?" God asked.

"Ain't no thing," Lucifer responded as they turned the corner. Already, they heard heated debating from the corner apartment, and recognized their peers by the differing accents and languages. "That mass annihilation scared the piss out of 'em; they're happy to be somewhere where things actually make sense. What about you?"

God didn't quite sigh, but there was a pang of regret. "It's sometimes tough. You were right, order does come with a price. We've got a long line, and some complaints, but I know we'll get there. All they have is time—something they didn't realize while they were here."

"Is your friend coming?" Satan asked with a twinge of jealousy.

"I hope so. We can't rewrite the rules without him. After all, he suggested the first rule."

Lucifer arched an eyebrow. "Being?"

God smiled as they reached the door and he turned the knob.

"'No Nukes.'"

*T*his story is an excerpt from Dan Barker's excellent book Godless: How an Evangelical Preacher Became One of America's Leading Atheists. *Dan is a former evangelical preacher who became an atheist and currently is co-president of the Freedom from Religion Foundation with his wife, Annie Laurie Gaylor.* Godless *begins as something of an autobiography and becomes a grand argument against religion, but in between is Chapter Nine. It's entitled "Dear Theologian," and appears as a letter from God in which he asks some deep philosophical and logical questions of his believer.* Godless *is an absolute must-read for any atheist — and should be for any theist — but "Dear Theologian" struck me immediately as one of the finest summations of what's wrong with those who believe. Dan has graciously allowed me to reprint it here.*

Dear Theologian

Dan Barker

Dear Theologian,

I have a few questions, and I thought you would be the right person to ask. It gets tough sometimes, sitting up here in heaven with no one to talk to. I mean really talk to. I can always converse with the angels, of course, but since they don't have free will, and since I created every thought in their submissive minds, they are not very stimulating conversationalists.

Of course, I can talk with my son Jesus and with the "third person" of our holy trinity, the Holy Spirit, but since we are all the same, there is nothing we can learn from each other. There are no well-placed repartees in the Godhead. We all know what the others know. We can't exactly play chess. Jesus sometimes calls me "Father," and that feels good, but since he and I are the same age and have the same powers, it doesn't mean much.

You are educated. You have examined philosophy and world religions, and you have a degree which makes you qualified to carry on a discussion with someone at my level — not that I can't talk with anyone, even with the uneducated believers who fill the churches and flatter me with endless petitions, but you know how it is. Sometimes we all crave interaction with a respected colleague. You have read the scholars. You have written papers and published books about me, and you know me better than anyone else.

It might surprise you to think that I have some questions. No, not rhetorical questions aimed at teaching spiritual lessons, but some real, honest-to-God inquiries. This should not shock you because, after all, I created you in my image. Your inquisitiveness is an inheritance from me. You would say that love, for example, is a reflection of my nature within yourself, wouldn't you? Since questioning is healthy, it also comes from me.

Somebody once said that we should prove all things, and hold fast that which is good. My first question is this:

Where did I come from?

I find myself sitting up here in heaven, and I look around and notice that there is nothing else besides myself and the objects that I have created. I don't see any other creatures competing with me, nor do I notice anything above myself that might have created me, unless it is playing hide-and-seek. In any event, as far as I know (and I supposedly know everything), there is nothing else but me in-three-persons and my creations. I have always existed, you say. I did not create myself, because if I did, then I would be greater than myself.

So where did I come from?

I know how you approach that question regarding your own existence. You notice that nature, especially the human mind, displays evidence of intricate design. You have never observed such design apart from a designer. You argue that human beings must have had a creator, and you will find no disagreement from me.

Then, what about me? Like you, I observe that my mind is complex and intricate. It is much more complex than your mind, otherwise I couldn't have created your mind. My personality displays evidence of organization and purpose. Sometimes I surprise myself at how wise I am. If you think your existence is evidence of a designer, then what do you think about my existence? Am I not wonderful? Do I not function in an orderly manner? My mind is not a random jumble of disconnected thoughts; it displays what you would call evidence of design. If you need a designer, then why don't I?

You might think such a question is blasphemy, but to me there is no such crime. I can ask any question I want, and I think this is a fair one. If you say that everything needs a designer and then say that not everything (Me) needs a designer, aren't you contradicting yourself? By excluding me from the argument, aren't you bringing your conclusion into your argument? Isn't that circular reasoning? I am not saying I disagree with your conclusion; how could I? I'm just wondering why it is proper for you to infer a designer while it is not proper for me.

If you are saying that I don't need to ask where I came from because I am perfect and omniscient while humans are fallible, then you don't need the design argument at all, do you? You have already assumed that I exist. You can make such an assumption, of course, and I would not deny you the freedom. Such *a priori* and circular reasoning might be helpful or comforting to you, but it does me little good. It doesn't help me figure out where I came from.

You say that I am eternally existent, and I suppose I would have no objection if I knew what it meant. It is hard for me to conceive of eternal existence. I just can't remember back that far. It would take me an eternity to remember back to eternity, leaving me no time to do anything else, so it is impossible for me to confirm if I existed forever. And even if it is true, why is eternal greater than temporal? Is a long sermon greater than a short sermon? What does "greater" mean? Are fat people greater than thin people, or old greater than young?

You think it is important that I have always existed. I'll take your word for it, for now. My question is not with the duration of my existence, but with the origin of my existence. I don't see how being eternal solves the problem. I still want to know where I came from.

I can only imagine one possible answer, and I would appreciate your reaction. I know that I exist. I know that I could not have created myself. I also know that there is no higher God who could have created me. Since I can't look above myself, then perhaps I should look below myself for a creator. Perhaps — this is speculative, so bear with me — perhaps you created me.

Don't be shocked. I mean to flatter you. Since I contain evidence of design, and since I see no other place where such design could originate, I am forced to look for a designer, or designers, in nature itself. You are a part of nature. You are intelligent — that is what your readers say. Why should I not find the answer to my question in you? Help me out on this.

Of course, if you made me, then I could not have made you, I think. The reason that I think I made you is because you made me to think I made you. You have often said that a Creator can put thoughts in your mind. Isn't it possible that you have put thoughts in my mind, and now here we are, both of us, wondering where we each came from?

Some of you have said that the answer to this whole question is just a mystery that only God understands. Well, thanks a lot. The buck stops here. On the one hand you use logic to try to prove my existence, but on the other hand, when logic hits a dead end, you abandon it and invoke "faith" and "mystery." Those words might be useful to you as place-holders for facts or truth, but they don't translate to anything meaningful as far as I am concerned. You can pretend that "mystery" signifies something terribly important, but to me it simply means you don't know.

Some of you assert that I did not "come" from anywhere. I just exist. However, I have also heard you say that nothing comes from nothing. You can't have it both ways. I either exist or I don't. What was it that caused me to exist, as opposed to not existing at all? If I don't need a cause, then why do you? Since I am not happy to say that this is a mystery, I must accept the only explanation that makes sense. You created me.

Is that such a terrible idea? I know that you think many other gods were created by humans: Zeus, Thor, Mercury, Elvis. You recognize that such deities originate in human desire, need, or fear. If the blessed beliefs of those billions of individuals can be dismissed as products of culture, then why can't yours? The Persians created Mithra, the Jews created Yahweh, and you created me. If I am wrong about this, please straighten me out.

My next question is this:

What's it all about?

Maybe I made myself, maybe some other god made me, maybe you made me—let's put that aside for now. I'm here now. Why am I here? Many of you look up to me for purpose in life, and I have often stated that your purpose in life is to please me. (Read Revelation 4:11.) If your purpose is to please me, what is my purpose? To please myself? Is that all there is to life?

If I exist for my own pleasure, then this is selfish. It makes it look as if I created you merely to have some living toys to play with. Isn't there some principle that I can look up to? Something to admire, adore, and worship? Am I consigned for eternity to sit here and amuse myself with the worship of others? Or to worship myself? What's the point?

I have read your writings on the meaning of life, and don't misunderstand me, they make sense in the theological context of human religious goals, even if they don't have much practicality in the real world. Many of you feel that your purpose in life is to achieve perfection. Since you humans fall way short of perfection, by your own admission (and I agree), then self improvement provides you with a quest. It gives you something to do. Someday you hope to be as perfect as you think I am. But since I am already perfect, by definition, then I don't need such a purpose. I'm just sort of hanging out, I guess.

Yet I still wonder why I'm here. It feels good to exist. It feels great to be perfect. But it gives me nothing to do. I created the universe with all kinds of natural laws that govern everything from quarks to galactic clusters, and it runs okay on its own. I had to make these laws, otherwise I would be involved with a lot of repetitive busy work, such as pulling light rays through space, yanking falling objects down to the earth, sticking atoms together to build molecules, and a trillion other boring tasks more worthy of a slave than a master. You have discovered most of those laws, and might be on the verge of putting the whole picture together, and once you have done that you will know what I know: that there is nothing in the universe for me to do. It's boring up here.

I could create more universes and more laws, but what's the point? I've already done universes. Creation is like sneezing or writing short stories; it just comes out of me. I could go on an orgy of creation. Create, create, create. After a while a person can get sick of the same thing, like when you eat a whole box of chocolates and discover that the last piece doesn't taste as good as the first. Once you have had ten children, do you need twenty? (I'm asking you, not the pope.) If more is better, then I am obligated to continue until I have fathered an infinite number of children, and an endless number of universes. If I must compel myself, then I am a slave.

Many of you assert that it is inappropriate to seek purpose within yourself, that it must come from outside. I feel the same way. I can't merely assign purpose to myself. If I did, then I would have to look for my reasons. I would have to come up with an account of why I chose one purpose over another, and if such reasons came from within myself I would be caught in a loop of self-justified rationalizations. Since I have no Higher Power of my own, then I have no purpose. Nothing to live for. It is all meaningless.

Sure, I can bestow meaning on you—pleasing me, achieving perfection, whatever—and perhaps that is all that concerns you; but doesn't it bother you, just a little, that the source of meaning for your life has no source of its own? And if this is true, then isn't it also true that ultimately you have no meaning for yourself either? If it makes you happy to demand an external reference point on which to hang your meaningfulness, why would you deny the same to me? I also want to be happy, and I want to find that happiness in something other than myself. Is that a sin?

On the other hand, if you think I have the right and the freedom to find happiness in myself and in the things I created, then why should you not have the same right? You, whom I created in my image?

I know that some of you have proposed a solution to this problem. You call it "love." You think I am lonely up here, and that I created humans to satisfy my longing for a relationship with something that is not myself. Of course, this will never work because it is impossible for me to create something that is not part of myself, but let's say that I try anyway. Let's say that I create this mechanism called "free will," which imparts to humans a choice. If I give you the freedom (though this is stretching the word because there is nothing outside of my power) not to love me, then if some of you, a few of you, even one of you chooses to love me, I have gained something I might not have had. I have gained a relationship with someone who could have chosen otherwise. This is called love, you say.

This is a great idea, on paper. In real life, however, it turns out that millions, billions of people have chosen not to love me, and that I have to do something with these infidels. I can't just un-create them. If I simply destroy all the unbelievers, I may as well have created only believers in the first place. Since I am omniscient, I would know in advance which of my creations would have a tendency to choose me, and this would produce no conflict with free will since those who would not have chosen me would have been eliminated simply by not having been created in the first place. (I could call it Supernatural Selection.) This seems much more compassionate than hell.

You can't have a love relationship with someone who is not your equal. If you humans don't have a guaranteed eternal soul, like myself, then you are worthless as companions. If I can't respect your right to exist independently, and your right to choose something other than me, then I couldn't love those of you who do choose me. I would have to find a place for all those billions of eternal souls who reject me, whatever their reasons might be. Let's call it "hell," a place that is not-God, not-me. I would have to create this inferno, otherwise neither I nor the unbelievers could escape each other. Let's ignore the technicalities of how I could manage to create hell, and then separate it from myself, apart from whom nothing else exists. (It's not as though I could create something and then simply throw it away — there is no cosmic trash heap.) The point is that since I am supposedly perfect, this place of exile must be something that is the opposite. It must be ultimate evil, pain, darkness, and torment.

If I created hell, then I don't like myself.

If I did create a hell, then it certainly would not be smart to advertise that fact. How would I know if people were claiming to love me for my own sake, or simply to avoid punishment? How can I expect someone to love me who is afraid of me in the first place? The threat of eternal torment might scare some people into obedience, but it does nothing to inspire love. If you treated me with threats and intimidations, I would have to reconsider my admiration for your character.

How would you feel if you had brought some children

into the world knowing that they were going to be tormented eternally in a place you built for them? Could you live with yourself? Wouldn't it have been better not to have brought them into the world in the first place?

I know that some of you feel that hell is just a metaphor. Do you feel the same way about heaven?

Anyway, this whole love argument is wrong. Since I am perfect, I don't lack anything. I can't be lonely. I don't need to be loved. I don't even want to be loved because to want is to lack. To submit to the potential of giving and receiving love is to admit that I can be hurt by those who choose not to love me. If you can hurt me, I am not perfect. If I can't be hurt, I can't love. If I ignore or erase those who do not love me, sending them off to hell or oblivion, then my love is not sincere. If all I am doing is throwing the dice of "free will" and simply reaping the harvest of those who choose to love me, then I am a selfish monster. If you played such games with people's lives, I would call you insensitive, conceited, insecure, selfish and manipulative.

I know you have tried to get me off the hook. You explain that Yours Truly is not responsible for the sufferings of unbelievers because rejection of God is their choice, not mine. They had a corrupt human nature, you explain. Well, who gave them their human nature? If certain humans decide to do wrong, where do they get the impulse? If you think it came from Satan, who created Satan? And why would some humans be susceptible to Satan in the first place? Who created that susceptibility? If Satan was created perfect, and then fell, where did the flaw of perdition come from? If I am perfect, then how in God's name did I end up creating something that would not choose perfection? Someone once said that a good tree cannot bring forth evil fruit.

Here is the title for your next theological tome: Was Eve Perfect? If she was, she would not have taken the fruit. If she wasn't, I created imperfection.

Maybe you think all of this gives me a purpose—putting Humpty Dumpty back together—but it actually gives me a headache. (If you won't permit me a simple headache, then how can you allow me the pain of lost love?) I could not live with myself if I thought my actions were causing harm to others. Well, I shouldn't say that. Since I think you created me, I suppose I should let you tell me what I could live with. If you think it is consistent with my character to tolerate love and vengeance concurrently, then I have no choice. If you are my creator, then I could spout tenderness out of one side of my mouth and brutality out of the other. I could dance with my lover on the bones of my errant children, and pretend to enjoy it. I would be very human indeed.

I have a thousand more questions, but I hope you will allow me one more:

How do I decide what is right and wrong?

I don't know how I got here, but I'm here. Let's just say that my purpose is to make good people out of my creations. Let's say that I am to help you learn how to be perfect like me, and that the best way is for you to act just like me, or like I want you to act. You goal is to become little mirrors of myself. Won't that be splendid? I'll give you rules or principles, and you try to follow them. This may or may not be meaningful, but it will keep us both busy. I suppose that from your point of view this would be terribly meaningful, since you think I have the power to reward and punish.

I know that some of you Protestant theologians think that I give rewards not for good deeds, but simply for believing in my son Jesus who paid the punishment for your bad deeds. Well, Jesus spent only about thirty-six hours of an eternal life sentence in hell and is now back up here in ultimate coziness with me. Talk about a wrist-slap! He was not paroled for good behavior—he was simply released. (He had connections.) If my righteous judgment demanded absolute satisfaction, then Jesus should have paid the price in full, don't you think?

Beyond that, it is entirely incomprehensible to me why you think I would accept the blood of one individual for the crime of another. Is that fair? Is that justice? If you commit a felony, does the law allow your brother to serve the jail sentence for you? If someone burglarized your home, would you think justice was served if a friend bought you new furniture? Do you really think that I am such a bloodthirsty dictator that I will be content with the death of anyone for the crime of another? And are you so disrespectful of justice that you would happily accept a stand-in for your crimes? What about personal responsibility? It is tough to open my arms to welcome believers into heaven who have avoided the rap for their own actions. Something is way out of kilter here.

But let's ignore these objections. Let's assume that Jesus and I worked it all out and that evil will be punished and good rewarded. How do I know the difference? You are insisting that I not consult any rule book. You are asking me to be the Final Authority. I must simply decide, and you must trust my decision. Am I free to decide whatever I want?

Suppose I decide that I would like you to honor me with a day of my own. I like the number seven, I don't know why, maybe because it is the first useless number. (You never sing any hymns to me in 7/4 time.) Let's divide the calendar into groups of seven days and call them weeks. For harmony, I'll divide each lunar phase into roughly seven days. The last day of the week—or maybe the first day, I don't care—I'll set aside for myself. Let's call it the Sabbath. This all feels good, so I suppose it is the right thing to do. I'll make a law ordering you to observe the Sabbath, and if you do it then I will pronounce you good people. In fact, I'll make it one of my Big Ten Commandments, and I'll order your execution if you disobey. This all makes perfect sense, I don't know why.

Help me out here. How am I supposed to choose what is moral? Since I can't consult any authority, the thing to do, it appears, is to pick randomly. Actions will become right or wrong simply because I declare them to be so. If I whimsically say that you should not make any graven or molten images of "anything that is in heaven above, or that is in the earth beneath, or that is in the water under the earth," then that is that. If I decide that murder is right and compassion is wrong, you will have to accept it.

Is that all there is to it? I just decide, willy-nilly, what is right and what is wrong? Or worse, I decide based on whatever makes me feel good? I have read in some of your literature that you denounce such self-centered attitudes.

Some of you say that since I am perfect, I can't make any mistakes. Whatever I choose to be right or wrong will be in accordance with my nature, and since I am perfect, then my choices will be perfect. In any event, my choices will certainly be better than your choices, you feel. But what does "perfect" mean? If my nature is "perfect" (whatever it means), then I am living up to a standard. If I am living up to a standard, then I am not God. If perfection means something all by itself, apart from me, then I am constrained to follow its path. If, on the other hand, perfection is defined simply as conformity to my nature, then it doesn't mean anything. My nature can be what it wants, and perfection will be defined accordingly. Do you see the problem here? If "perfection" equals "God," then it is just a synonym for myself, and we can do away with the word. We could do away with either word, take your pick.

If I am perfect, then there are certain things that I cannot do. If I am not free to feel envy, lust, or malice, for example, then I am not omnipotent. I cannot be more powerful than you if you can feel and do things that I cannot.

Additionally, if you feel that God is perfect, by nature, what does "nature" mean? The word is used to describe the way things are or act in nature, and since you think I am above nature, you must mean something else, something like "character," or "attributes." To have a nature or character means to be one way and not another. It means that there are limits. Why am I one way and not another? How did it get decided that my nature would be what it is? If my "nature" is clearly defined, then I am limited. I am not God. If my nature has no limits, as some of you suggest, then I have no nature at all, and to say that God has such-and-such a nature is meaningless. In fact, if I have no limits, then I have no identity; and if I have no identity, then I do not exist.

Who am I?

This brings me back to the conundrum: if I don't know who I am, then how can I decide what is right? Do I just poke around in myself until I come up with something?

There is one course I could pursue, and some of you have suggested this for yourselves. I could base my pronouncements on what is best for you humans. You people have physical bodies that bump around in a physical world. I could determine those actions that are healthy and beneficial for material beings in a material environment. I could make morality something material: something that is relative to human life, not to my whims. I could declare (by conclusion, not by edict) that harming human life is bad, and that helping or enhancing human life is good. This would be like providing an operation manual for something I designed and manufactured. It would require me to know all about human nature and the environment in which you humans live, and to communicate these ideas to you.

This makes a lot of sense, but it changes my task from one of determining morality to one of communicating morality. If morality is discovered in nature, then you don't need me, except maybe to prod you along. I saw to it that you have capable minds with the ability to reason and do science. There is nothing mysterious about studying how humans interact with nature and with each other, and you should be able to come up with your own set of rules. Some of you tried this millennia before Moses. Even if your rules contradict mine, I couldn't claim any higher authority than you. At least you would be able to give reasons for your rules, which I can only do by submitting to science myself.

If morality is defined by how human beings exist in nature, then you don't need me at all. I am off the hook! From what I have read, most of you have your feet on the ground with no help from me. I could hand down some stone tablets containing what I think is right and wrong, but it would still be up to you to see if they work in the real world. I think we all agree that grounded reason is better than the whim of an ungrounded deity.

This is a wonderful approach, but what bothers me is that while this may help you know what is moral in your environment, it doesn't help me much. I don't have an environment. I'm out here flapping in the breeze. I envy you.

Nor does the humanistic approach help those of you who want morality to be rooted in something absolute, outside of yourselves. It must be frightening for you who need an anchor to realize that there is no bottom to the ocean. Well, it's frightening for me also. I don't have an anchor of my own. That's why I'm asking for your help.

Thank you for reading my letter, and for letting me impose on your busy schedule. Please answer at your convenience. I have all the time in the world.

Sincerely,

Yours Truly

W hat would an anthology of speculative, atheist-centric fiction, designed to have genres to appeal to everyone, be without an adventure story? Dan Thompson's is set in a dystopian future where the forces of religion are crusading to convert or destroy nonbelievers. It's a fun adventure tale set in a grim world where it's science combating religion, reason against insanity, and freedom fighters versus oppressors. And the battles for the survival of the heroes' ideals against the evils of religion are fought on the high seas, with Dan's extensive knowledge of old-style sailing ships. Bring on the naval warfare! The future of the entire world is at stake...

A New Broom

Dan Thompson

Severed human heads stared sightlessly at the shuttered windows of the buildings surrounding Tarragona's plaza, each decaying remain spiked on one of hundreds of tall poles planted in the paving. Some of the men in Sam Thorne's landing party swore godless curses at the gruesome display but most were struck speechless.

"The Brotherhood," their guide, Franco Ortiz, whispered. "Since they conquered Catalonia, the Brotherhood has been busy converting the heathen." He pointed to the rows of heads. "They are the ones who were too devout in their beliefs to accept God's Hand as the True Faith; Christians, mostly, and a few Jews and Muslims."

He led them to a corner of the plaza, where a large pile of broken machinery glinted in the moonlight. Suspended above the shattered brass, steel, and cast-iron apparatus, a wooden cage hung from a timber frame, holding the rotting remains of a man. Above his empty eye sockets, wisps of gray hair waved in the gentle breeze. White bones poked through tattered strips of cloth and flesh.

"Professor Morgan," Ortiz said. "When the Brotherhood discovered the Difference Engine in his workshop, it outraged them. Technology is the Great Evil. Science caused the Cataclysm. That's what they preach. When they found a working computer! Well, you can see for yourself."

The eruption of the super-volcano at Yellowstone had buried North America in ash and quickly killed millions. The dense clouds of ash that were blown into the atmosphere circled the world and brought a volcanic winter that lasted for years. The darkness, the cold, and the acid rain that fell from the black skies caused mass extinctions of plant and animal life. Ninety-five of every hundred humans on Earth died of starvation, disease, or at the hands of other humans in those terrible years. The survivors might have kept the machinery of civilization running, but rumors that the Cataclysm was a man-made creation, triggered by scientists' meddling with nature, spread nearly as fast as the ash clouds. The terrified and angry survivors smashed machines, burned books, and lynched anyone associated with science. A two-hundred-year Dark Age settled over the world. Now, a few isolated nations like Hypatia struggled back to civilization.

Anger froze Thorne. His people had stories that said computers had once changed the world. It would be generations, at least, before they could build one. They'd only recently rediscovered electricity. But then they got word about the Babbage Machine, a computer that they could build. Hypatia's leaders believed gaining it worth the risk of sending a ship, even though they had so few. They had placed their hopes and trust in him. They desperately needed an advantage in a world full of enemies that hated them because they refused to bow down to superstition. Now that hoped-for edge was nothing but a broken promise.

"Damn them to their own hell!" Thorne swore. He was too late. They'd made the long voyage through packs of icebergs drifting down almost to the Equator and a fierce storm off the coast of Africa that nearly sank them. Now he risked himself and his men in an enemy-occupied city—all for nothing. With Morgan dead and the Difference Engine destroyed, he'd failed his mission.

"It was horrible." Ortiz was still talking, quietly, staring at the cage. He hadn't heard Thorne at all. "They let him die of thirst. I came every day but I couldn't help him. I wouldn't let the *señorita* come here at all."

"You did well, friend." Thorne placed a comforting hand on the slight man's shoulder. He felt Ortiz trembling; whether from rage or sorrow, he didn't know. "Now, let's get away from this stinking place."

Ortiz led them to a large house just off the plaza. Inside, he lit an oil lamp, illuminating a large room furnished with comfortable-looking chairs and a table. Large, dark oak shelves lined one wall, filled with books in leather bindings and even a few with the colorful paper covers common before the Cataclysm. Thorne heard a soft scuffing sound and turned to see a young woman coming down a curved staircase of the same polished dark oak as the furniture and bookshelves.

She had raven-black hair woven in a heavy braid, and her face held an olive complexion. Dark eyes, a patrician nose, and a full mouth graced an oval face. A tight Catalonian dress showed to advantage her voluptuous figure. She was beautiful. And she held a small flintlock pistol in her right hand, pointed unwaveringly at Thorne's chest.

Carmen Morgan aimed the pistol at the big man standing next to Franco. Tall, nearly two meters, and broad-shouldered, he had long, dark-brown hair tied in a sailor's queue and a full but neatly trimmed beard. A wide-brimmed hat shaded cool, gray eyes. His deeply tanned, weathered face gave a false impression of age. She decided he wasn't more than five or six years older than she. She didn't doubt for a second that he was in command of the small band of tough-looking men.

He spread his arms, holding his empty hands level with his broad shoulders, and bowed slightly from the waist. "Samuel Clemens Thorne, commanding the Hypatian Navy schooner *Jefferson*, at your service, ma'am."

Carmen felt relief. The Hypatians were here, at last. And this Captain Thorne, there was something reassuring about him. She lowered the gun to her side. "I am Carmen Maria Morgan y Diego. Franco, take the Captain's men to the kitchen and get them something to eat. The Captain and I must talk."

Her loyal retainer led the sailors out, leaving her alone with the Hypatian officer. Carmen laid her pistol on the oiled-wood top of a sideboard and opened the lead-glass doors of the cabinet. "Would you care for some wine, Captain Thorne?"

"No thanks, señorita, I don't drink."

She poured herself a glass of the sweet, red wine for which Tarragona had long been famous, even before the Cataclysm. "Tell me, why are you here? All that my father said was that Hypatians would come."

"Apparently your father had been in communication with my government for some time. When the Brotherhood of God's Hand invaded, he asked to be taken to Hypatia with his computer. I received orders and piled on the sail. I'm deeply sorry we didn't get here in time."

BOOM! The door vibrated to a powerful blow and Carmen and the Captain turned toward it, startled. Another blow shattered the iron lock and the door flew open, sagging on its torn hinges. Thorne reached for his sidearm but stopped as a half-dozen men rushed in, their muskets raised and cocked. Carmen had forgotten her pistol and now was frozen by the sight of the man who stalked into the room after the soldiers. Taller even than Thorne, he was slender in comparison. He wore a black ankle-length robe with the hood thrown back to reveal pale skin drawn tightly over a narrow, bony face and white, bowl-cut hair. A wide leather belt supported a sheathed sword and a holster for the pistol he pointed at them.

"Corporal," the cadaverous intruder said in Spanish with a heavy Italian accent, "get their weapons. Then take your squad and secure the other infidels." He motioned with the pistol. "I'll take care of these two."

He strode up to the two prisoners as the soldiers hurried out of the room. His manner was tightly controlled but a small look of satisfaction crept into his expression. "I have been watching you, señorita. I knew you weren't as innocent as you pretended. Blood will tell. Let me introduce myself to your visitor. I am Brother Ignacio de Briganti, Inquisitor for this province." He turned to Thorne. "Who are you and what are you doing here?"

"The name's Sam Thorne. My business is my business."

Sounds of breaking crockery came from the kitchen, followed by silence. De Briganti pointed with his chin in that direction, "My men have taken yours into custody, Señor Thorne. I think your business is mine as well."

"Do you know this person, señorita?" Thorne asked.

An image flashed in Carmen's mind, one of de Briganti smiling as his men dragged her sweet, loving father, a man who had never harmed a soul in his life, from their home. Tears of rage blurred Carmen's vision. Carmen spat at his feet. "This swine killed my father."

De Briganti smiled and opened his mouth to respond, but her revulsion at his very presence overwhelmed her. Without warning, Carmen threw her glass at his face and it shattered. He screamed, staggering back, his hands flying up to his face to wipe the broken glass and burning liquid from his eyes.

Sam Thorne jumped, tackling the robed Brother. They went down in a tangled mess and rolled across the floor. Sam felt arms like steel cables wrap around him. The slender monk was surprisingly strong but Sam outweighed him and he used that extra mass and his own considerable power to shift their positions.

The rank smell of an unwashed body and garlic-tainted breath wafted around him as they struggled for advantage.

He broke the other man's grip and pinned him against the floor. De Briganti still had his pistol and pushed the barrel into Sam's side. Somehow, Sam got his hand on the pistol just as de Briganti pulled the trigger.

The hammer snapped against the web of soft flesh between Sam's thumb and finger. Sam grimaced but just slugged de Briganti three times, slamming his head back against the hardwood floor with each blow.

Sam stood up as Carmen grabbed her pistol off the sideboard and aimed at the rear doorway, ready for the Brotherhood soldiers to come charging in from the kitchen. Instead, a tough-looking, older Hypatian cautiously poked his head around the door frame. "You okay, Cap'n? We took care of those fellas back here."

The sailors quickly bound the unconscious invaders. Besides a few bruises, the Hypatians were unhurt. After a few minutes, and a helpful kick in the ribs from Carmen, de Briganti came around. He stared at Thorne, his dark eyes burning with unfathomed hatred.

"You better kill me, infidel," De Briganti snarled. "If you don't, I swear by God's Hand that I will hunt you down. I will follow you to the ends of the Earth, even into the heart of your unholy country if I must!"

"I'm tempted, Brother, but we don't kill prisoners," said Thorne. "I'll just have to take my chances. O'Brien, gag 'em. Señorita Morgan, please gather your things. I failed to save your father; I'll be damned if I leave you here to deal with this scum."

Carmen kicked de Briganti again, hard, and smiled slightly at his pained yelp. "Yes," she said, "this is no longer home."

Carmen Morgan insisted they stop at her family's *masia* south of Tarragona. They had the cover of darkness for the first part of the trip but the sun was well up when they reached the country farmhouse. The old farmer and his wife and son who ran the estate for Carmen were startled by the sight of a band of armed men marching up the dirt road, but the presence of Carmen and her explanation that they were friends calmed their fears. With the sailors settled and out of sight, she motioned for Sam to follow her.

"Come, I have something to show you," she said and led him up the stairs of the farmhouse and into a bedroom. She hid a smile when she saw Sam blush at the sight of the tall, ornately carved bed, but gave him no time to think. She went straight to a large wooden wardrobe against the far wall. She tripped the secret latch and, with a soft click, the whole wardrobe swung away from the wall.

In the exposed chamber beyond sat a long chest of oiled mahogany bound with tarnished brass straps. Sam knelt beside her as she lifted the lid. Inside lay the drawings for both the Difference Engine and for Babbage's more advanced design, his Analytical Engine. Carmen told him how her ancestor had brought the Difference Engine south from England to escape the advancing glaciers, to be guarded by her family for two hundred years since the Cataclysm.

She spread the aged rolls of paper on the bed and watched his expression. She could see a darkness pass from his face and his shoulders straightened slightly, as if a weight had been lifted from them. She felt happy, the first time since her father's murder, to know that she had eased his burden.

"You didn't come just to rescue me and my father, did you?" she asked. "You came for these?"

"You're right," Sam admitted. "Hypatia has many enemies, especially the nations under the sway of the Brotherhood. We're an abomination in their eyes because we're freethinkers, because we place reason above faith. Since our enemies fear science, our technological lead has kept us free. The capability contained in these plans, and the principles we'll learn from them, may ensure our survival."

"I give them to you. It's what my father wanted and now I want it, too," Carmen said. "I have something else that I think may help you in your fight, but it is important to me whether you can use it or not. Can you take it with us, too, *por favor?*"

"If it's in my power, I promise you'll have it," Sam swore.

Sam Thorne wondered what he was in for as he followed Carmen to the entrance of a cave in a bluff behind the *masia*. He'd made a promise, and he would keep it if at all possible. He just hoped whatever the young woman cared so much about would fit on the ship.

Inside, the cave was large and dry. Carmen stood, beaming, beside a construction of light wood covered with varnished cloth. Sam walked around it, his eyebrows drawn together in puzzlement. The machine, if that's what it was, looked vaguely familiar but he couldn't quite remember why.

"All right, I give up. What is it?"

"It's a glider. I designed and built it." Carmen radiated pride in her accomplishment. Sam's continuing incomprehension deflated her slightly. "It's an aircraft, it flies through the air. They had flying machines before the Cataclysm."

"You're serious, aren't you? This thing really can fly?" But even as Sam asked the questions, he knew the answer. He saw it then, the shape of the wings connected to the control surfaces by trusses made of slender wood members. The details of the construction were vastly different but the overall shape was like pictures of airplanes he'd seen in ancient books.

"Yes, I'm serious. I've flown it, several times, from the cliff above the cave. This is my work; I want to take it with us to Hypatia."

"Of course we'll take it. This is at least as important as the computer," Sam said and he meant it. The glider and the practical knowledge of flight it represented were likely to be more immediately useful to Hypatia than the plans for the computers.

* * *

Sam's crew found the glider easier to move than they had supposed. Carmen had designed the wings to come off for the trip up the cliff, and the whole thing didn't weigh a hundred pounds.

It was a great relief to be back in his ship. With fair winds and clear skies, they set course for the Straits of Gibraltar. The *Jefferson* was a two-masted topsail schooner. She displaced one hundred eighty-five tons with an overall length of one hundred fifty-five feet and was ninety-six feet on deck. Her main mast towered ninety-five feet above the water. She could carry ten thousand square feet of sail. Her long, sleek, low hull was built of Southern live oak and her raked masts and yards were white pine. Miles of rope supported and controlled the masts and yards, the standing rigging painted with black tar to protect it from the elements.

But dimensions and materials didn't really describe the ship. Those things, combined and worked by the skilled hands of men, became a complex creation that had grace and strength beyond any single component. She was a thing of beauty, dancing across the waves with the wind filling her sails. Sam loved the feel of the deck beneath his feet, the constant motion of the sea and the vibration from the rigging. He savored the aromas of wood, tarred rigging, and the sea, so different from the strange alien smells on land or even the shore. A ship was never quiet. The hull creaked, the rigging groaned, water rushed along the hull, and the wind whistled and roared. It was all music in his ears, making him feel at home again.

He showed Carmen around, proudly pointing out the schooner's advanced technology, like canned food and the spark-gap radio. With her, he wasn't embarrassed to confess his love for his rakish ship and her crew.

But he wasn't so unaware that he spent all their time talking about the *Jefferson*. Gentle questions about her life in Catalonia, her father, and his work drew her out. He was especially interested in how she came to build the glider. He enjoyed the way Carmen's face lit up when she described finding a decaying remnant of a book about aircraft—how, with her father's encouragement, she had built first models and then more and more sophisticated, full-sized craft.

It was obvious to Sam that Carmen loved flying like he loved sailing. He even tried to imagine ways to combine the two, flying aircraft from ships. The idea seemed too farfetched and impractical to discuss with anyone, but he enjoyed the mental exercise.

They were beating to windward on a port tack. The Cape of Tortosa was barely visible off the starboard beam. A shout from the masthead dispelled his relaxed mood.

"Deck there!" the lookout shouted down from the crosstrees. "Sail off the starboard bow."

"Can you make out what she is?" Thorne called through cupped hands.

"Aye, Cap'n, I can see her plain. She's a lateener, a big one."

Thorne climbed halfway up the mainmast shrouds and hooked an arm through the ratlines. He pulled his prized binoculars, a family heirloom, from their case and looked out to the horizon. He gently twirled the knurled focusing knob and a large xebec sprang into crystal clarity. Ports for ten guns a side pierced her garishly painted bulwarks, twice the *Jefferson's* armament. Thorne slid down a stay, one of the many heavy, tarred ropes steadying the mast, to the deck. They had some time until they closed the distance. He had Shapleigh, his first officer, send the hands to their noon meal.

The xebec's long, shallow hull and huge, triangular lateen sails made her a fast and maneuverable opponent. But the schooner was fast, too, and her fore and aft rig and deeper keel made her more weatherly. The Brotherhood's ship had the weather gauge and was trying to force him on to the lee shore. He had to seize the initiative. With a mile of water between the ships, he sent the crew to quarters.

"Up your helm!" Thorne shouted. "Hands to braces and sheets!"

The schooner's bowsprit swung through the wind. Her huge booms swept across the deck, their momentum carefully checked by sailors hauling on the sheets. Immediately, the xebec came up into the wind, paralleling his maneuver. Now both ships were sailing toward the distant north coast of Africa on converging courses.

Thorne noticed that Carmen Morgan was standing behind the wheel, trying to look small. He called Tommy Hayashi, the cook's helper but today serving as a powder monkey, to him. "Señorita, Tommy here is going to take you down to the cable tier. I'm afraid no place on board is completely safe, but that's the best I can do."

"Please, Captain," Carmen protested, "I prefer to stay on deck with you. I am not afraid."

"No, miss, I didn't reckon you were, but I'd feel better if you were below. Please, do it for me." *Because I cannot bear the thought of you getting hurt,* Sam thought.

She nodded in reluctant agreement and followed Tommy down the companionway.

The distance between the two ships closed to five hundred yards, too much for the squat carronades that lined the bulwarks. For the long, eighteen-pounder pivot gun mounted amidships, though, it might be possible. Thorne called to Jameson, the eighteen's gun-captain.

"Jameson, I'd be obliged if you would blow away that fella's rigging."

Jameson smiled. "Aye, aye, Captain. That we will."

The gun crew hauled on the gun's tackle and swung it around to point over the starboard gunwale. Jameson stood behind the gun, sighting down the barrel. He spoke quietly to his men, who made small adjustments to the gun's alignment with iron crowbars. Jameson waved everyone back, stood off to one side, and waited for the ship's uproll. He jerked the lanyard and the gun roared. A shaft of fire and smoke flashed from its muzzle and the big gun recoiled back on its slides. Thorne had his binoculars out, watching for the shot's fall. The sea spouted a few yards from the xebec's bow.

Even before the shot had landed, the gun's crew had it sponged and reamed and were starting to reload. The xebec's side billowed smoke and, seconds later, the sea around the schooner erupted. Sea water sprayed over the deck. A crash forward and a high-pitched scream meant at least one shot had hit.

When the spray settled, Thorne saw Adams, his second officer, leaning over a sailor with a three-foot splinter sticking out of his side. Another seaman sat nearby, grasping his right wrist with his left hand. Blood spurted from the mangled stump. Both men were silent in shock as their shipmates carried them below to the surgeon.

Jameson took careful aim and fired his second shot even as the xebec fired another broadside. Moments later, the xebec's foresail yard swung wildly as the ball found its target. The xebec's crew scrambled to repair the brace cut by the shot and in minutes had the sail back under control. But the Brotherhood ship had lost way and the schooner pulled ahead. Thorne thought it was time to make the next move.

"Men!" he shouted. He spoke in a calm, confident voice when he had their attention. "In a minute we're going to come about and run across the xebec's bow and rake her. Take your time, make every shot count. Remember, we're all infidels to them. Ask the bosun if you want to hear how the Brotherhood treated infidels in Catalonia." He saw grim nods of agreement.

"You're free men of Hypatia and a match for any superstitious slaves of the Brotherhood," he finished. "Let's hit them hard and send them crawling back to the Araxes River."

An enthusiastic cheer rang out. The gun crews slapped each other on the back, confident in their ability.

Tommy came up the companionway with a leather cartridge case in each hand. "Tommy," Thorne asked, smiling at the boy's concentration on his important job, "did you get Miss Morgan in the cable tier all right?"

Tommy flushed, "No, sir. She just wouldn't go. She's in sickbay, helping the surgeon with the wounded. Said she wanted to do something useful."

"I'm not surprised," Thorne said. He felt a flash of admiration for her bravery. "You did fine, Tommy, carry on."

Thorne's experienced eye measured the separation between the ships, their angle of approach and relative speeds. Finally, something clicked and he shouted the order.

"Helm up! Handsomely, now." The schooner's bow swung around and the sails boomed as they filled with wind on the opposite tack.

"Run out your guns!" The gun crews hauled the tackles and the black muzzles poked through their ports. The gun captains knelt behind their guns, their fists in the air to show they were ready.

The *Jefferson* raced toward the xebec. Thorne worried that he might have mistimed the tack, but no, as the distance closed he could see that they would just miss the enemy ship's bowsprit.

"As your guns bear!" he shouted. "Fire!"

Now! The schooner's bowsprit crossed the xebec's centerline. Almost instantly, the sharp crack of the nine-pounder bow chaser rang out, followed by the deeper sound of the foremost carronade firing. One by one, the other three carronades and the pivot gun fired into the xebec's bow as they crossed. In seconds, it was over. The *Jefferson* was past, the end of her mainsail boom clearing the xebec's bowsprit by inches.

Everyone was looking sternward, holding their breaths. Then a cheer rose, long and lusty, as the thinning smoke showed the mastless xebec down at the bow. Her stern lifted, and the enemy ship slipped beneath the waves.

The men of the *Jefferson* laughed or stood silent, waved their hats in the air or retreated from the mass of men gathered by the rail, each expressing in his own way the fact that they'd survived one more time. Suddenly, a deafening crack sounded. The *Jefferson*'s foremast, weakened by an unnoticed hit, tilted slowly, and then collapsed across the deck in a huge tangle of ruined rigging and broken spars.

The black schooner shuddered to a halt as the dragging wreckage acted like a huge sea anchor. The crippled ship drifted before the wind, helpless. Her crew began working at a feverish pitch to make repairs. Their lives and the future of their nation depended on their effort.

While they worked through the night, the wind died. The morning found the *Jefferson* with a new foremast jury-rigged but no breeze for her sails. Her crew lay about the deck, sweltering in the harsh Mediterranean sun, when the lookout reported two ships on the horizon.

Thorne climbed to the crosstrees with his binoculars. He saw two galleys, double-banked oars churning. He estimated they were making two or three knots. They were probably out of Acuna. The rowers would be tired after such a long pull, but they could still reach the *Jefferson* in seven or eight hours.

Sliding down a stay, he jumped to the quarterdeck, calling for his officers. As they gathered, he noticed that Carmen was again on deck, standing by the aft rail.

"Gentleman," Thorne said, "this is the situation. We are becalmed with two war galleys approaching. We can't maneuver. Each of those ships mounts a pair of twenty-four-pounders in the bow. They can row around to our stern and bow and pound us into flotsam. I'm looking for ideas."

"Well, sir," Shapleigh said, tugging at his blond mustaches as was his habit in thought, "we can put boats in the water and use them to turn the ship so that our batteries will bear."

"Good idea, Mister Shapleigh." Thorne had already considered that but didn't want to inhibit their thinking. "That will let us engage one of the galleys. Now, let's come up with a way to counter the other. Talk to your sections. We'll go to quarters about an hour before the galleys are in range. Dismissed."

"Captain," Carmen joined him when the others had dispersed, "is there no way to escape?"

Thorne shrugged. "The wind could come up at any time. We can easily outsail galleys. If it doesn't, I guess we'll have to fight."

"If I could just get my glider in the air," Carmen said quietly, as if thinking out loud, "I could drop something on them before they could shoot at the ship."

Thorne's head whipped around, his attention suddenly totally focused on his beautiful young companion. "What was that? Could your glider really get to the galleys while they're still out of range?"

"Yes, I think so, if I could get into the air with enough speed to gain altitude. I can't count on finding any thermals in these conditions, but yes, it might be possible."

Thorne's thoughts struggled with each other for a moment. On the one hand, he needed any advantage he could lay to hand if they were to win through this situation and survive. On the other hand, he realized now that he was in love with this woman, even though they had been together a very short time with little chance to get to know each other. It didn't matter; he loved her. He was as certain of it as he was that the sun would rise. And if he loved her, how could he let her take such a dangerous chance?

And just as certainly, he knew that he must. It was her right to defend herself and them all, as surely as it was his. He could not deny her that.

"Carmen, I haven't mentioned it because it seemed foolish, but I've been thinking about how to launch your glider from the ship. Just daydreaming, but it might work. Mister Shapleigh," he called to the first officer, "bring the bosun, the carpenter, and the gunner down to my cabin in fifteen minutes. Let's go, Carmen, we have some planning to do."

The *Jefferson's* builder never would have imagined her in her strange new configuration. Carmen Morgan marveled at how quickly the schooner's crew turned their captain's ideas into physical reality. Dozens of men worked like demons, and Carmen could only watch in awe. Saws ripped through planks and beams of wood, and hammers banged. Ropes were strung in ways she could barely follow. She quickly became involved in modifications to her glider as equipment was brought up from the ammunition magazine. The activity was furious and then, suddenly, it was done.

A timber A-frame supported the main boom parallel with the deck. Short slats nailed to the bottom of the massive spar gave it the look of a horizontal ladder. A lubberly looking arrangement replaced the normal rigging. The mainsail gaff extended over the ship's side with a spare anchor hanging from a block at its end, eighty feet above the water. The line from the anchor ran down to a snatch block on the deck, from there to a block at the end of the boom, and back to a sled resting on the slats, straddling the spar.

Her glider sat on the sled, attached by a hook that would release when the sled reached the end of the boom. The schooner's technicians had hurriedly modified the glider. Clusters of signal rockets, minus their explosive charges, hung under each wing. The gunner had gingerly hung nets of napalm-filled grenades from the sides of the small craft's cockpit. Sailors in wooden sailing ships feared nothing more than fire, so they handled the flammable liquid with great caution. The cutter and the whaleboat were in the water, to pick her up after the flight or to turn the ship if she failed.

Thorne strode over to where she stood next to her aircraft. "Carmen, I wish I could go instead," he said.

She looked up at him and saw the tenderness and concern

in his eyes. She didn't know exactly when she'd fallen in love with him, but there was no denying it. She reached up and touched his cheek. "Captain... Sam... that is gallant but silly. You outweigh me by at least thirty kilos and even if that weren't a consideration, I've flown before and you haven't, remember? Now help me into the cockpit."

He picked her up and dropped her into the cramped compartment. Carmen fastened the buckle of her restraining belt and tested the glider's controls. The ailerons at the ends of the huge, fabric-covered wings flapped up and down when she moved the stick. The rudder at the rear of the fuselage and the forward-mounted canard elevators worked perfectly, too.

"I'm ready," she said. Sam leaned over to check her safety belt. She put her arms around his neck and pulled him close to give him a long kiss. "For luck," she said. The crew cheered, but neither one of them really noticed. Sam stepped back and the carpenter handed him a hatchet. He looked around to see that everyone was clear.

"All right, on the count of three!" Thorne hollered. "One... two... three!"

The razor-sharp blade sliced the rope holding the sled. The anchor dropped. The line whined through the blocks. The glider accelerated toward the end of the boom.

Carmen concentrated on the tasks that had to be done in the right order in the next few seconds. Halfway down the boom, she closed the switch that ignited one of the clusters of rockets under each wing. The thrust slammed her back in her seat. She felt a jolt when the glider left the end of the boom. She pulled pack on the controls, sending the temporarily powered aircraft into a steep climb.

One rocket failed to fire, but since the other five in the cluster had, she could compensate for the unbalanced thrust. The rockets burned out after fifteen seconds and she pulled the pin that released the spent casings and ignited two more sets of rockets. When those had finished, she dropped them and the radio battery that had supplied the current to ignite them. She let the glider continue to climb until she felt the first hint of a stall. She leveled out and flew directly toward the two galleys that were now less than two kilometers away.

The napalm grenades were a standard Hypatian weapon. Normally, the user lit the short fuse just before throwing it. For this mission, the *Jefferson's* gunner added a glass jar containing a length of burning slow match to each net of grenades. As the glider passed over the leading galley, Carmen could see the crew looking up in amazement at her nearly mythical machine. Some soldiers on the quarterdeck lifted their muskets and fired, but the shots missed widely.

Carmen released a net of grenades and watched them arc down to strike the foredeck of the galley. The ceramic grenades smashed and sticky fountains of jellied petroleum sprayed all over the ship. The glass jar containing the slow match burst at the same time, and the hot ember at the end of the match ignited the napalm. The ship erupted in walls of searing flames. The sailors' worst fear became reality. Sun-dried timbers burned and crackled, feeding greedy flames that raced up the tarred rigging. Canvas sails exploded and varnished spars burned like kindling. The napalm had splattered across the crew, too, and fire burned them as well. Their screams pierced the roar of the fire and Carmen shuddered at the sound.

In seconds, a raging conflagration consumed the ship. Looking over her shoulder as she flew toward the next galley, Carmen saw explosions blast apart the bow of the burning ship. The fire had reached the ammunition brought on deck in preparation for bombarding the Hypatian schooner.

The second galley was starting to turn away. The double banks of oars churned the water into white foam. Carmen swooped low and saw a tall, black-robed figure shouting at the galley's officers. De Briganti—he must have ridden through the night to roust out the galleys while the *Jefferson* repaired her battle damage.

There had seemed no choice but to leave with Sam, but now she felt gladness that doing so gave her another chance to finish de Briganti, She released a net of grenades as she passed over the galley.

Carmen brought the glider around in one last graceful turn. She had neither enough speed nor altitude for another pass. A spreading inferno engulfed the deck of the galley. De Briganti stood at the very stern. He grabbed the stock of a swivel gun mounted on the gunwale. He had to know the flames would reach him in seconds, but he aimed the gun and fired at the glider. A swarm of grapeshot tore through the glider and Carmen felt it lurch, then spin out of control. The sea seemed to rise to smash her out of the sky and everything went black.

Light, shining in her eyes. She opened them slowly and saw Sam and Dr. Polowczyk, the schooner's surgeon, leaning over her.

Sam took her hand. "How are you feeling?"

"A little groggy, but all right. Was I shot?"

"No," Polowczyk said, "just banged up in the crash. And you swallowed some seawater before the cutter got to you. But you'll be fine, just rest." The doctor stood, stooped in the low space between decks, and opened the cabin's door. "I'll check in on you later," he said and left the two alone.

"What about de Briganti?" Carmen asked. "Is he dead?"

"If he was aboard one of those galleys, he is. They both sank. We picked up a few survivors, but de Briganti wasn't among them. The wind came up a few hours after you crashed, and we're through the Straits. We have clear sailing back to Hypatia."

Carmen looked up through the cabin's skylight. Far above the deck, a sailor hung in a rope sling, tying a broom to the very top of the mast. Sam followed her gaze.

"It's an ancient naval custom," he said. "A broom at the masthead signals that we've swept the enemy from the sea. I like to think that for us, it has another meaning, too. It's a new broom, sweeping out the old world to make room for a new one."

Sam leaned down and kissed her. "There's still a lot of work to do to make that world. I'd like us to do it together."

"Yes, Sam, I'd like that, too. Take me home."

*T*here's nothing like a story set in a dystopian future in which the world has become a ruthless theocracy, where religion is in charge of our lives and destinies, and we must adhere to what the religionists demand, with serious penalties if we don't. And such a theocratic dystopia is all the more fascinating when those who don't believe as the majority does dare to oppose the religious fanatics who run the show and suffer the consequences. If this sounds a lot like real life, remember that the difference between our real world and the terrifying society Corwin Merrill presents here is that we still have a choice, and the religious zealots can no longer torture or execute us for blasphemy. But it hasn't been too long since they were actually able to do that, and if common sense and reason don't continue gaining ground, what Merrill postulates in this story might well come to pass.

The Word Is 'Freedom'

Corwin Merrill

They pursued him through the deluge, mindless crusaders with a purpose. He'd been able see lights behind him across the fields for the last hour, but in the past five minutes he'd been able to hear them. The mad, howling storm was so intense that to hear them at all meant they were dangerously close.

Horizontal rain stung his face like a plague of locusts. He leaned into the screaming wind, squinting, hand out to break the rain from his eyes, and pushed onward. He couldn't be captured. If they acquired what he carried, so many would suffer.

He stole a look over his shoulder. Beyond the rise were the faint glows of many lights. He stumbled on the muddy gravel but kept moving. They were damn close, and he was so tired. He'd barely slept at all in the past five days. His body ached and cried out in its exhaustion for him to stop, to just collapse and let sleep overtake him. He couldn't let that happen.

*　*　*

"How do we know he has it, Captain Gramwell?" the nervous young man hollered over the storm.

"Another of his kind told us all about it," Gramwell hollered back in the dimness of their lights. "It's amazing what those barbarians will say when you drive a few steel spikes through their bodies."

"I wonder what's taking the skimmer so long," the kid said.

Gramwell smiled. "You tired of this, kid?"

"No, sir," the kid said, but his face said otherwise.

"Not discouraged from the rain and the wind?" Gramwell asked with a sardonic grin. Rain smacked his wrinkled face; wind whipped his soaked hair around. He was the only one in the group not wearing any headgear. The rest of them were bundled up as if ready for an Arctic trip. "Not tired and hungry and wishing you were dry?"

"I suppose I am, sir," the kid yelled. "But I want to see him caught."

"As well you should," Gramwell said with a chuckle. "And we'll get him, son. We have to. He carries something we need. So all of you remember," he said, raising his voice, "as tempting as it is, keep this one alive—and don't damage him. We don't know where it's hidden."

"Sir, the skimmer is on its way," came a voice from the liquid darkness, and Gramwell smiled with satisfaction.

He broke the rise and saw it. Straight ahead, nearly invisible in the black torrent, he saw the dark outline: the forest, several hundred feet away. A surge of hope exploded in his heart like a firecracker and he staggered drunkenly forward. If he could break the treeline before they topped the ridge behind him, he'd be safe. Without dogs or air support, they'd never track him in there. His heart was like a woodpecker trapped inside a tree. His lungs felt like swelling balloons, full of chilly air and cold water. If all he got out of this were pneumonia, he knew he'd be lucky.

His foot suddenly hit an unseen rock and he went over the way they'd toppled what was left of the Washington Monument when he was eight. He hit the ground sprawling, cursing the precious lost seconds.

He clambered to his feet and snapped a look back as he staggered into a clumsy sprint. He couldn't see their lights behind him. The trees loomed close before him. He was going to make it. He ran again, fast and awkward, feeling like the scarecrow in a movie he'd seen as a child. It was banned now, like most movies—especially a fantasy like that, full of magic and all. The censorship was such a tragedy—

The sky lit suddenly up above and before him. He yelled in anguish, skidding to a stop as the massive hovercraft roared into view over the treetops and dropped sharply between him and the woods. Blinding spotlights targeted him as if he were some overrated stage performer. The thirty-foot, silver-domed skimmer's sensors were locked on and he knew it wouldn't lose him. He watched helplessly as it lowered to the ground, blue-glowing pulse guns emerging from their compartments with hydraulic whirs.

He stood in the driving rain, pelted as if by countless nails, hands up and fingers at his temples, waiting for the end. That was standard procedure. He only hoped they opened up good, and aimed above his shoulders. That ought to destroy his cargo.

Behind him, the voices were getting louder. He looked over his shoulder to see the searchers herding toward him like excited cattle. He spun back to the hovercraft, eyes wide.

"Do it!" he yelled above the roar of the storm, keeping his hands at his temples. "DO IT!"

They did it.

He was on cold concrete, still wet. Every joint was stiff. Every muscle ached. He had a pounding migraine. He tried to sit up and could only groan in pain.

"Morning."

He rolled sideways, pushed himself painfully into a sitting position. He was in a jail cell, barely eight feet on a side, without any beds or mats. A single dim overhead light down the hall weakly illuminated the cell through the thick bars. Distant voices were barely evident.

"How long?" he asked, hoarse and raspy.

"About ten hours." He was a young man, blond and athletic, dressed in a black prison jumpsuit. He sat in one corner with an arm resting on an upright knee. "It was late last night. They didn't even get you dry clothes. What'd you do, anyway?"

"What's your name?" he asked.

"Nice dodge. I'm Thomas. You?"

He regarded the kid for a moment, then answered, "Clevalis."

"Can't say I've ever heard a name like that."

"No. My parents created it."

"Something wrong with James or Peter or Matthew, or any other normal name?"

"Yes. They're Christian names."

Understanding crossed Thomas's face like a dark cloud over the sun. "I see. You're one of *them*."

"Interesting way of putting it. What 'them' are you talking about?"

"You're Godless," Thomas said, visibly astonished. "That's why they treated you so badly. They're never nice to sinners in here, but you... they dumped you in here like... garbage." He said the last word as if he'd actually tasted it.

Clevalis winced as he leaned against the wall. The concrete was rough, but the cold felt good against his burning back muscles. "You think I'm garbage, kid?"

"Doesn't matter to me. Matters to the Church. I'm not sure why I deserved you as a roommate, but if you don't mess with me, I'll stay on my side of the cell."

Clevalis cocked his head curiously. "That's quite judgmental for someone also in here for breaking a moral."

"My immorality doesn't compare to yours."

"Do tell."

Thomas shrugged. "I was caught stealing."

Clevalis raised his brow. "Oh, not just any moral—you broke a Commandment. They'll crucify you for that."

"Just for a few hours, and no spikes."

"Ah, yes—typical Christian hypocrisy. The Church has decided God's will: Stealing gets you strapped up for a while, but not honoring God is punishable by death."

"That's because 'Thou shalt have no other gods before me' is first on the list. You broke the primary Commandment."

Clevalis laughed, shaking his head. "So much for 'judge not, lest ye be judged.' Anyway, the logic is flawed. Being an Atheist isn't the same as having another god, you know."

Thomas blinked. "Being a *what?*"

"An Atheist—you know, godless types. But I suppose they don't teach you about that."

"They sure don't, mister."

"So how many times have you been up on the cross?"

"Is that your business?"

"I'm trying to make it my business."

The kid considered it. "This will be my fourteenth. But I've never been spiked. They've all been minor thefts... well, I got caught lying once when I was in school, and I skipped daily service once a few years back and got caught."

Clevalis gave a low whistle. "You don't learn, do you?"

"I just have a... theft problem. I don't get caught often. I have some nifty tech gear that usually gets me out of trouble."

"Tech gear is very immoral for citizens to possess," Clevalis said. "You get caught with that..."

"No kidding. The only reason I've gotten caught at all is because I didn't want them to see me using my tech gear." He shrugged, smiling under his blond mop. "So once in a while things go wrong and I get tied up for a while."

"So what's your tech gear?" Clevalis pressed.

Thomas shook his head. "Sorry, I don't tell anyone that." He shifted uncomfortably on the floor, changing which knee was up and leaning the opposite way. "So why are you locked up? They usually crucify you guys immediately."

"I'm a special Atheist."

Thomas grunted in amusement. "That's an oxymoron. What's so special about you?"

"I'm sure you wouldn't care."

"Hey, you wanted to make things your business. Now it's my turn."

Clevalis nodded with a raised brow. "Fair enough. I have a cybernetic implant in my body. The Church wants it."

"So why don't they just kill you and take it?"

"They don't know where it is. It's microscopic. It could be anywhere. They don't dare risk damaging it. But soon, an expert with the right equipment will be here to find it. Then they'll spike me."

Thomas was visibly interested now, leaning forward a bit, eyes slightly wider than before, mouth slightly open. "What's in that implant?"

"Names," Clevalis said. "Names of Atheists hidden in society, pretending to be just like you. People whose lives will be ended if they're discovered."

Thomas scoffed. "Well, you're asking for it, you know. Your beliefs are clearly against the morals of the Church. All you have to do is accept God when you're up on that cross tomorrow and you'll be spared."

"That will never happen," Clevalis said through gritted teeth.

"Why not?"

"Because I don't believe."

"Why not?"

"We could debate this all day," Clevalis said. "My clock's running down, kid; I don't have time to try to stir up the logic and reason I know is buried in that head of yours somewhere."

"Maybe you're not clear on this," Thomas said carefully. "As soon as they get the implant, they'll string you up on a cross and they'll pound spikes through your hands and feet. They'll leave you up there for an hour, a day, a week—however long it takes. It's not going to be some anti-Church statement. It's not going to make you a martyr, because nobody will care. It's going to be painful and terrible and will result in your death. So give them what they want and convert, man!"

Clevalis chuckled. "I can't give up my intellect in favor of fairy tales—not even to save my own ass."

Thomas shook his head in disbelief. "Then... lie! Just tell them you believe. Hell, I don't think anyone should be tied up on a cross for stealing or lying, but man, I tell them that's what I believe. You just have to play the game their way if you wanna live. After all, if you have Atheists living in society who are pretending to be like us, why can't you do the same?"

"The mindlessness never ceases to amaze me," Clevalis said, closing his eyes and leaning his head heavily back against the cold wall. "Listen to yourself, will you? Preaching about how righteous you are and how terrible godlessness is... talking about what's good and what isn't... and at the end of it all, advising me to lie about believing to save my ass—and telling me how you do the same. If you could truly hear how ridiculous you sound... maybe you'd learn to think differently."

"Captain Gramwell?"

Gramwell looked up from his paperwork at the face of the cop leaning in his doorway. "Go ahead, officer."

"Bringing the prisoner, as ordered."

Gramwell's face hardened. "All right."

The young cop came in, Clevalis in tow and in handcuffs.

Two other cops followed. The office was spacious, the far wall open glass; the spires and bell towers of countless cathedrals standing tall in the backdrop of the cloudy sky could be seen for miles. The walls were adorned with the decorations Clevalis expected: Christ on the cross, a painting of the Last Supper, a few assorted Psalms, portraits of Church leaders. Bookcases full of Bibles and other religious texts lined every wall.

Clevalis, now in a prison-issue black jumpsuit, took it all in as he was led before the monstrous mahogany desk. Gramwell, decked out like the officers in his dress whites, blue field with a superimposed red cross huge on his chest, leaned back in his chair and regarded the prisoner for a few long moments.

"You sad bastard," Gramwell finally said. "Standing there in your godless glory, nothing but a filthy animal. Running free in our great society, corrupting the lives of good Christians... running from the acolytes as they chase you all over God's Creation. Pitiful, Clevalis—shameful and embarrassing."

"I'm not ashamed or embarrassed," Clevalis said quietly.

Gramwell rocketed forward in his chair, slamming both hands on his desk with a resounding smack. The white-clad officers jumped at the sudden sound. Clevalis didn't flinch.

"*I'm* ashamed *because* of you!" Gramwell snarled, his dark face a mask of rage. Age lines in his face hardened into steel grooves. "I'm embarrassed that you're living in my world. I'm offended by the very smell of you, you evil little punk. You and your kind disgust me."

He calmed abruptly, smiling lightly and clasping his hands before him. "But that can all be past you. Everything can change. We give you people a chance—the chance you're deserved as a child of God. Officer, get this man a book."

The first cop scrambled to a bookcase behind him, fished out a volume, and scurried to the desk. He set it down, bowed his head briefly with his hands together before him, then backed off to his original position.

Clevalis regarded the book, disinterested. It was big, thick, and white, with black letters emblazoned across the cover:

THE HOLY BIBLE
THE PERFECT AND DIVINE WORD OF ALMIGHTY GOD
NEW MODERN CHRISTIAN AUTHORITATIVE
ULTIMATE FINAL EDITION REVISED
VERSION 12, REVISION D

"That is a Bible," Gramwell said. "It will be your very own Bible when you leave here. It will be your personal under-standing of God's word and His will, carried with you every-where you go, for consultation whenever you need it—if you make the right choice. That choice is this: You place your hand on this Bible and proclaim acceptance of Jesus Christ as your Lord and Savior. Then, like any good citizen, you'll have a Guardian Angel device implanted in your body. That will en-able us to keep track of you, in case you're ever led astray."

Gramwell smiled, leaning back in his chair once again, visibly pleased with himself. Clevalis regarded him with the same neutrality he'd exhibited since being brought in. "So are you ready to make that choice?"

"I see no choice," Clevalis said in monotone.

"Then open your eyes, boy. You choose what I've told you, or you go to the cross. Now, for a lot of things, we just tie them up for their sins and let the catcalls and thrown stones teach them the error of their ways; but not for you Atheists. Disbelief is the worst offense, and we'll spike you for it. We'll nail you up there and let you bleed to death. So that's your other choice, Atheist... and from where I'm sitting, the first one is a whole lot better."

"That's no choice," Clevalis said. "That's the Church forc-ing people into submission. That's the Church controlling eve-ryone—do it their way or die."

"You're starting to catch on," Gramwell said, his face hardening again.

"I'll never surrender intellect and reason in exchange for mindless child beliefs," Clevalis said. "I choose crucifixion."

Gramwell's eyes darkened and he said through clenched teeth, "What the hell is it with you people? All you have to do is make the right choice and you'll live, boy! And you're not protecting anyone—our specialist will be here tomorrow morning and we'll find that implant and have those names. Then, it won't matter if you accept God or if you die screaming in agony on that cross like a stuck pig. And when we find the rest of the Atheist scum, they'll all face the same choice as you—become members of Church society or die bloody deaths!"

Clevalis regarded him coolly, lips pursed. "If that's what we have to endure for exercising the free will your own God has given all of us, so be it."

"Don't you blaspheme my religion," Gramwell hissed.

"How am I blaspheming? It's your own rules!" For the first time, Clevalis was showing emotion beyond his stony face and flat voice. "Free will is guaranteed by your God—regardless of who we are. And nobody but God is supposed to pass judgment. Yet the Church has molded society into its own will, not God's—made all the decisions, spoken on behalf of God, interpreted everything to its own benefit!"

"You're Satan, quoting Scripture to your own purpose!" Gramwell said, gripping the arms of his chair with hydraulic fingers. His nostrils flared; his eyes were flame.

"And you're a hypocrite," Clevalis said, shaking his head. "All of you... nothing but an army of mindless hypocrites. Robots reciting what you've been told to believe, ignoring logic and reason when you can't explain your way around the fallacies and contradictions of your worshiped mythology."

"That will be all," Gramwell said, still holding his chair arms in death grips and trembling with anger. "Take this God-less scum back to his cell."

* * *

"Good thing you have that implant, or they'd have roughed you up," Thomas said to him later. "They usually do."

"That's the 'convert or we'll beat you until you do' technique," Clevalis said from his corner of the cell. He lay on his back, one arm over his eyes, and chuckled. "You seem like a reasonably intelligent guy, Thomas. You mean to say you can't see how silly that is?"

"I never said it wasn't silly," Thomas said. "I told you before I don't agree with everything the Church says. It's just that... I believe in God and you don't."

"That's not the point. Your religion supports free will and your Church doesn't."

"I support free will. Heck, I've made free choices to break more morals and Commandments than anyone I know, but that doesn't mean I don't believe."

Clevalis looked from under his arm at him. "Okay, I'll go out on a limb. There's no way I'm ever going to accept your god or your religion, or this fascist society that requires me to do so. Knowing that, do you think I should be allowed to live free or should I be put to death?"

"What you're really asking," Thomas said slowly, "is whether I think anyone, regardless of beliefs, should be allowed to live in our society without Church control."

Clevalis smiled. "Like I said, you're a reasonably intelligent guy."

Thomas returned the smile. "You're pretty sharp yourself, for a disbeliever."

Clevalis grunted his way into a sitting position, legs crossed, and leaned forward with his elbows on his knees. "So how about it?"

"Well, first off, I think you're wrong to disbelieve. I can't imagine how you're unable to see the truth."

"I believe as I do because I've used logic and reason to

direct my life," Clevalis said. "Now tell me how *you* believe what you do."

Thomas shrugged. "I was brought up that way. I learned from my parents... from living in our society. It's all around us... it's in everything we do."

There was a long silence in the dark cell. Thomas and Clevalis stared at one another for the long moments; Thomas' face blank and searching, Clevalis' anticipatory. Presently, understanding washed over Thomas and he smiled weakly. "I get it. You're saying I believe because I've been programmed to believe."

Clevalis shrugged. "I'm not saying anything. I just asked a question. You're the one making the connections."

"Well, it isn't like that."

"Maybe not. But it was nice to see the intellect that I know is hiding in that head of yours kicking in for a brief moment."

Thomas glared at him. "So you want to know if I think Atheists should be allowed to live."

"I already know your answer," Clevalis said.

Thomas rolled his eyes. "So now Atheists are mind-readers, I suppose."

"I don't need to be. You're not a mindless robot like the rest of them, Thomas. There's a stronger humanity in you than most of the believers in this society — certainly more than those who run it. I can see the good in you as clearly as I can see the senselessness, the hypocrisy, the evil in the Church."

With that, he returned to his prone position on the cold concrete floor, arm back over his face. Thomas watched him, mouth agape, anticipation still coating him like a glass shell. Finally, he said, "Well... what do you think I was going to say?"

"You think Atheists should be allowed to live as Atheists," Clevalis said simply. "You think it's a tragic injustice for them to be forced into your beliefs. You feel it the same way you feel it's a tragic injustice to be strung up on a cross even for lying or stealing—and the way you feel it's a tragic injustice for the Church to pervert your religion into a society of people afraid to be who they want to be."

Thomas thought for a moment before saying, "You seem pretty sure you have me all figured out."

"It's obvious to me," Clevalis said.

Thomas dreamed he was running, barefoot, from the acolytic police. They were chasing him through the streets of the cathedral-populated city. No matter where he ran, people crowded on the sidewalks shouted insults and threw stones. Some of the faces were people who were sure of themselves in their righteousness. Others were far more doubtful—insulting and stoning because they knew they were supposed to. In the crowds were plenty of metallic robots, too.

"Thief!" they screamed at him.

He ran faster, but his pants were loose and trying to fall down. He hauled them up and kept running, but there were always people—and there always acolytes not far behind. They commanded that he stop. He tried to fly, but of course he was barefoot and beltless.

Eventually the crowds thickened and spilled off the sidewalks, and his path down the street narrowed. Soon the road was completely blocked by thousands of people pointing fingers—all accusing, all judging, all condemning.

"I need to fly!" he hollered to the heavens, hoping his God would hear him. He tried to leap into the air, tried to fly without his gear, but he fell to the ground and collapsed in a heap.

The acolytes were upon him, beating him to the ground. He begged for them stop, but there was no mercy for one who had broken a Commandment—and run from those who would take the Lord's vengeance on His behalf.

He was hauled up to a cross that standing in the street behind him, and they lashed him to it with the restraining straps—wrists and arms, ankles and legs, torso and neck. He struggled the whole time, but the crowd liked it when he did. They cheered, drunk with satisfaction. Everyone loved a good show of barbarism.

"Thief!" they all screamed in primitive ecstasy.

"You are charged with breaking the Commandment against stealing," Captain Gramwell called out, and the crowd roared its approval. "And with possession of immoral tech gear enabling you to escape your crime scenes."

Then the cops stepped up with steel spikes and mallets, and Thomas began screaming again: "It's just stealing... they never spike for stealing... *it's just stealing!*"

"You are also charged with violating the most important Commandment of all," Gramwell bellowed, and suddenly his eyes glowed red and horns sprouted from his temples. "For committing the ultimate mortal sin, violating the Commandment that prohibits having other gods before Him, the penalty is death."

The crowd went insane. Thomas was thunderstruck. "But I *believe!*" he hollered above the intense noise. "You've got it wrong! I *believe!*"

"But you've been listening to an Atheist," Gramwell said, and with that they drove the first spike through his hand.

Thomas woke with a violent shudder and stifled cry. It was dark in the cell, even darker than usual. At night, they killed the main lights down the hall and left just the emergency lighting.

"You okay?" came a soft voice from the darkness.

It took his muddled brain a moment to focus. "I'm fine," he said shakily. "Just... bad dream."

"What were they doing to you?"

"Who?"

"The Church. 'It's just stealing, they don't spike for that,' and other stuff. What did you do to deserve spiking?"

"If you must know, I was charged with violating the First

Commandment... for listening to *you*."

Clevalis whistled lightly. "Well, I don't think they spike for that in the real world — *yet*."

They lay quietly for a few minutes, until Thomas' eyes had adjusted to the darkness. He said, "So what does this specialist do to you when he arrives in the morning?"

"He'll use a tech device to scan me. In five seconds they'll know where it is."

A few silent moments passed before Thomas said, "You were right in your assessment of me. What they're doing to Atheists is wrong. What they do to liars and thieves is wrong. Just about everything they do is wrong. I want to believe, I want to *keep* believing... but the Church has twisted everything."

"It's hard to expect anything less from the followers of a religion filled with contradictions and illogic."

Thomas sighed, exasperated. "I'm trying to communicate with you, and you're crapping on my religion — and you're not backing your mouth up with any facts. Give me some examples of how my religion is contradictory and illogical."

"I could give you a thousand, but I'm due to be crucified in a few hours; so I'll leave you with one good one: If God is all-powerful and perfect, why does he need to be worshiped?"

"How is that contradictory or illogical?"

"Because he either needs people to worship him, in which case he isn't all-powerful; or he wants people to worship him, which makes him vain and thus imperfect. An all-powerful, perfect God who wants or needs *anything* is nothing short of a totally illogical contradiction."

"We can't presume to understand God's reasoning —"

"But there isn't any gray area here — he either needs or wants worshipers. No Supreme Being, no Creator, would ever have needs or wants. Is there a Higher Power? I don't know. Maybe, maybe not. But if there is, I'm certain it doesn't need worshiping."

Thomas sighed again. "I admit there are a lot of holes... and I've questioned them myself, believe me. And points like those make me question everything about the Church and society."

"As well it should. Now I have a question for you."

"Okay."

"Are you gonna tell me about your tech gear?"

Thomas laughed aloud. "No! What makes you ask that?"

"Well, you have my curiosity," Clevalis said. "I'll be dead in a few hours, and before I go, I'd like to know what nifty, immoral tech gear you have. I mean, who am I gonna tell?"

"Sorry, man," Thomas said with a grin.

Clevalis chuckled. "Can't blame me for trying."

"Tell me something about the names of the Atheists in your implant... why carry them at all? Why put them at risk?"

"There are lots of us. The Church can track every other form of communication, but we need to coordinate somehow. It's a necessary risk."

"But why live with us like they do? The cause seems so hopeless... why live among us, risking their lives?"

"Because everyone should have a choice," Clevalis said. "Every human should choose for himself and not be forced into anything—not Christianity, not Atheism, nothing. Not long ago, there were many other religions on this planet. Now there's only one, because the Church runs the world and nobody has a choice. We live among you because this is our planet, too. We work to educate others. Eventually, we hope people will unite against the Church and make Earth once again a world where everyone can choose to follow any religion—or no religion. That's the way this planet has to be."

"But the Church is too powerful and far-reaching," Thomas said. "Your cause is beyond hopeless. There's a word for why you do what you do. That word is 'insanity.'"

"No," Clevalis said, "the word is 'freedom.'"

*   *   *

They lay in silence for several hours while Thomas thought. The only sounds in the dark were the distant murmurs of their jailers, several corridors away. The ventilation system moaned faintly. Somewhere nearby, Thomas could hear the light sobbing of another dissatisfied customer. Finally, he said, "Where's the implant?"

Clevalis looked at him in surprise. "It doesn't matter. They'll find it soon enough."

"I'm serious. If they'll find it anyway, why won't you tell me?"

Clevalis scrunched his brow. "You won't tell me about your tech gear... why should I tell you about my implant?"

"Give up on the tech gear, Clev," he said, irritated. "Just tell me where the damn implant is."

Clevalis regarded him a few moments longer, then sighed. "All right. They'll have it soon anyway. It's in my right index fingernail, near the tip. Just have to cut the end off."

"I want you to give it to me."

Clevalis gave a start. "What?"

"Tear the end of your nail off and give it to me," he repeated. "I've been awake half the night thinking about this. I don't know what I believe right now, but I do know the Church is wrong. If there's a God, I'm sure this isn't something he'd condone. I can't let you go out there with the names of all those people — not when I can do something about it."

The next morning, their wrists and ankles were shackled and secured together with belly chains, and they were escorted outside to the prison's crucifixion yard. Decorated with three dozen crosses, the yard looked like a field of giant daggers. Already, six moral-breakers were tied up on crosses, enduring the taunts of the crowd. Several dozen citizens were beyond the fence, letting the sinners hear their thoughts on the sins. An occasional stone was lobbed over the fence, but nothing like Thomas knew it soon would be — especially with an Atheist being spiked.

"This is it," Clevalis whispered, nodding toward a group of guards coming toward them. "Better not look like you're friendly with me."

Led by Captain Gramwell, the guards escorted a plain-clothes tech over to them. "This is the one," Gramwell announced as the tech readied a hand scanner. "Let's get this over with so I can get on with these crucifixions. You planning on repenting while you're up there, Clevalis?"

"No," Clevalis said quietly. "And there's no implant to find. You were misinformed."

The tech smiled smugly. "We'll see about that."

"Don't bother," Thomas interrupted. "He's gotten rid of the implant."

Everyone looked at him in surprise—especially Clevalis. Gramwell stepped up, nose to nose with Thomas. "You're a known thief and a liar, Thomas. You'd better not be lying now."

"I'm not—I swear to God," Thomas said. "The implant was in his right index fingernail. But he chewed off the end so you wouldn't find it."

"You backstabbing bastard," Clevalis breathed incredulously.

Thomas ignored him as the tech hurriedly scanned. The guards grabbed up Clevalis' hand and produced the proper finger. Clearly, the end of the fingernail had been recently chewed off. The tech looked up, eyes wide. "I'm not reading any implants in this man's body."

Gramwell turned angrily to Clevalis. "Where is it?"

Clevalis gave no reply, and Thomas said, "He'll never talk, Captain. But I can tell you where it is. He flushed it this morning. I'd have told the guard, but I didn't know he was going to do it. They returned him after a visit to the toilet and he told me."

Clevalis looked astounded. Gramwell ordered one of his

officers, "Shut down the sewer systems. Take the tech down there to scan for it." To Clevalis, he said, "All this does is delay our finding the implant. You're still dying today, you Atheist scum."

"What about me?" Thomas interjected. "If it weren't for me, you'd never know where to look. You might have scanned him and assumed he never had the implant at all. I've now made it possible for you to find the Atheists living among us."

Gramwell sighed and nodded. "All right. You'll get no pardon, but your punishment is hereby commuted. But don't expect any 'get out of jail free' cards from me in the future."

"I appreciate that, sir," Thomas said, and extended his hand. Gramwell regarded it for a moment before taking it. Thomas pumped it heavily with a huge smile. "However, I have had the unpleasant task of being stuck for two days in a tiny cell with this Atheist scum, listening to his godless propaganda." He gestured out at the crucifixion field. "I'd like to be the one to lead him up the steps to the cross—and the one to drive the spikes through his body."

A slow smile crept across Gramwell's face, and he nodded. "A fitting duty for a repentant man such as yourself, Thomas. So be it."

"Thank you, sir," Thomas said with a broad smile, and then he gestured down at his prison blacks. "But can I change back into my own clothes first?"

By the time Thomas had returned in his street clothes, all seventeen sinners—besides Clevalis—had been strung up on crosses. Thomas stood, silent and stoic, next to the still-chained Clevalis.

Captain Gramwell was on the loudspeakers, playing to the huge crowd outside the fence. "We have one more for you today, citizens... one that will make your faith in Almighty God ever stronger!"

The crowd roared its approval. Clevalis leaned his

head toward Thomas and whispered, "What the hell are you doing?"

"You don't believe in hell," Thomas said with a smile.

"Here we bring you a Godless soul!" Gramwell hollered, pounding the air above his head with a fist. "Captured while trying to destroy your right to know the truth—an Atheist spy!"

They screamed. They cheered. They waved arms in the air.

"Citizen Thomas," Gramwell said, "take the prisoner to his cross."

Thomas gripped Clevalis' arm and strode forward. Clevalis stumbled along clumsily in all his chains. The crowd, like some beast with hundreds of voices, cheered them on as they mounted the steps.

"I hope there's something I'm missing," Clevalis said.

"You won't miss a thing," Thomas said.

The punisher, all in white, waited above. The binding straps were attached to the cross, but the punisher held a mallet in one hand and three gleaming, stainless steel spikes in the other. When they reached the top, he handed the tools to Thomas and prepared to bind Clevalis to the cross. Thomas stopped him with a raised hand.

"You can spike him," the punisher said, "but I'm required to strap him."

"I know," Thomas said. "Just give me your mike. I want to speak to the crowd first."

The punisher passed over his handheld microphone and Thomas keyed it up. The loudspeakers squeaked and the crowd obediently quieted like a flock of sheep. Gramwell regarded him from across the yard with a satisfied smile.

"Citizens," Thomas announced, "I stand before you now to do my duty in punishing this Atheist."

"Spike him!" someone in the crowd yelled, and others echoed his sentiment.

"But I say it is not our place to decide the fate of others—

that falls only to God, and we cannot presume to know God's wishes."

"What is this?" Gramwell hollered out.

"It isn't our right to put a man to death for being an Atheist," he yelled over the microphone. "So I will not participate in the crucifixion of this man—instead, I will set him free."

"Enough!" Gramwell cried. "Punisher, strap this blasphemous Atheist-lover to the cross!"

The punisher growled and advanced. Thomas whirled about, dropping the mallet and two of the spikes, lunging with the third. The punisher yelped in surprise, leaping back to avoid being skewered, and toppled over the edge.

"Guards!" Gramwell screamed, and a dozen uniformed officers dashed across the yard toward the stairs. The crowd lost its collective mind now, screaming in its displeasure. Several people began trying to scale the fence.

"One more thing," Thomas hollered, holding a silver and gold watch high in the air. "Lose something, Captain Gramwell?"

Gramwell realized and frantically checked his empty wrist. Thomas stepped close to Clevalis. "Hang on tight," he warned.

"You're crazy," Clevalis said, grabbing on.

"I must be," Thomas said, getting a handhold on Clevalis' belly chain as the guards thundered up the stairs toward them, and then he hit the hidden button on his belt buckle.

His boots kicked in and the pair shot into the air high above the crucifixion yard, the startled guards, the prison, and the city. The sounds of the screaming citizens below were quickly lost as they antigravitated. His passenger hung on for all he was worth, but the antigrav field handled them both easily.

Clevalis yelled, "Antigravity boots!" He laughed insanely. "I'd say they're definitely against the morals!"

"They certainly are," Thomas said as they flitted quickly

through low clouds and broke into the endless blue sky. "And that's not all. What good are antigrav boots without a flight belt?"

Thomas kicked his feet at different angles, leveling their trajectory. Clevalis wrapped his legs around Thomas' as Thomas thumbed other hidden controls on the belt and they rocketed away to the north.

"North to the Atheist lands?" Thomas asked.

Clevalis nodded. "First order of business will be to remove your Guardian Angel so they can't track us." He laughed. "You amaze me. I knew there was something special about you, but this... thank you."

"It's my pleasure," Thomas replied as they soared on invisible wings toward the horizon. "You were right about freedom, Clev."

"So are you thinking differently about your beliefs?"

"I don't know what I believe," Thomas said, "but I know things need to change."

They flew off into the heavens, angels happily cast out.

*I*f one thing can be said about Earl Lee, it's that he's a funny guy. I challenge anyone not to chuckle throughout this story, which is a parody of The Screwtape Letters. C.S. Lewis, author of the original, claimed to have been a young atheist — reportedly angry at God for not existing — before rediscovering Christianity. That sounds a lot more like a young Christian being rebellious to me, but since C.S. can't debate the point, we'll move on. Earl seems to be the opposite of C.S.; he appears downright jovial that God doesn't exist, and happy that the True Believers give him so much material to work with. There's plenty of absurdity to be found in theology, and Earl probably could have sustained this parody to a novel's length, but we'll settle for a shorter form here.

The Screwletter Tapes:
Messages from Heaven...
to a 21st-Century Christian

Earl Lee

PROLOGUE

These phone messages are from the private voicemails of Cardinal Joseph Ratzinger, known affectionately to his closest childhood friends as "Wurmig." These voicemails were transcribed in 2005 and inadvertently preserved in the Vatican Archives for the benefit of future generations of Christian scholars. And now that Cardinal Ratzinger has become the Pontiff, these messages take on a whole new importance.

Who is the person who speaks on the voicemails? In the context of his messages the author claims to be "Archy" who is an "Angel of The Lord" or alternatively a "Holy Inquisitor." His identity is uncertain, and some skeptics have claimed that he could be just a lowly priest or even a lay person who is mentally ill — although that cannot be determined from the context. In any case, his phone messages to "Wurmig" provide a new theological insight into the "The Heavenly and Angelic Hosts" who watch over us.

Several Christian theologians are already describing these messages as the most significant event in the history of the Christian church since Pope John XXIII opened the secret letter from Our Lady of Fatima, on 17 August 1959, and then discovered that the envelope contained the lost laundry list of Pope Pius XII, from Easter 1944.

— The Editor

THE VOICEMAIL MESSAGES

Message #1: Television and Popular Culture

"You have reached The House of Ratzi. Sorry I can't answer the phone right now, and my assistant is always under a Bishop these days. But your call is very important to me, so please leave your message after you hear the beep...."

[BEEP!]

"Hello.... Wurmig, is that you? Pick up, please. Come on, pick up.... Oh, Damnation, I hate these things. But... oh well,... here goes."

[Noise in background as a wooden chair is adjusted on Linoleum.]

"My Dear Wurmig,

"After the visit of Our Beloved Pope, *George 'n Ringo...* Ha! Ha! That joke always gets me. Here, let me start again...

"After Our Beloved Pope John Paul visited the United States last winter, I decided that it was My duty as an Angel of the Lord... and as an officially lay'd leader of the Holy Office of the Inquisition... to visit a group of churches in the St. Louis area to see how Our Master's message was received.

"I was led to believe that the United States was a very liberal country. I was expecting the city of St. Louis on the Mississippi River to be very much like Paris on the Left Bank of the river Seine. But much to My surprise and delight, the people I met were all staunch conservatives in their religion. I am told that this is a fairly new development, and it is one that is very much to Our liking.

"The growing social conservatism in the U.S. is a hopeful trend, especially as conservatism lends itself to an unflagging belief in religious rites and traditions—that is, to traditionalism in general and *in situ*. And this trend helps Our Holy Cause.

"I know you are very concerned about the fact that many millions of Americans watch television and get all their news and opinions from that source. But not to worry. Years ago there was a leftward bias in the news, especially during the Vietnam War era, but that old liberalism has dissolved into a stew of bad memories. For example, Dan Rather is no longer an anchor on network TV news. Instead, people listen to Bill O'Reilly and Ann Coulter and Rush Limbaugh, *bless their souls*, not to mention the consistently Rightward message of all Our good friends at the Fox News Channel—*May the Saints Preserve Them in Their Sanctity and Holiness.*

"Almost all of the major talking heads are on Our side now, like Pat Buchanan and Mike Huckabee. Pat has always been a strong Defender of the Catholic Faith, and Mike is a Holy-owned subsidiary of the Southern Baptist Convention. None of the more left-leaning news commentators is willing to challenge Us!—at least not directly. They know that Our Defenders stand ready to inundate their bosses with angry letters and threats to boycott their sponsors. We are masters of the poisoned pen and the rumor mill. We don't have to worry about mere facts because We can bombard Our enemies with iron-balled opinions. The Church Canon stands always forever ready, and The Holy Church will always be triumphant! Their mere scientific facts and secular truths fall before Our lightest shadow, and the power of Our True Truth—meaning the Only Begotten Truth of the Saints and the Scriptures—it overawes them all.

"Yes, there are several new evangelical rationalists who have entered the fray, including Richard Dawkins, Sam Harris, Christopher Hitchens, and a few others. But, after all, We survived Thomas Paine and Voltaire, who were far more popular than these guys and spoke directly to the unwashed masses. We easily defeated them, so why worry? People aren't interested in rationalism anymore. And the number of people who read these skeptics can't begin to compare with the millions who spend their evenings watching our religious programs on television. And I'm not just talking about *The 700 Club* or the old nun with the enormous wart. I'm talking about prime-time network television.

"Millions of people enjoy *The Ghost Whisperer,* and *Medium,* and *Pet Psychic,* and *Ghost Hunters,* and *Paranormal State,* and *Most Haunted*—not to mention all the movies about the supernatural, like *The Sixth Sense,* and *The Legend of Hell House,* and *13 Ghosts,* and *The Amityville Horror,* and *Stir of Echoes.*

"And that doesn't even begin to cover the popular teenage movie series, like *Poltergeist,* numbers one to three; and *Nightmare on Elm Street,* numbers one to eight; and *Friday the 13th,* numbers one to eleven; and *Witchcraft,* numbers one to twelve (and it's not just about watching naked witches cavorting across the screen). And then there's *The Prophecy,* numbers one to three, and *The Howling,* numbers one to four. And, of course, there is My very favorite movie series of all time: *The Exorcist,* numbers one to four. There are thousands of other films that help Us by promoting a belief in the almost unlimited powers of The Supernatural.

"Oh yes, and there is also a wonderful new TV show called *Supernatural* where two brothers from Kansas hunt down and destroy the evil Demons. Young Sam and Dean commit credit-card fraud, petty thefts, and frequent fornications—and, believe it or not, these handsome young 'good ol' boys' are allied with The Angels. They are on Our side! Every week they capture and torture the evil demons—burning them with Holy Water, shooting them with rock salt, stabbing them with sacred knives. I would never have believed it if I hadn't seen it myself. How perfectly Medieval! I think that this show is one of My favorites, and many of Our lesser Angels are quite the fans of the actor Jared Padalecki! (I sometimes wonder if he can feel the press of angelic lips on his face, his lips, and etc.) But enough said about that.

"In most of these TV programs and movies, the Evil Supernatural Powers are forced to submit to the Spiritual Authority of Our Holy Church. Our Priests are on display, fighting against Evil, 24/7, like Arnold Schwarzenegger in *End of Days*. Occasionally Our side is defeated, usually because of the interference of secular authorities; and, of course, then Evil triumphs. This is as it should be. After all, no one is safe when you rely on the secular government for help. The innocent believers need Us to save them!

"In these films people are taught to believe that their only hope for survival against these supernatural onslaughts is through the power of The Church. They may rely on the power of prayer for their daily needs, but in The End Times the only power that can save them is, of course, the power of The Holy Roman Church itself. A willingness to supplicate oneself before The Church is the only way to escape the power of The Forces of Evil.

"These films and movies outnumber, by far, the television programs and films that promote Realism and rational thinking. Except for a few detective shows and medical dramas, Our friends control television with almost no rebuttal at all. And when a television show has a major character who is a pure rationalist—like *House*, or *Monk*, or *The Mentalist*, or *CSI*—well, in these situations Our friends at the networks make sure that the rationalist "hero" of the tale is emotionally crippled (or even physically crippled) by the loss of a loved one. After all, these atheists and rationalists do not have the 'sure and certain hope of the resurrection' to rely on, as We do. And so

Death is always a traumatic and destructive event that poisons their lives and grinds their souls under the wagons of chaos and the wheels of empty existence... at least that's Our line, and We're sticking to it.

"Even more important, these television programs serve to distance people from real life. While the rationalists and materialists can only offer them plain carrots and peas, our priests can hold in front of their eyes The Holy Peace and The Great and All-Powerful Carrot, which stand just inside the Brass Doors of The Holy Church. By that I mean their belief in the supernatural makes it easier for Our priests to lead them in Our Holy Processions, to lure them with an orange and green papier-mâché Holy Carrot, mounted on a stick. We can jiggle our paper Carrot and make blood come miraculously from its sad potato eyes. They only need to believe and stretch out their hands to grab the... ooops, missed it again! Maybe next time...

"The mass of people live today in conditions of abject poverty. In the past We have always been able to use this to Our advantage. A person who struggles from day to day, trying to find enough food to eat, does not focus his mind of the great social and political issues of the day. Instead, he bows his head before the Might and Glory of Our Lord, and he prays hard — on his knees — and begs for Our Help... well, not so much the help of the priests or the Church — after all, he's not a complete fool — but he prays for help from Our Glorious Lord in Heaven.

"Remember, it is not in Our interest to try to improve the daily lives of individuals. After all, recent surveys show that the most deeply religious and conservative people are also the poorest people. In the U.S., for example, the vast majority of the poor are either Catholics or they are members of Baptist churches. As you go up the social ladder, the wealthier Americans are usually members of more liberal churches, like the Lutherans and the Episcopalians.

"Why would We exert Ourselves in trying to improve the lot of the poor — who will be with Us always, anyway — when

We know that, once they escape poverty, they will become Anglicans or Presbyterians or, even worse, Unitarians! Once they have a little money in their pockets, they get educated and they have free time to think about social issues and politics and sometimes, God forbid, they even join labor unions! Their lives and ideas become secular and distant from Our will. We must instead work to preserve their honest poverty while also nurturing their spiritual well-being.

"It is for reminding us of this that We owe a debt of thanks to Mother Teresa, Our Blessed St. Teresa of Calcutta, who ministered to the poor—but without doing anything that might improve their impoverished condition. And she did this while also collecting vast sums of money in donations to her religious order, the Missionaries of Charity. Our beloved Teresa preached her belief in the spiritual goodness of poverty, and she worked hard to evangelize among the poor. Teresa's main concern was for their immortal souls, not their daily bread. And when ambulances were donated to their Order, the nuns converted the ambulances into limos for themselves. Just imagine the Holy Chutzpah! The insolence, the audacity, the impertinence! To collect hundreds of thousands of dollars for the poor, and to then just keep the money and put that money in a bank for the benefit of her Holy Order. It takes Our breath away. If only the whole world could be a gigantic Calcutta of purest faith...

"Perhaps that is too much to hope for. But if the whole world could be like Calcutta... or at least more like New Orleans... wouldn't that be wonderful!

"Fondly,

"Archangel 'Archy' Screwletter."

Message #2: Christian Art and Entertainments

"Sorry I can't answer the phone, and my assistant has his mouth full right now. But your call is important to me, so please leave your message after you hear the beep."

[BEEP!]

"Wurmig, are you there? This is Archy. Pick up, please. Tell the kid who works for you to take the banana out of his mouth and answer the phone! Come on, pick up... Oh, Hellation... well, here goes."

[Noise in background as a squeaky office chair is dragged across carpet.]

"There!

"My Dear Wurmig,

"While visiting St. Louis, I happened to see a roadside billboard advertising a place called The Precious Moments Chapel & Gardens. This appeared to be some kind of theme park located a few miles west of St. Louis and, best of all, like Heaven it offers free admission. You know what a sucker I am for places with the free admission. And so, as an officially lay'd leader of the Holy Office, I immediately decided to go visit this chapel and examine its theological soundness.

"What was even more intriguing about this place was the fact that the billboard proclaimed that this Precious Moments Chapel was 'America's Sistine Chapel.' Amazing!

"Of course I have already visited the Sistine Chapel in Rome, many times; and so the chance to see its artistic rival was just too much to pass up. I still remember My first visit to the Sistine Chapel, so many years ago. The city of Rome is immensely beautiful, as you already know. And the Chapel itself... *wunderbar!* As you enter the stony portal and see the splendid paintings and feel *l'érection d'un Dialogue spirituel en massif,* deep within your soul... well, let's just say that it is an experience that no one would want to miss.

"I believe that all of us—even the highest archangels—we all have this great Spiritual Emptiness, deep within, that only a God can fill. And so, to experience once more the strong Embrace, and then the Entrance of *l'érection massif...* it was all just too much to pass up. I haven't felt this way since I visited that church in Rockford, Illinois. You know the one. It's the church with the gigantic half-Gothic, fully-tumescent spire built of glass and brick. This is TruChristian Art (my new idea for 'branding' our most holy art treasures).

"So I bought a ticket for a tour bus going to The Chapel. Surprisingly, I ended up traveling with a busload of Mormons from Nauvoo and retired folk who were fresh from a casino on the Mississippi. As the bus sailed along Highway 44, heading west toward a small town called Carthage, Missouri, I carefully observed all the billboard signs. Believe me, as I flew along the highway I became more and more hopeful about the future of the Christian faith. It seems as if every road sign along the highway was another advertisement for pure, delightful Christian entertainment.

"In some town called Branson, they have a Shepherd of the Hills theme park and outdoor theatre. Evidently, they show a Protestant Christian play based on a novel by Rev. Harold Bell Wright. The play boasts 'more than eighty performers, forty horses, a shootout and a fire'! This certainly must be worth seeing. Branson also boasts other features, including a musical play about Noah's Ark, complete with hundreds of animals! It's called *Noah: The Musical,* and it has a life-size replica of Noah's Ark which protrudes out into the audience, so they can all see and even smell the family-friendly realism of Noah and his Blessed Ark.

"And there were road signs for The Righteous Brothers, The Days of Praise Tour, The Spirit of Christmas, and even The Osmond Brothers! Honestly, tears come to My eyes just trying to remember the serene purity of the Osmond boys, from the last time I saw them in Las Vegas.

"Even more remarkable is the fact that in a town nearby, called Eureka Springs, they have an outdoor live-action performance called 'The Great Passion Play.' It takes over four hours to perform because it follows the last days of Jesus! They also have a Bible Museum, a life-size recreation of The Holy

Land, and a Creation Science Museum where people can see how humans and dinosaurs once lived together in harmony. I've heard that the dinosaurs actually wear saddles! Just thinking about it brings the purist joy to My soul. My heart leaps up, as the poet Wordsworth said. And to top it all off, they have a ten-foot section of concrete from the Berlin Wall. It is meant to celebrate the Triumph of Godly Capitalism over Atheistic Communism.

"And that's not all! They have a gigantic concrete statue called The Christ of the Ozarks. Can you imagine! A sixty-seven-foot statue of The Christ overlooks this amazing valley of wonders, and the healing springs of water flow through it, blessed by the enormous Shadow of Our Lord. Just the thought of it reminds me of My visit to Brazil last year for Carnivale.

"I was tempted, I was very sorely tempted, to turn aside and visit these Great Wonders. But, after all, My goal was to see the astonishingly beautiful Precious Moments Chapel & Gardens, and only after doing that could I imagine visiting the lesser artistic and religious glories of the Ozarks.

"On the way there, the bus stopped at a small town called Delight, Missouri. It is, or I should say *was*, a bump in the highway with an official population of 8,324 people. It is where the road from Cabool meets Highway 44. This is where the tour bus stopped, and we had the chance to buy some lunch. As I stretched My legs and aired out My wings—a bus full of old folk can get a bit gamey—I noticed that a newspaper stand offered free copies of the local newspaper. And you know what a sucker I am for the free stuff.

"So I began to read the shopper's guide, and especially a front-page article about the Delight city government. Apparently a local minister had asked the city government to place a Ten Commandments marble monument on the front lawn of the courthouse. The city leaders, believe it or not, voted not to permit the monument, citing some mythical 'separation of Church and state' issue! They had the boldness to suggest that the monument be erected, instead, on the church lawn across the street from the courthouse. The supernatural arrogance of these fools!

"I read the article again and again. I felt the blood boil in My Seraphic sinus tissues (this is always a very bad sign, as you know) and steam began to rise from My wings and jets of flame flew out of My mouth and nostrils. The smell of burning sulfur filled the air.

"Before I even realized what I was doing, I had laid waste to the entire city. The Heavens rained down Fire and burning Asphalt (good quality brimstone is hard to get these days). Jets of Heaven's Fire crashed down from the skies. There were flames and smoke and the cries of women and the gnashing of teeth!... well, to be honest, it happened so quickly that there was very little wailing—only a surprised "Whaaa!?!" was uttered as the women and the men were instantly consumed in flames and quick-fried where they stood. The effect was like that of napalm poured onto human flesh. Some of the bodies heated so quickly that they literally exploded from the expanding hot air in their lungs. The body of the local grocer was mashed into the trunk of an elm tree, and there was a rather sad and oily expression on what was left of his face. One of the angels told me that the grocer was a refugee from Iraq who had narrowly survived the bombardment on Highway 80, during the siege of 1991. He had come to Delight, Missouri for his health.

("To be honest, I should mention that I was assisted in destroying Delight by many angels and even a few mortal souls who joined in to help. Special Honorable Mention should go to Saint Colonel Sanders, who personally directed much of the frying and broiling, and to Our Sainted President, Ronald Reagan, who stuck a fork in them afterwards.)

"Where the public library once stood was only a pile of shabby books—their pages charred and smoking—and it reminded me of that time in Alexandria when we burnt the library for, I think it was, the third or fourth time. I think it was in 391 or 392 maybe. But the flames were spectacular! All the togas and sandals flying through the air and catching fire, just like in Cecil B. DeMille's *The Sign of the Cross*.

"The destruction of Delight was both horrible and fascinating to watch. Buildings were smashed and even the very bricks and stones were wrenched apart by the force of Heaven's Wrath! In a matter of minutes the entire city was consumed in Heavenly fire! And then there was the deathly quiet.

"In those few seconds a rain of severed arms and legs and even a few severed heads began falling from the sky. The old folks from the tour were terrified, and they quickly scurried back onto the bus for shelter. Blood and Death now walked among them. And it rained on them, too. And that was followed by The Silence.

"And then the grim quiet was broken as the howling of dogs, the screeching of cats. And the lowing of the bovine beasts was heard, and this sad sound was carried along by the wind across the fields of grass.

"I stepped back onto the bus, as it quickly pulled away from the Conoco station. I had been so blinded by anger that I forgot to get my senior coffee and my Big N' Tasty hamburger, with no pickles, at the McDonald's next door.

"As the bus pulled onto Highway 44, the entire city of Delight was sucked into a vortex and collapsed into a hole in the Earth, drawn down to the very bowels of Hell itself.

"Yes, yes... I know that I'm supposed to look for a hundred good men, or failing that, ten good men, or even just *one* good man before unleashing Heaven's Heavenly Wrath on a City of the Unjust—like this one. But I just couldn't help myself. And even now hundreds of Angels are flying around, trying to repair the hole in the Human Timeline. By the end of the week, no one will know that the city of Delight even existed. All human records were destroyed, every bit of paper mentioning the city was subtly altered or, failing that, they burst into spiritual flames. Soon no one will remember that Delight or any of its residents ever existed. The tax rolls in Jefferson City, Missouri, will be adjusted to show that the whole area is undeveloped land.

"The only survivors of the flaming holocaust were the pets and farm animals. They have, of course, seen this many times before. From their place on the eternal stage, the animals seem to understand the nature of this human tragedy, and they accept this much the same way that they accept their unnatural relationships with their two-legged masters.

"And hundreds of angels carried away the souls of the 3,821 innocent children and babies who died that day in the firestorm at Delight. Dozens of angels worked very hard to catch all the bloody Unborn as they fell from the sky. Their souls will, of course, go directly to Heaven... do not pass Go, do not collect ten thousand sins. And I almost—I emphasize *almost*—felt a twinge of guilt for having deprived them of the chance to grow into adults and fully experience... well, the fully human experience.

"Human existence is often described as being a combination of ignorance, fanaticism and anxiety, and daily life is said to produce a trance-like state burdened with despair. Even so, we must let them grow in The Spirit, even as their feet are planted in the crapola of Earthly pain. We must gather souls to Heaven, by way of Our gentle guidance.

"In My last message, I perhaps went on a bit too much about carrots and sticks. We must progress beyond such primitive methods for converting the unbelievers. In the old days it was considered okay to use a sword to convert the heathens, but these days it is a lot harder to get away with that kind of stuff—at least in Europe.

"Nowadays we have to rely on advertising and making a good impression on the churchless. We can try to get 'em in that front door with promises of free rice, but that only worked in China, and not even there anymore. Now you have to convince them they want to be there in church, at least once a week. Even if it's only for the AA and the Christian Singles meetings. These days it's all about the benefits. And if a young virgin ends up with a hangover and dose of gonorrhea after going to church, well, that's just how it works—sometimes there are a few broken eggs.

"Yours Fondly,

"Archangel 'Archy' Screwletter."

Message #3: Christian Religious Sites—
Come Ninevah, Come Delight

"Sorry, I can't come to the phone right now, and my assistant is busy planting a fig tree in the back yard. But your call might be important to me, and so please leave your message after you hear the beep."

[BEEP!]

"Wurmig, is that you? Pick up, please. Hello... come on, pick up... O, Holy Fermentation! I hate these answering machines. Oh well... here I go."

[Noise in background as a wooden ladder on wheels is pushed along a library wall.]

"My Dear Wurmig,

"After My releasing of Heaven's Fire against the town of Delight, Missouri, there was quite an uproar among the lesser Angels, and Holy Heaven to pay. I am now forbidden to smite any town with a population of more than five thousand! Can you believe it! I, who smote the great cities of Aacorpophilia, Ambergris, and Anthraxica... and even Zinevah and Zondervahn! I, who have rendered a hundred thousand human corpses with the twitch of my left eyelash, I am now forbidden—forbidden!—to smite any town of any significant size without first getting the proper permissions and filling out the necessary forms... in triplicate! Oh, how The Mighty have fallen.

"It was one of those spotty Angels, the short one with the irritating voice and the peculiar lift in his right eyebrow. The one who always seems to be winking at you. He is the one who always delivers Heaven's Judgments.

"In the old days We had none of this secrecy. We went out of Our way to make sure everyone knew Who had done the smiting and why they were smote. When I demolished West Nineveh in a whirlwind of flame and smoke, you can believe Me that everyone across the river in East Nineveh knew the reason why. I'm sure you know the old story:

"The Prophet Jonah was walking through the streets preaching against the sinfulness of the people when the residents began taunting him and throwing feces off of the roof in his general direction. Normally, I am slow to wrath. And this act would not have resulted in immediate punishment. As I walked along, I was considering turning the cows' milk bad or perhaps causing the Tigris River to run red with the blood of a few dozen innocent first-born residents. And as I carefully considered the options, a bucket of rotten eggs was tossed on my head and my wings were covered in disgusting smelly yolks and broken eggshells.

"Back in the old days, I was a lot more patient than I am today. The city would have probably gotten off with a stern warning — probably a systematic cleansing from 353,231 cases of running diarrhea, combined with a plague of pus-filled sores and the occasional case of projectile vomiting. But no! — they just couldn't let it go. They were determined to humiliate poor Jonah, an Officially Recognized Prophet of the Lord God Jehovah, and no argument or reason could deter them. And then they threw rotten eggs on Me! The supernatural arrogance of these fools!

"It was then that I recalled the prophecy of the destruction of Nineveh that is written in the Book of Nahum 3:6: 'And I will cast abominable filth upon thee, and make thee vile, and will set thee as a gazingstock.' Yes, it was already clear from the writings of The Prophet. The people of Nineveh had dared to turn the tables on us... to make Me a gazingstock... can you believe it... a gazingstock! They were already doomed in God's book and by the prophecy of Nahum. It was therefore left up to Me to make good on his prophecy.

"My wings began to shudder uncontrollably, and then to vibrate. A dozen angels flew down and grabbed Jonah and carried him away to safety. And then... well, you know the drill. I laid waste to the city (no pun intended) and a hundred thousand souls were carried off to Hell, which in those days was just a little place — not much smaller than Australia. Well, actually it *was* Australia up until about 1350 B.C., but then the space shortage caused Heaven to open an annex of Hell in an uninhabited part of West Texas. Even today when you visit West Texas you can still detect the faint odor of human pain and suffering, mixed with something like burning tires, and sometimes a burnt curry smell with a dash of Old Spice.

"And that was the end of West Nineveh.

"I'm sure you know how it is. Back in the day no one would dare question My Authority. But now every sub-sub-Angel thinks it's his responsibility to second-guess my decisions. Even so, I'm not sorry about what I did. People who defy the Divine Will deserve whatever punishment that befalls them.

"If you are ever in Missouri and traveling down Highway 44, you can look for an exit with an abandoned Conoco station and a McDonald's, both standing alone on a high hill. That is all that is left of Delight, Missouri. If I had my way, this high spot should stand as a perpetual reminder of the physical Death and the certain spiritual Annihilation that awaits the Heathen in the flames of Hell.

"Yours Fondly,

"Archangel 'Archy' Screwletter."

* * *

Message #4: Christian Cleansing Technology

"Sorry, I can't come to the phone right now, and my assistant is busy pollinating the rose bush in the front yard. But your call may be important to me, and so please leave your message after you hear the beep."

[BEEP!]

"Wurmig, is that you? Pick up, please. Hello... oh, well... here I go...

"My Dear Wurmig,

"The next stop on Highway 44, after Delight, was at a small town called Mt. Vernon. We were still heading toward Carthage and the Precious Moments Chapel, where they have free admission to see the wonderful ceiling that rivals the famous Sistine Chapel in Rome. I was very hungry by then, but I was able to finally get my senior coffee and my Big N' Nasty hamburger, with no pickles, at the McDonald's in Mt. Vernon.

"As the bus pulled back onto the Highway, I detected a familiar odor. Moving down the aisle toward me was a rather bulky form, but it was the odor that hit me first—the smell of boiled cabbage, vinegar, and sausage. Yes, it had to be the Angel Stercutus. He was obviously sent here, by Heaven, to keep an eye on Me.

"Back in the third century, old Sterquilinus was a Roman rain god. The Romans prayed to him so that he would bring the gentle rains to their fields of wheat, their grape vineyards, and their olive trees. He was also known for doing a little fertility-god work on the side. He could be counted on to spread manure on your garden; and, if you were particularly reverent, he would come to your house at night and piss on your rose bushes.

"Sterquilinus was a fairly popular god to the Romans, early on, and he generally tried to avoid politics and religious disputes. But as the early Christians gained in political power, Sterquilinus decided to convert to Christianity; and Heaven was quite happy to make him an official Angel. His name was changed to the Roman-sounding 'Stercutus' and, as part of the deal, the High Priestess of his cult—who I think he was dating at the time—was given an extreme makeover and she became the Blessed Saint Margaret, the Patron Saint of Fertility. I think her Saint's day is celebrated on the twentieth of July. You probably weren't aware of this, but that kind of supernatural wheeling and dealing was fairly common in the old days, especially among the pagan gods in the area around Antioch and Ephesus. Not so much anymore.

"Anyway, the Angel Stercutus plopped down in the seat next to me. He bellowed out 'Hi! Screwy, how's the old tricks?'

"Stercutus always was one of those 'hail fellows' you read about in Shakespeare. He could have made a wonderful Falstaff in one of the plays. But I don't think Stercutus and Shakespeare could have known each other, or even been on speaking terms. The fact is that Stercutus considered himself to be a great Patron of the Arts, but in fact his taste was horrible. He was incapable of recognizing True Religiosity in art, and he always went for the gaudy, the vulgar, and the popular. He was a true Arse Poeticus. The last time I saw him, he was playing in a Christian grunge band in Salem, Oregon, in 1999. As usual, he had leaped onto a trendy idea just as it was going out of fashion.

"Stercutus was a rather large Angel, probably the size of St. Chris Farley (whereas I am a bit smaller, about the size of the actor Claude Rains, or perhaps Jude Law—except in those parts where I tend to resemble Tommy Lee). But Stercutus took up a good deal of space on the bus seat next to Me, and I had to manipulate space-time, just a bit, in order to get comfortable again.

"It was another thirty miles to Carthage and the wonderful Precious Moments Chapel. And so I was doomed to listen to Stercutus go on and on about his collection of signed Stephen King first editions, his collection of Frank Sinatra clown paintings, his collection of Elvis Presley's prescription bottles, his collection of Troll dolls from the 1960s, his collection of Pet Rocks from the 1970s, his collection of MC Hammer CDs from the 1980s, his collection of Vanilla Ice posters from the 1990s, and on and on and on.

"Meanwhile, about three dozen angels were passing among the other passengers with their collection plates. The angels were busily doing Brain Wipes on the passengers, trying to remove all memories of the destruction of Delight. Of course, this also meant cleaning the blood off of their clothes and removing any stray body parts that had fallen from the sky. For example, a Mennonite woman had a single human finger sticking up from her hat—looking like a tiny horn—until an angel removed the finger, delicately, and placed it in one of the collection plates.

"All in all, the older Mormons seemed to take this experience in stride. The Angels generally like dealing with Mormons, even if they are a bit dull... or maybe I'm thinking of the Jehovah's Witnesses... but anyway, the Mormons sat very still as the Angels passed the lily-white cleaning rags through their ears. It's actually fairly easy. You just stick the tip of the rag in one ear—kind of like threading a needle—and then you pull it out through the other ear. An experienced angel can whip his rag through a human brain like a magician pulling a tablecloth off of a table without moving any glassware. All the bad memories are easily removed by the Holy Cloth, but unfortunately the cloth is badly stained by the old bad thoughts and has to be taken to a laundry. I'm sure you know about that wonderful laundry in Turin. They do very good work in cleaning Our dainty tidy whites, and they add just the right amount of starch.

"The old people from the casino in St. Louis were a little more fidgety. I think this might have been a first time for most of them... I mean the whole Brain Wipe experience. The angels call them BWVs—or, Brain Wipe Virgins—and the whole process is a lot trickier, especially with the old ones. Their brains tend to be clogged up with a lot of old memories, and with some of them you have to use two, or sometimes even three Holy Cloths! And a few of them tend to twitch, and sometimes their legs jerk and they start kicking. Three years ago this elderly dentist from Genoa started kicking, and he caught the Angel Nuttbutter in the groin with a solid shot. It took four angels to hold the old guy down while they finished the Brain Wipe. And then the Angel Nuttbutter grabbed the old guy and kicked him in the groin a couple of times before returning him to his shop. But these things happen. As they say in Heaven these days, 'You can't make an omelette without busting a Nuttbutter or two.'

"Yours Fondly,

"Archangel 'Archy' Screwletter."

Message #5: The Precious Moments Chapel

"Sorry, I can't answer the phone right now, and my assistant is always digging in the garden these days. But your call is probably important to me, and so please leave your message after you hear the beep."

[BEEP!]

"Hello... Wurmig, is that you? Pick up, please... become a, come a, come a, comedian. Come on, Wurmig, pick up... oh, Fiddle-Styx!"

[Noise in background as a wooden crate is moved across a concrete floor.]

"My Dear Wurmig,

"Having to ride on the bus next to the Angel Stercutus was an ordeal, but it was worth it when we finally reached the Precious Moments Chapel & Gardens. As the tour bus pulled into the drive, I saw the beautiful metalized statues which stood on the edge of the pool and fountain. But before I get past the old folk exiting the bus, Stercutus had already waddled over to the deluxe fountain and the glorious bronze (or maybe brass) statues gathered around a lugubriously dark and unreflective pool.

"Stercutus began to gush incoherently about the beautiful pool and statues. It was hard to appreciate the sublime beauty of the figures in the context of his constant chatter, but soon the ordeal was over and we entered the doors of the Welcome Center. The long hall led directly to the official gift shop, which was filled with hundreds of collectible figurines. A sign proclaimed that these figurines were available nowhere else. Once again Stercutus began to blather on, this time over the beauty of the Pocahontas figurine; her large bulbous head sat dreamily upon a tiny body, with large black braids cascading down from her mottled Indian headband. Her skin color was, perhaps, a shade darker than the Gretel (and Hansel) dolls, but her enormous full dark eyes quite literally drew you into her tiny soulfulness. I admit, she was hard to resist.

"We spent perhaps an hour in the gift shop, where Stercutus 'ooohd' and 'aaahhhd' over all the porcelain figurines, from George and Martha Washington and Betsy Ross—who is in the Famous Women series—to the Heroes of the Old Testament collectible-plates series. But I was really and truly amazed by the sheer number of Angel figurines and dolls—of all sorts—and even a poster of an angel sitting on a cloud and talking into a cell phone, evidently advertising the new Precious Moments cell-phone service. Unbelievable!

"Soon we made out way out of the gift shop and into the great hall. As it happened, it was about a week before Christmas and our old friend Santa was sitting in his gigantic chair, listening to a child ask for gifts, while a young female elf took their photo. I knew that Stercutus and Santa were friends, from back in the old days when they were both pagan gods. I imagine they met at several ancient covens and perhaps even shared a bowl of mulled wine or a flagon of mead on the festive occasions of the Roman Saturnalia and the winter solstice.

"Stercutus nodded to Santa, and Santa — smiling broadly — nodded in return, with a wink and a chuckle. Then Stercutus said, 'He's not looking so good this year. But, of course, he's had a very hard life. The wear and tear of Christmas is really taking its toll.'

"'What do you mean?' I said, a bit offended at his tone.

"'Well, you wouldn't know it to see him now, but back in his youth Santa was — as the kids say — really rather buff. He was once a solid one hundred ninety pounds soaking wet in his leather jerkins, but the years of persecution really wore on him. The Christian church in Norway pursued him and persecuted him for centuries. And after St. Olaf ran the pagans out of Norway in 1024, he threw Santa into prison — well, it was all too horrible to imagine... especially for a pretty young boy like Santa.'

"'Wait! What are you suggesting?' I said.

"Stercutus snorted and said, 'Well, how do you think he got the name Nichol-as? Anyway, he put on a lot of weight while he was in prison, and he was only released after promising to become the spiritual representative of Christmas throughout the world. He is a unique being, because he possesses and is possessed by every human who puts on the Santa costume. Poor Santa shares his spiritual nature with many good men... but there are thousands of the alcoholics, and the impoverished and homeless share his soul, too. After eight hundred years of this, it can get very difficult, and a being like Santa has mental problems that we can only imagine.'

"Stercutus and I left the hall and walked down the garden path to the Precious Moments Chapel. And — amazingly enough — there we met St. Roma. Many centuries ago, she had been the Municipal Spirit of Rome, but after the conversion it was decided, On High, that she would have to leave Rome and become the Patron Saint of some other town. It was decided that she would rotate her time among all the towns of Roman descent. And so today she was the Patron Saint of Italy, Texas, a small town south of Dallas, and just down the road from Willy Nelson's ranch. As we approached Roma's presence, we could see that she was drinking water from a clear plastic bottle. It was 'Willy Water' — the official water of Willy Nelson, with his 'Always on your mind' taste. Clearly she had a 'product placement' deal.

"Roma wore the traditional black nun's habit and a leather thong — and very little else. The Archangel Michael, years ago, described Roma as all the street whores (male and female) who ever plied their trade in Rome, rolled into a ball and given one pair of shapely legs and six pairs of fishnet stockings.

"As we approached Roma, she barked out the order, 'Hon, get my cigs.' A tiny capuchin monkey suddenly sprang up her backside and, swinging from one breast to the next, found a pack of Camels and a lighter wedged into a roll of fat near Roma's armpit. Roma lit up the cigarette, and as we walked up, she recognized Stercutus. She smiled, pressed her enormous breasts together and did a shimmy for his (and hopefully not my) benefit.

"'Hey Sterquilinus, how's tricks?' she bellowed, and then flicked an ash from her cigarette onto the bald head of a nearby Mormon elder. The female Saint and the Angel exchanged pleasantries, and we discovered that St. Roma was here to see the famous chapel, too. The town of Carthage had applied for a new patron saint, and — amazingly — Roma was in the running for that honor. I tried to ignore their chatter, but then I noted a condom wedged into a roll of fat on her thigh. It was used. I knew that Roma — as a supernatural being — could not contract a venereal disease. So I assume the condom was her boyfriend's idea. No point taking chances. (I guess maybe old Willy must be smarter than he looks.)

"A tour guide appeared — thankfully — at that moment and diverted my attention to the interior of the Precious Moments Chapel. The walls and the ceiling were, indeed, decorated with dozens of PM figures. The characters from the Old and New Testaments lined the walls, their bulbous heads and enormous eyes smiling and enjoying God's favor, here in His sight. Yes! This was TruChristian Art, if ever I have seen it, and the child-like faith reflected in their faces filled me with Love and Compassion for all Mankind, and even Womankind, too.

"At the right side of the vestry, a series of clouds were lifting the souls of children into the heavens. Each cloud was like a fluffy elevator, carrying the children skyward. And at the top was the City of God and Jesus, himself, talking to a small child. The child seemed to be explaining something to Him.

"And so sometime next week you should receive a letter with My Official Certification that this wonderful Chapel is the spiritual equal of the Sistine Chapel in Rome. Both St. Roma and the Angel Stercutus have offered to co-sign the document, if you so wish.

"Yours Fondly,

"Archangel 'Archy' Screwletter.

"P.S.: Roma says 'Hi!'"

EPILOGUE

This ends the phone messages from Archy Screwletter. Apparently Cardinal Ratzinger changed his phone number and no further messages were recorded. We can always hope that Archy can use his heavenly contacts to get the Pope's new number for his private line, but until then this is the end.

— The Editor

*T*his first volume of Atheist Tales *wasn't trying to highlight American-only writers, but it did mostly end up that way. The exception is Marianna Manns, a young Canadian woman who has presented us with a fascinating religious dystopia that could feasibly be in our future. But unlike many dystopian tales such as this, Marianna has given us a story that transcends the church taking over; rather, she gives us a very different, and very original, reason why. Can religion be faulted for becoming the overlords of the world and humanity when its reasons go far beyond simply the tenets of its faith?*

From Above

Marianna Manns

The unrelenting sun scalded the crowd of worshipers that had gathered to listen to the Messengers. It was only once a week that anyone faced the intensity of midday; except for days of temple, citizens rested while the sun was highest in the sky. They would not complain of their personal ordeal—the poor with their bare feet blistering on the baked ground and the rich with sweat soaking their silk garments—for the wealthy and the poor served alike. On one day of every week they knelt outside the temple like equals.

It had been the Messengers who decided that fortune had no place in the sacraments. "The Gods reward those who follow their laws," they said, "regardless of standing." Those who were privileged enough to indulge in luxuries on any other day found no favour at the temple. They knelt outside on the ground next to the poor, albeit with palm-fiber sandals to protect their feet and heavy veils covering porcelain skin.

Everyone knelt in silence, stone-like and still, their heads bowed. Enduring the steaming temperature, the stifling air, the blinding sun, and the stinging sand, not one person so much as whimpered in discomfort. All wore faces of stone as they awaited the ceremony.

A boy called Sajha knelt in the front row, staring down at his sun-stained toes. Like those around him, his face did not display the pain of sitting stiffly in an awkward position while the skin on the bottoms of his feet baked beneath him. He tried not to think about his flesh cooking as if on a charred iron grill, but images of thick, blackened slabs of meat kept squirming into his head.

Instead of supporting him in his crouched position, his calloused hands were crossed over his chest. It was a struggle of will to keep them there as his calves began to cramp. He had lived for sixteen years under the reign of the Messengers. If the Gods willed him to kneel in wait for an indeterminate amount of time without moving a muscle before each ceremony, then he would. But even the Gods and their Messengers could not prevent his bitterness. He was still human.

Sajha hoped that his thoughts were not reflected on his face. He had never been given any indication that the Gods could access his mind, but if the Messengers saw his displeasure his family could lose its favour.

His family flanked him on both sides, a devout group of workers strong of body and of faith. They served the Gods and were rewarded for it. Sajha's sister, Aalya, had recently been granted permission to study at the temple of the Messengers. It was an honour for their family, bringing them a scholarly status. Sajha had also benefited personally from her elevation.

It was unheard of for a well-off young lady like Jade to speak with him, but Sajha had mustered up the courage to at Aalya's acceptance ceremony. Jade was a daughter of one of the Messengers, and looking across the crowd at her now, Sajha felt that she was wrapped in mystery. Her hair had a red sheen to it, and her skin was a light cream, hardly touched by the sun. Her eyes did not wander the crowd as his did. She stared straight ahead to the dais at the foot of the temple, where the Messengers would stand, with a knowing look in her almond-shaped eyes. Jade was not mystified by the Messengers, which made sense, being that she was the daughter of one. Her pride and confidence left him bewildered that she would converse with him.

Yet at Aalya's acceptance ceremony, while the early guests waited in a shadowy alcove on the side of the courtyard, Sajha had made an effort to work his way toward her. Jade had looked regal and omniscient that day as well. He had searched his brain for something to say to her, but was speechless until she spoke.

"That is your sister. Your family must be proud."

Sajha was surprised at her confidence and way of speaking. There was no questioning inflection in her voice, and he was put off guard, but eventually replied, "Yes, they are."

"They have good reason. The Messengers choose few disciples." Jade glanced into the bright courtyard to where Aalya was preparing for her initiation, a look of genuine concern in her eyes. "You will help her with her studies, I am sure? Some are unable to take the strain of being chosen by the Messengers."

"I will."

"She will do well, then," Jade replied. Then, as suddenly as the conversation had begun, she had picked up her skirts of undyed cotton and whisked herself away.

Remembering the conversation set Sajha's heart pumping. He wished he had said something more intelligent or interesting, and he replayed the situation over again in his mind, imagining all the things he could have said to impress her. More than once he thought of what it would be like if he had been chosen to study with the Messengers.

The memory faded from his mind as the Messengers approached. The soft swish of robes and the plodding of leather-shod feet penetrated the silence. Seven figures, clothed in simple white, took lengthy, measured strides towards the centre of the crowd. Men and women alike wore their hair long and looked majestic despite modest garbs. They took in the crowd with steady gazes, their faces impossible to read.

The Messengers spoke as one, their words unified eerily in a single voice made up of a variation in timbres and pitches, yet clear and distinctive. "Today the worshipping of the Gods must be delayed to contend with an issue that has come to their attention." The voices were expressionless, revealing nothing, but Sajha's breath caught in his chest at their words.

"There has been a violation of the will of the Gods that must be dealt with swiftly and effectively. A third child has been born to a family, in direct disobedience to the Gods' will. This growth in population is unacceptable, but the children will be raised by the Messengers of the Gods, cared for by the generosity of the State. This is a place of honour for them, but penitence must be paid by their antecedents."

They turned as one towards the temple and motioned for the crowd to look upon the lawbreakers, a pair of married merchants, who were escorted by one unarmed guard. Fear was evident in their faces but they did not try to escape. They walked bravely to the dais and knelt before the Messengers.

Their obedience was surprising to Sajha, who felt that he would fight defiantly even if he had broken the rules. He understood that the Gods' laws were for the benefit of their society, but as he imagined himself before that dais all he could envision was a struggle, to put all of his physical strength to hindering his assailants. He would scream and beg for mercy, for the crowd around him to rise against this brutal authority.

Yet in all the oppression he had seen in his life, never had a victim pleaded. They always accepted their fate peacefully. Most said it was the will of the Gods, or the power of the Messengers, that strengthened people as they faced their punishment. The couple knelt with careworn faces raised, dignified, toward the sky.

The Messengers spoke in their unnatural harmony: "It is the Gods' wish that you receive this punishment and restore the order that your actions have corrupted. You do well to accept your punishment."

The pair before them stiffened and fell to the ground, faces completely relaxed in the peace of death. They did not utter a sound suggesting pain or fear, and the cause of death was not evident. The crowd was just as still, for they had seen such rituals hundreds of times. Sajha was young enough to wonder what strange magic the Messengers possessed and whether they could use it however they wished. Fearfully, he imagined the Messengers disobeying the Gods and using their powers to control his people.

The continuation of the ceremony drew Sajha's mind from its fantastical scenarios. Even as the corpses were being dragged away, the children were brought through the crowd, the eldest carrying a newborn infant. The Messengers hid nothing, it seemed. Or perhaps, as Sajha thought bitterly, they paraded certain atrocities to keep others hidden in plain sight.

Though their skin was tanned and cracked from hard outdoor labour, the two elder children wore faces as pale as fresh milk. They bore their fate as stoically as had their parents. Their eyes were fixed on the Messengers without flinching. What sorcery kept the children from mourning the loss of their mother and father? Sajha remained in a shocked daze through the rest of the proceedings. He watched as the children were initiated into the Messengers' service, and as the eldest publicly accepted their offer of care. But Sajha was not watching what occurred in reality; he saw the events of his mind's eye unfold before him.

He imagined the boy calling out in a rage that transcended his humanity, his arms swinging wildly to beckon the crowd to join him in his vengeance before streaking towards his parents' murderers. While one hand struck out at the closest Messenger, the other searched the prophet's robes until it found a sacrificial knife and plunged the blade into the feebly protesting man's chest. But then, surely, the sky would darken as the sun would be blocked out by the Messengers' shadow magic and the Gods themselves would arrive, surfing gales of wind or appearing in clusters of exploding sparks, and, assuredly, all would be punished. Perhaps, Sajha thought as he returned to the reality, the boy was as afraid of the consequences as he.

Similar ideas played their way through his inner vision even after the children took their places kneeling. The weekly ritual of Curing followed the punishments.

Citizens who were sick came forth in an orderly queue and were fed strange concoctions which usually healed them instantaneously. The mixtures were a secret from the Gods. Only occasionally did people get violently ill, and in that event the Curing occurred only partly in public. Injuries were also dealt with out of sight, and few knew how the more serious wounds were healed.

When the last were cured, the ceremony turned to meaningless rituals that bored Sajha. Prayers, repeated by the masses, were followed by handholding throughout the crowd, the lighting of a single candle and its dousing by a few gentle drops of water. Finally, there was an admonition from the Messengers to lead auspicious, good lives, following the laws of the Gods. Sajha supposed that the Messengers were symbolised by the healing rain, and a disobedient citizen by the flame of destruction. A similar fire burned in his gut.

His unease was extinguished by relief as soon as he was allowed to stand. He stretched his muscles and headed along with the crowd to the water trough.

He was met there by a familiar face. Upon seeing Aalya, his thirst was forgotten. Sajha pushed through the crowd to the girl, a slightly more feminine and shapely reflection of himself. Her hair now grew past her shoulders, a thick mass of ebony, and a change since the days when she had worked the fields with it cropped well above her stubborn chin. They shared the same heavily lashed, inquisitive eyes. As they embraced, the tension in Sajha's grip betrayed his agitation to his perceptive sister.

Her eyes became concerned as they drew apart. "My brother, what troubles you?"

Sajha looked around the crowd of thirsty worshippers and wondered whether this was a safe place to speak freely. No one was paying them any mind and it would be less suspicious to stay here than to sneak off. Drawing close enough to Aalya to speak softly into her ear, he was unsure of what to say even to someone he could trust completely. Perhaps his suspicious thoughts should not be vocalised at all.

Slowly and deliberately, he finally managed to say, "I feel... unsettled by the execution today."

He was appreciative that Aalya kept her face as smooth as still water. She did not look up at him and replied while hardly moving her lips. "We all doubt the Messengers sometimes, but they always work for the greater good."

"I know why they did it, but there is something so... inhuman about it."

"The Messengers serve a higher power, one that is not human but has our best interests in mind. The deaths here today were in service of a greater purpose, one which we cannot understand. The mystery in their ceremonies comes from this benevolent force. You would do well not to question it."

Sajha had never heard anyone talk like this about the Gods, as if they were entirely unlike human people and impossible to understand. Something Aalya had learned since becoming a disciple must have changed her perspective. "There is something you are not telling me," he said.

"No, I mean it. The Messengers work for something no one can comprehend. This became clear when I first stepped inside the temple. There is more to their magic than we see. I'm not certain I can describe it."

"Please try," Sajha said. "I need your reassurance."

Aalya hesitated. "Well, the inside of the private chambers is like nothing I have ever imagined. I don't mean ceremonial decorations and great treasures; it's not like that. It's like nothing you'd see in the village, the marketplace, the farming houses, or even the richest homes. A cold light illuminates the classrooms, and there's nothing there made of wood, stone, cloth. They make things out of glass that's never burnt, and so clear there's never a trace of colour. And everything is perfectly clean without a single grain of sand or smudge of dirt. In some of the rooms there are strange things that work on their own, like magic, even when no Messengers are there."

In her fervour, she'd regressed from learned scholar to excited farm girl. Sajha could tell that this had been bothering her for some time. "We're not supposed to talk about any of this, not even to our families — as if they could understand it." She drew closer to him and whispered, "They teach us to make the Curing potions, but we don't know what they're for. I think some aren't for healing sickness at all."

Sajha's eyes grew wide. "What do you suppose they're for?"

"I don't know, but they only bring a few types to the Curing ceremony. The rest go to the Messengers' private inner sanctum. There were rumours today that the man and woman who were executed were brought from there. It is not the first such rumour."

"You were telling me how this all came from a benevolent force acting for the good of humanity," he said.

Aalya's shocked expression told him that, in trying to prove her point, she had talked herself out of it. She shook her head as if to dislodge those ridiculous notions. "You're right. Forget what I've said. We can't understand the Messengers or the Gods. But their actions improve our society."

Sajha was impressed at how quickly Aalya had talked herself back into her safe beliefs. Perhaps, he realised, the Messengers had not chosen her as a disciple for her hunger for knowledge, but her naivety. He let his disappointment with her play across his face as he turned and walked away. The Messengers were not the only ones capable of manipulation. Even if Aalya convinced herself that all was well, Sajha knew that this would gnaw at her. For the next week, Sajha would be unable to do anything, while Aalya would decide where her loyalties lay.

Another sizzling day held the next week's ceremony. Sajha knelt in the front row, his muscles locked and unwavering. A week of gruelling labour and steady routine had quelled his rebellious spirit. Now the only thing bothering him was his uncomfortable stance. He took deep breaths and tried to clear his mind, but he had never been good at that. Rogue thoughts darted out of the shadows when he least expected it, such as a musing as to what effect his glare had had on his sister.

He also could not keep his mind off his family. With Aalya living in the temple, Sajha was an only child. He was growing out of a difficult youth, and learning to take over his family's land was causing him to become like his kind and noble father, Rahka. Kneeling beside him, Rahka's face was sun-stained and ragged, stretched like thinning leather. It was deeply wrinkled around eyes that once may have gleamed inquisitively, but that light had long since faded. Rahka worked hard to remain in the Gods' favour, teach his children right from wrong, and protect his family from the Messengers.

Once, when Sajha was a boy, he and a few other children sneaked into the temple, and Rahka had talked the Messengers out of punishing him. Sajha didn't know what had happened, but he was sure he had been old enough to remember. He could see the outer hall in his mind's eye: a shadowy entranceway into dark catacomb passages. There was a feeling attached to the perception. They had been young and adventurous, loud and boisterous, but upon entering the temple they were filled with awe and a tingle of fear that brought silence. Everything about marching up those sunlit stone steps was clear in his mind—the excitement and curiosity, the heat on his skin before the relief of cool darkness, and even the packed sand under his fingernails—but past those doors he could form only a single picture. The entrance hall was dimly lit with an unidentifiable light source, ancient and imposing. Age-old artefacts hung from the walls. He felt he must have been there a long time, more than long enough to run through the catacombs with his friends, but all that remained for him was a single frozen image.

Then he was out in the sun again, his father's farmer arms defending him. He had never heard the man speak so desperately. "Please don't take my son," Rahka had pleaded. "We are servants of the Gods. We exalt them. We teach our children to serve, O Prophets of the Infinite. It will not happen again. Please do not take him from us."

Sajha could remember all of that clearly. His father's arms had shaken and one tear had run down his stone face as he bowed to the ground.

Finally giving up on his meditation, Sajha decided that focusing on something else would keep the bodily pain at bay. His concentration was unwavering as he mentally recited the lessons. "Barley and wheat are planted before the rain season. They are harvested in the spring and offered to the Gods. Barley can stand harsher conditions. We are lucky to have enough rainfall to cultivate wheat; we trade surplus with nearby communities. When there is drought in summer, the yield is low. We use irrigation from the diverted Gadi Whazza stream to help the vegetables and legumes. We must make sure that the stream can replenish itself faster than we use it up." Then there was something about renewable sources and returning nutrients to the soil. That part made so little sense to him that he could not memorise it, and it seemed like there were holes in the teachings.

Luckily his break in concentration did not lead to more pain, for just as he gave up struggling to remember something about nitrogen-fixing or salinity, the Messengers arrived. Their communal voice rarely conveyed any emotion, but today they sounded sorrowful.

"There has been another transgression. We are disappointed that so many crimes have been committed in recent weeks. To prevent further breaking of the Gods' laws we wish to remind all citizens that while crimes against individuals can often be resolved peacefully, crimes against the state require justice against the guilty. Disobeying any of the Gods' laws, therefore, is punishable by death.

"The law restricts dangerous research and development by unlicenced parties. Those with technological-studies licences are subject to the limitations imposed by the Gods.

"Yesterday a group of researchers was discovered in the outer sanctum of the temple. They were using the tools provided for peaceful, sustainable development to construct weapons far too malevolent to be permitted. Such weapons could be used to wage war and kill hundreds of people who are simply trying to live harmoniously with us, destroying the planet's beauty at the same time.

"To prevent this dangerous advancement in technology, the Gods have ordered that we, their Messengers, pay retribution to those who have threatened our way of life."

As the offenders reached the dais in the centre of the crowd their dead eyes made Sajha think of Aalya's speculations about strange medicine and a mysterious inner sanctum. Had the men before him come from the Messengers' private room? Their helpless, gaunt faces suggested so.

The Messengers conducted a sort of simplified trial before the people of Gaza. "Do you admit to researching dangerous weapons?"

The men responded in a chorus similar to that of the Messengers. "I do," they all said calmly.

"Do you understand the necessity for your execution, and recognise the infinite Gods as your lawmakers and judges?"

Again they replied uniformly, "I do."

"Do you submit yourself now to their judgment?"

"I do."

The words made it effortlessly from their mouths. They did not even choke. Each fell to the ground with truly dead eyes.

Sajha found that he was calmer after this execution. If the men accepted that they deserved to die, then so be it. They had admitted freely to committing the crime. Hadn't they? Again Sajha's imagination ran off with him. He had seen that the Messengers had the power to kill and to heal; perhaps they could also control people. But if the Gods were truly benevolent, they would not give such powers to their governors. Perhaps it was the potions, then. Perhaps the Messengers had learned how to make concoctions for purposes other than those intended by the Gods. If that were so, it would mean that the Messengers could kill whoever they wanted without the Gods' approval. Going against the Gods in this way would surely bring trouble to Sajha's people.

As always, the ceremony went on as the bodies were dragged away. It was time for the weekly Curing. Not a step was missed in the routine. The Messengers called up the citizens in line, questioned them about their ailments, took some strange measurements with instruments that were inserted into mouths and ears, and administered the medicine with a blessing. When they were all done, a blessing was said for the health and benefit of all.

Then it was over again. Again Sajha was parched, but he knew he would not drink until he had spoken with his sister.

This time his parents had spotted Aalya first and were greeting her excitedly. Their mother wanted to know all about her lessons, what could be revealed at least, and their father made sure she had everything she needed. Rahka's chest swelled visibly with pride.

While she was with their parents, Sajha felt a firm arm

ushering him away from his family. Jade led him to a bustling part of the crowd. Even surrounded by sweaty peasants he could make out the rich fragrance of spices trailing after her.

As she stopped, he found that she made an effort to stand next to him, rather than facing him. "Your sister does not wish to speak of it, but she conveyed your sentiments to me."

She spoke at a perfectly audible volume so that he did not have to watch her lips. In return, he avoided looking at her, but he thought that must look even more obvious. His eyes were drawn to her and it was to be expected that a boy of his age gawk and stare at her beauty.

When he did not answer she continued. "Aalya will not tell you, but she saw the men who concern you going into the inner sanctum. And I saw one more leaving than went in. Rumours also only counted four researchers, yet five were executed. I think a man was killed for a crime he did not commit."

Sajha's eyes were wide, and before she could continue he was calling for action. "The Messengers have gone too far if they are covering up the true reason for an execution. That is murder. We have to expose them."

"We must be cautious. If I am to go against my own father, I must be sure."

"There's no time," Sajha protested. Plans were formulating and playing out before his eyes, and the best plan, albeit the most reckless, would not even involve Jade. If all went well, anyway. "I will take care of it. You will not have to betray your family."

Before she could say anything else he was wading through the sea of people, back toward the dais. His heart was pumping madly and he knew his plan was just as mad. But something had to be done. He would turn around the evils of the Messengers and lead his people to a new way.

Gathering up all of his courage, he began to yell at the top of his voice. "It is just meant to control us all! It is not real. Do not trust them!" His thoughts tumbled out over a thick, parched tongue and quickly gained in volume. Before he realised what he was doing, various theories of deceit and treachery were spewed from his mouth. The crowd around him spread out to clear themselves of any blame and many fell to their knees facing the Messengers.

Some of the Messengers turned towards him. Oddly, he did not feel as though he were any peril, but more like a child about to be punished for shouting the truth when the truth was not appropriate. Like such a child, he stood defiantly with hands on hips. A guard grabbed him from behind and put him in such a tight hold that he could not struggle in the least, and the leader of the Messengers revealed himself by speaking alone.

"This boy has shown disrespect to the Gods and their prophets. However, it is evident that he is quite mad. We will confer directly with the Gods to determine, with their counsel, whether we must take his life as punishment for treason."

Without his chorus, the man's voice was sharp as a knife and far more threatening.

Sajha sat blindfolded with little room to stretch his legs, as he had for seven days. He knew how much time had passed only because a rough voice had barked that today was his execution day. But he did not plan to die. His plan was a simple act of will, requiring only that he refuse to stand acquiescently before the Messengers while they brought about his untimely demise. Whatever they did to make the others abandon themselves in their final moments would not work on him. His will was strong.

It was also strong enough to block out ideas of all of the things that could go wrong. Sitting in that cramped position in the complete dark for so many days, he had had plenty of time to construct scenarios, most of them involving his own death. But today he would not waver.

The door creaked open. One pair of hands reached for his

blindfold while another took Sajha's hands and pulled him up. The blindfold was off. His enemies surrounded him on all sides. And there was that cold, alien light Aalya had described. He was deep inside the temple, perhaps in the inner sanctum.

The Messengers wore solemn faces that suggested disappointment, but Sajha met their deceitful eyes with an unruly glare. After a week living in a cupboard, his glower was probably not as fierce as he imagined it to be, but gaunt and bony. The image weakened his resolve a little bit and, as if sensing the shift, the Messengers chose that moment to move him to the centre of the room. They sat him down on an armchair, and metal cuffs snapped shut over his wrists to hold him securely. Aalya had not been lying when she said that everything was unnatural, from the lights to the shiny green material that coated his chair.

The Messengers had been watching him take in his surroundings. He refused to ask them a single question, certain that they would feed off his insecurity. He knew he had to be unwavering. Finally the leader from the last ceremony stood in front of the white wall and spoke.

"We have hoped that in the past few days you have had time to reflect on what you have done. Only that can prepare you for what we are about to show you."

Reflect on what he had done? Had there been any moisture in his mouth, Sajha would have worked up every bit of precious saliva and spewed it across the man's face. Instead he spoke through a parched throat. "I have done nothing but speak the truth."

"It was my daughter who informed us that your faith was wavering. Jade is very good at ferreting out those who doubt our ways, so that they may be brought back to the truth."

Jade. The name cut deeply. His heart bled for the betrayal. The man must have seen Sajha grimacing, for he added, "You must forgive her. You see, one day she will replace me. Currently, it is her job to ensure peace and stability in our world."

But Sajha could not forgive her for fooling him. He had been so certain of her good character, her integrity, but he had forgotten that he barely knew her. He had imagined her to be brave, strong, and virtuous, and she had used this fantasy to earn his trust—then betray him. This he would not forgive.

"You are here for the truth to be revealed," said the lead Messenger. Sajha nearly snorted with disdain before the Messengers walked behind him, and was left to deal with Jade's duplicity.

The lights faded completely. In the middle of the floor before Sajha, a fire sprang up without apparent cause or sustaining fuel. Only it was not exactly a fire, but a brilliant orange ball caked with grey smoke that had been preceded by a thunderous boom. Had he not been strapped down, Sajha would have leapt from his seat and run, all thoughts of Jade abandoned. But then he realised that while the combustion was only a few feet away from him, he felt no heat. Somehow the Messengers had conjured up an image of an explosion.

The first boom was followed by many others, some with a backdrop of a blue sky and impossibly tall structures crumbling over an impossible number of people who were tiny and scattering like ants. At first this supplemented his feelings of anger and pain. One ball of fire enveloped a sea of green trees. Three-dimensional images showed the impact of a bomb throwing a crowd of people helter-skelter in all directions, or a building coming down on top of its occupants, many of them rushing down flights of stairs to get out. Such violence and death Sajha had never encountered, and it dwarfed the evils of the Messengers. But he supposed that was the point.

Next there was an image of a village quite like Sajha's own. Adobe buildings a few stories high were surrounded by sandy roads. The chaos in the streets drew Sajha's attention. An explosion demolished half of a mud-brick home, but the men surrounding it were preoccupied. They were fighting, hiding behind whatever shelter they could find, and loud bangs preceded many of their deaths. They fell to the ground, clutching hearts, arms, and legs, and spewing blood from wounds that appeared from nowhere. Every man in the street fight fell, dead.

Next he saw a young woman who looked more like what he expected to see in his village, only she spoke in a language he could not understand. She was talking in an animated voice as if to herself. Large white letters appeared before his face, he assumed to translate her speech.

"We cannot resort to mass weaponry. This is not our fight. They say we should attack while they are weak, but this will only lead to a war we cannot win." Her eyes were pleading.

They were replaced by determined and hateful eyes set in a pale face that surely had never seen the light of day. "We must take back our country, whether by expulsion or extermination, so that we may focus on our family lives and personal livelihoods. This has gone on far too long. Racial mixing is weakening the gene pool and undoing the Gods' work of ethnic division. The inferior and the sinful are infesting our lands. A pestilence is upon us, and soon too will the Gods' wrath be."

Then another man appeared. His skin was much darker than any Sajha had seen or thought possible. "The death toll has risen to seven million dead in this civil war. Reports claim that the terrorist attack today was unprovoked. Retribution will be had against the so-called Nationalists."

The man was replaced by more images of fire, explosions so big they were enveloping entire cities, smoke raising high into the sky. Piles of human bodies wearing blood-soaked clothes sprawled on the floor before him. With one final boom it was over and he saw the barren land he was so familiar with. No green, no sea of trees, no anthills full of people. Just desert. Everywhere.

Then it was gone. When the lights returned, Sajha realised he was shaking. He blinked away tears before the Messengers had made it around the chair to see him. Again, one spoke alone.

"Now you see our past, what we are trying to prevent. History is doomed to repeat itself, they used to say—but not if history is erased. Not if no one remembers.

"The means are important too. Nuclear weaponry is a dangerous tool that killed millions at once, and it was a double-edge sword. Everyone involved suffered. From the moment of its creation, mass destruction was inevitable. So we, the survivors, prevented it from being reinvented. Any technology that could yield information toward nuclear power will never be permitted. And we slowed development altogether. Now do you understand, Sajha?"

Chastened, the boy nodded. The world he had seen was far worse than the one he lived in. He submitted. Then he sought some answers. "Who was that angry man, the pale one?"

"In the hologram you saw a man of great wisdom." A hologram, they called the image. But their strange magic seemed unimportant now. Sajha discarded the thought as the Messenger continued. "He was the inspiration on how to implement peace. It was his belief that conflict could be avoided if people who were different from one another were kept separate. If each group kept to its own territory, they could have their own rules without interfering with each other."

It made sense, keeping different peoples divided. "I understand," he said.

"I knew you would. You are an intelligent boy, and our forefathers knew what was best for our people."

"Forefathers? I thought the Gods knew best."

The Messengers exchanged glances. Then words were exchanged.

"It's too late for him anyway," said one.

"Let him hear the truth first," agreed a second.

The leader conceded and turned back to Sajha. "It is time you knew. Before I tell you the truth, think of everything we do for the benefit of our society. Think of how we control technology, consumption of resources, the population, crime—even small things like greed, violence, disorder. You see how it is crucial to name the Gods our lawmakers. In truth, it has been over a thousand years since the Gods have spoken to a Messenger. They do not guide us day to day, but we follow their teachings and have faith that we are doing what is best."

"The Gods do not speak to you? They did not tell you to kill anyone who finds out the truth?"

"They guide us only with their principles, laid down before all of this chaos. But no, they do not give us direct orders. We make the decisions and use the people's beliefs for order. Can you blame us, Sajha? The people are more receptive to our laws if those laws come from an omniscient being."

"If the Gods have not spoken to anyone in a thousand years, how do you know they exist? That their principles are still valid?"

"We have faith." The man stepped forward, knelt before Sajha, looked into his eyes as if they were those of a child. The answer seemed weak, but what did that matter compared to the destruction Sajha had just witnessed?

"Extreme measures must be put into place to maintain peace," the man went on. "One of those measures is the pretence of the Gods' guidance. To keep up this illusion, you must be punished publicly for treason. There is no other way."

Sajha nodded again. They were right. This was beyond his individual desire for survival.

He did not object when one of the Messengers came forward with a long, thin needle and injected him with some unknown potion. Normally such a foreign, threatening object would have frightened Sajha, but he was deep in thought.

"Sajha, in one hour you will be brought before your people and you will die to protect them. The poison already courses through your veins. You cannot fight it now. If you are ready, we will escort you to a place where you may come to terms with your decision privately."

Again the boy nodded, berated by having been so certain he was right, only to find out he had been wrong. And it had cost him his life.

Sajha stood in that same dark chamber in the temple — the one from his childhood of which he could only remember a single picture from one precise angle. He had a moment to look around and create a memory. The mud-brick walls were carved with thick symbols that meant nothing to him. He had learned to read, but these must have been an ancient script. It was there that they left him to think.

The decision was his. He could still follow his plan and defy them openly. But who was he to decide the fate of his people? The Messengers claimed to know the history of the world. He knew only the brief glimpses that they allowed him, and even that was enough to see. Those who had died before him must have agreed. There was far less death this way.

His people would develop slowly with the Messenger's ideology in mind. They would live peaceful lives without pain and violence. The Messengers were right. The past was hidden by lies, but those lies protected the future.

The fires and bombs were etched on his eyelids so that each time he even blinked he saw the horror. He envisioned the bodies of his family and friends strewn on dusty streets, covered in scorch marks and abrasions. He saw his father lying face-up on a pile of corpses. Dead eye sockets haunted him. This was the repeated history the Messengers were preventing.

No longer did Sajha see himself fighting the Messengers for his survival. He would accept his death as a tribute to the world he had known. He would bow his head before them and submit. For the greater good.

The longer they left him alone in that room, the more justified he felt his decision was. Many objections occurred to him, but he brushed them aside as the selfish desire to live. He deserved to die for attempting to disrupt the Messengers' peace. He would die with his head held high like so many before him. They had all realised the good of their sacrifice too.

The objections slowed and his mind calmed. Going back to examining his surroundings, he felt a new peace within himself. His eyes traced the shapes in the wall. Calmed now, his youthful curiosity took hold of him and he stepped down the corridor. The dark passageway beckoned him, and any fear was easily overcome. In less than an hour he would be dead.

The carvings began to change as he walked along the corridor. No longer meaningless symbols, they were now shaped like naked, faceless men standing with arms and legs spread wide, heads sideways in profile. They were all carved figures the colour of the sandy walls. But then there was a little man painted with red dye, and a few columns over, a yellow one. Several rows up a carving had been filled in with dark-brown paint. Still most of the figures were the colour of sand. He was walking beyond the candlelight now and darkness hid their colour. When it became light again, he found that more and more of the carvings were painted. The corridor ended. The wall at the far end was covered with the little dark-brown man -shapes, and no others. They reminded Sajha of the man from the Messengers' illusion, the one whose skin was darker than he had thought possible by the sun. Idly, he wondered why he had never met anyone like that.

He should have had a feeling as if he had been here, at the end of this corridor, before. Nothing was familiar but it should have been. A memory had slipped out of him somehow, and he did not know why. Seeing the place again should have brought it back.

In search of his lost memory, he took another desperate look around. He peered more closely at the carved and painted men, ran a finger along the grooves in the stone, stood on his toes to inspect the highest corner and crouched to look at the lower. There at the bottom of the outer wall he found writing that he could understand in a square that looked as if it had been drawn in wet sand by a thick finger. In the box were four little men, one of each colour that appeared on the wall. Words were written next to each. It was a symbol legend, indicating that each little man stood for one thousand of each colour. At one end there were hundreds of figures of every colour, and at the other, only of sand. Sajha shivered at the feeling of foreboding this place had suddenly filled him with, though he did not know why, and after a moment he returned to the temple gate.

Just as he had every week of his life, Sajha knelt in the noonday sun before the Messengers. There were only a few differences today. For one, it had been years since Sajha had been so full of faith and trust in his leaders. For another, his pulse was slowing and he knew that they had killed him.

He had passed Jade on his way out, and merely nodded at her. After the horrors of the hologram, her crime seemed quite trivial.

The Messengers were informing the crowd of the Gods' decision. Sajha would be struck down by their power as punishment for heresy. Across from him, Sajha's family knelt. They were remaining calm and held together. His death would save them.

But his father did not look as if he wanted to be saved. Rahka's eyes were darting between his son and the Messengers as if seeking resolution.

Sajha decided not to look at him. As the Messengers delivered a speech about the Gods' goodness, he let his eyes wander the crowd. At least dying in this way he would be surrounded by everyone he had ever known and loved, and knew that they were safe.

He paid little attention to the speech, but the words hummed in the back of his head: "This boy has spoken ill of the Gods. He submits today to their will. He understands his mistake."

The people Sajha loved so much, descendants of a terrible past, looked upon him impassively. Every golden-brown face was framed by straight, dark hair, while the rich spattering the crowd wore veils to cover fair cheeks and curls of every colour, both natural and unnatural. Some of them shared the Messengers' creamy skin.

It was something Sajha had never paid any mind to, but now the gathering of worshippers resembled the countless unpainted men on the brown temple walls, and he wondered again why there were no men with skin as dark as the man on the hologram.

"His mortal sacrifice is an act of faith in the Gods' ways."

And what did the other colours mean? It looked as if the only survivors of the Messengers' war had been pale-skinned. And the lightest were the most privileged today. He had always thought the poor were darkest because they spent the most time working in the sun. Now it seemed to Sajha that perhaps it was the other way around. Perhaps they were poor, and spent the most time working in the sun, because they did not have fair hair and skin.

It certainly fit the pattern that Sajha looked out upon, and the pattern on the temple wall. The Messengers were counting how many of each colour remained. Then they divided the survivors among those they deemed superior and inferior.

Sajha's breaths were coming with difficulty now. "This boy repents for what he has done," the Messengers were saying. It was hard to concentrate on the words. The outer temple filled his mind, the absent memory, the needle that had sent a timed poison into his veins, the painted men.

"Now you see his faith has been restored. His brave acceptance of the punishment for heresy shows that he believes in the Gods and their wishes."

The executed had all been darker of skin. He had never seen a man so dark as on that holograph. The darkly painted men were all gone. Realization crashed on him in the final moments of his life and he was overcome by fanaticism.

"He kneels here with no binding chains, no knife at his throat, ready for the Gods' magic to take him."

He did kneel before the Messengers unbound, head held high, but he had one last weapon to use. He looked past the Messengers to his father. Rahka was breaking, his deepest fears unfolding before his eyes. Sajha spoke loudly, breathlessly. "I've been poisoned. And deceived." It was all he could get out. Pleading eyes begged his father to understand and to act. Just before he fell, Sajha saw his father stand. The threat of the Messengers' power gone, a wave spread across the crowd as the oppressed got to their feet and began to crash upon their oppressors. Struggling, he took one last breath, and the scene went dark.

*D*avid Fitzpatrick is a delightful surprise. Just when you think he is going to zig, he zags. And when you think he will zag, he zigs, and then he zigs again. This story is a delicious send-up on wankerish books like The Bible Code *and the many "End of Days" fantasy books. Not a story for the faint of heart, the plot is a breath of fresh air pumped into us with a gas mask at one end and a tire pump at the other. I'm sure you'll enjoy that filling sensation as he mocks the irrational thinking of The Religious.*

— Earl Lee

Unlikely Messengers

David M. Fitzpatrick

The bitter January cold stabbed like frozen needles into Mitch Jensen's face as he hurried through the night. A wind whipped down the street, as invisible and unrelenting as an angry poltergeist. He wasn't dressed for this kind of weather, and he could already feel his aching lungs constricting, but then the city manager had made it sound like nothing short of an emergency. He'd even left his Bible on the front seat of his car, just so it was easy to keep his hands pulled inside his coat sleeves. He brrr-ed aloud against the cold and mounted the steps to Bangor's City Hall. He'd never been there at two in the morning.

The lights were on and a waiting city cop opened the door for him. Jensen felt the welcome blast of heat in his face.

"Morning, Pastor," said the cop, whose name tag said he was Officer Guilford . "Cold night for this."

Jensen shivered, pausing to haul his inhaler out of his jacket pocket and take a puff. "That it is. So what's this about?"

"I'm just supposed to let you folks in," the cop said. He

motioned for Jensen to follow.

"What other folks?" Jensen asked as they headed up the stairs. He puffed again on the inhaler, and felt his lungs relaxing. Oxygen was good.

"Lots of your religious colleagues," he replied amidst the hollow echoes of his boots thudding in the stairwell. "I guess this one needs a bunch of different faiths."

"What happened?" Jensen pressed as they stopped at the top of the third-floor stairs.

Guilford's brow furrowed on his solemn face. "I was told not to talk about it, but... one of my officers found him in Bass Park, near the Paul Bunyan statue. He was dazed and not dressed for this weather. And when Officer Dickerson saw... the *thing*... well, he called Chief Cullen, who called the city manager, and here we are. You'll see soon enough."

They entered the third-floor hallway and there was Officer Dickerson, a grizzled, heavyset city patrolman. Like Guilford, he looked distracted.

"The last one," Guilford said to Dickerson.

Dickerson looked Jensen up and down. "Kinda young for a priest, aren't you?"

"Actually, I'm a Methodist minister."

"Oh, sorry — I don't go to church much." A weak laugh stumbled out. "Although I guess I'd better start. Anyway, they're down the hall — city manager's office."

Jensen could feel the cops' eyes on him as he headed for the open door. This was easily the strangest trip he'd ever taken to City Hall — not like council meetings or registering his car. Suddenly, he thought about that Bible he'd left in the car, and he was gripped by the idea of running back for it. Then he fought the urge; it was really cold out there.

He found the city manager at the receptionist's desk, slumped back, looking dazed. There was a flat-panel television on the wall, where a CNN anchor was delivering the latest headlines at low volume. The city manager regarded Jensen and said, "They're in there." He motioned to his own office. CITY MANAGER WILLIAM STINSON, said the nameplate.

"Bill, what's this all about?" Jensen asked, leaning over the desk.

Stinson smiled. "It's a miracle, Mitch."

Jensen sighed and straightened up. "I hope so. I'm very tired and I have to deliver a sermon in a few hours."

"Skip church," Stinson said. "You'll soon be delivering a sermon to the whole world."

The time for mystery was over. Jensen spun about, headed for the office door next to the wall television, and threw it open. And he froze in his tracks.

The other clergy looked up at him with deadpan stares. Father Murphy from St. Andrew's, not wearing a crucifix or carrying a rosary, was there. Rabbi Sidney Levy from Temple Beth Yushurun, with his braided beard, stood next to him. There was Reverend John Clark from Sunbury Baptist in a jogging outfit instead of his usual polyester three-piece. Finally, there was the normally elegant Amelia Largay, minister of the Brewer Unitarian Universalist Church, who wore jeans and a T-shirt and had a mass of disheveled blond hair haphazardly tied back in a scrunchie.

But they were all an afterthought compared to the man seated in front of the city manager's desk, whose attire was completely inappropriate for a subzero January night. He wore loose-fitting gray shorts with the blue University of Maine "M" on them, a Red Sox 2004 "World Series Champions" T-shirt, and green L.L. Bean slippers. He wasn't even wearing a hat—but he did indeed have something on his head, so to speak.

He looked up with dazed, mournful eyes, regarding Jensen's bulging eyes and sagging jaw. The guy was thirty-ish, and could have been a banker or a millworker, a lawyer or a convenience-store clerk. He was an everyman—except for the ghostly apparition hovering above his head.

"My God," Jensen breathed aloud.

"That was our consensus," Amelia said.

It was a giant ring, a foot in diameter, hovering magically a few inches above the man's head. It glowed with a soft light, and Jensen could almost see glimmering rays emanating from it. It seemed to be spinning ever so slightly, shimmering like polished gold. Without a doubt, it was a halo.

In a weak voice, the man said, "I just don't understand."

Jensen's legs felt like immovable pillars of salt, but he struggled forward, breathless. The closer he got, the more the halo seemed to shimmer and rotate. The man angled his head to keep his pleading eyes on Jensen, and the halo angled with him. Jensen reached out, and his hand felt warm and tingly as it passed through the halo. He pulled his hand back and said, "What's your name?"

"Mike," he said, and his voice was tired and slightly hoarse. "Michael Barry."

"When did this appear?"

"I don't know. I was home watching TV, and the next thing I knew, the police were talking to me and I was in the park, freezing, with this thing over my head." He looked at Jensen, with a helpless expression. "What the hell is it?"

"It's a halo, my son," Father Murphy proclaimed. "A symbol of sainthood."

"I'm no saint," Michael said. "I'm anything but."

"No — halos are just artistic representations; they aren't supposed to actually be visible," Jensen said. "Triangular halos are used in representations of the Trinity. A circle with a cross represents Jesus. Rings like yours are for saints — who must be dead and later canonized in your faith, Father."

"While square halos are often depicted on unusually saintly people who are still alive," Murphy said, "you're right that they're not supposed to be visible in life."

"Not so fast," Rabbi Levy said. "In Exodus, it was said that when Moses came down from Mount Sinai he had a glowing or radiant face. Jerome mistranslated this as 'his face was horned'—an unfortunate image, considering Satan's usual depiction."

"I wouldn't call it a mistranslation," Father Murphy said. "It's a misunderstanding of the metaphor."

"I'll have to go with my Catholic colleague on this," Reverend Clark announced with an upraised hand. "Saints are products of Christianity. Holy indeed was Moses, but certainly he isn't—"

"Oh, stop it with the televangelism," Amelia Largay said, rolling her eyes. "If halos only appear in art, then why does Michael have one?"

"There *is* a belief that saints have halos during their earthly lives, and that the truly pious could see them," Father Murphy said. "In other stories, the saint-to-be could be seen with an aureola, a glowing energy radiating from his body."

"Fanciful stories made to fit Catholic beliefs," Rabbi Levy snapped.

"This isn't limited to Catholicism or even to Christianity," Father Murphy shot back. "Halos, nimbuses, and other divine glows predate Christianity; they can be found in ancient Rome, Greece, India, Egypt. And not just gods—even kings were so depicted."

"Are you implying that this isn't a holy event?" Reverend Clark said.

"Not at all. Our Jewish friend is, because his half-complete, Old Testament faith doesn't feature such things."

Levy began muttering Yiddish epithets, but Jensen interrupted him. "Okay, everyone, let's put the brakes on the holier -than-thou debate," he said. "Clearly, this requires unity of our faiths, not division."

"Excuse me," Michael said quietly.

All heads turned to him in surprise, as if suddenly remembering the man with the halo was still there. He said, "All this arguing about halos doesn't answer why I, of all people, have one."

Jensen took a deep breath. "I apologize, Michael. We're all just as stumped as you are."

"I'm not stumped at all," Clark trumpeted. "My boy, the reason is clear: You're a saint on Earth, sent by God to bring His message to us! The Almighty has chosen you as his new prophet on this Earth. Hallelujah and praise Jesus!"

There was a long silence before Amelia said, "What did I tell you about the televangelism, Reverend?"

"Even you and your pseudo-Christian ways can't refute my logic," Reverend Clark said, and Jensen knew he was right.

"There's no other explanation," Jensen said. "Michael, we can't guess why, but it seems clear that you're God's chosen messenger."

"It's a glorious honor, son," Father Murphy said, resting his hand on Michael's shoulder. "Finally, God will speak to us again—through you."

"But that can't be right," Michael said, and his halo sparkled as he shook his head.

"Why can't it?" Rabbi Levy asked.

Michael looked from face to face, finally locking eyes with Jensen. "I'm an atheist."

The room fell into stunned silence. Jensen stared back at Michael's blue eyes, incredulous.

"I spent my life in various Protestant denominations, but eventually I decided I couldn't believe all the silliness and hypocrisy," Michael said. "I started attending meetings of the local chapter of United Atheists, and I've found all the answers with science and reason. But now this..."

He trailed off, his head bowing to the floor. The halo remained solidly fixed in place, giving Jensen his first good view of it from the top, and it was beautiful. He could see subtle hints of silver sparkling as the shimmering golden ring spun slowly in place. It was almost impossible to resist reaching out and touching the ethereal phenomenon. It was as if the halo beckoned to him.

"I can feel it," Amelia said, stepping up beside Jensen.

He turned to her. "Spiritually?"

"No—I can feel it physically. It's like a wave pulsing through me. If I close my eyes and listen, I can even hear it."

He looked at her dubiously, as did the others.

"Go ahead, all of you," she said. "Close your eyes. Listen to it."

Jensen closed his eyes and, judging by the silence in the office, he guessed everyone else had, too. The faint glow of the halo barely permeated his eyelids, seeming to be everywhere within his otherwise-dark world. He felt the wave Amelia had described, flowing through his entire body, over and over.

Then he heard it. Faint, nearly imperceptible, but clearly there was a sound. Unmistakably, it was a voice—no, a chorus of voices, all speaking together. Maybe there were several choruses saying different things. He strained to hear, and began to make out the voices. At first he thought they were too faint or garbled, but he realized they were in another language.

"Why, that's incredible," came Father Murphy's soft voice, and Jensen's eyes snapped open. Everyone stood in awe.

"Did you hear that?" Amelia said excitedly. "I clearly heard voices, but I didn't understand them."

"I don't think anybody would," Rabbi Levy said. "I'm a student of many languages, and I can tell you this is like nothing I've ever heard."

"It's the language of God," Reverend Clark said. "The words of Heaven. Those were angels we heard, cherubim and seraphim singing to us."

Amelia didn't tell him to cut the televangelism this time.

"It makes sense," Jensen said. "God willing, it's the only thing that makes sense."

"But why an atheist?" Father Murphy said. "Why would God choose someone of no faith?"

"We've all questioned our faiths at one point or another," Jensen said. "Maybe this is God's way of testing

Michael's faith."

"I can't believe such a miracle is solely to test one man's faith," said Rabbi Levy. "No, this is something far greater. The voice of Heaven? The coming of a Messiah? A beacon to shine as irrefutable proof of God? Perhaps all of those."

"So... what do we do?" Michael said.

Jensen felt the smile crawling over his face even as his chest tightened with all the excitement. "We tell them," he said, hauling his inhaler out again.

"Tell who?" Amelia asked.

Jensen turned to her as he puffed another dose of the medication, his eyes gleaming like the halo over Michael's head. "Everybody. Call them all. This is the holiest of all things, happening right here in our little city. We're on the front line of this incredible event, and we're going to stun the entire world."

Just then, the door flew open, and City Manager Stinson was there, eyes wider than ever. He looked caught between utter terror and overwhelming excitement.

"I think you'd better come see the TV," he said.

The men had names like Matthew, Adam, Luke, and Michael. The women had names like Mary, Ruth, Esther, and Eve. They were found all around the world, wandering and unable to recall how they'd gotten there or what had happened to them. And they all had halos. And they were all atheists.

Bangor shared the stage with cities, towns, and villages mostly in North America, but there were halos all around the world. After the initial hubbub in Bangor had subsided, Jensen had headed home to plant himself in his La-Z-Boy and watch the worldwide coverage. It was early afternoon when his doorbell rang, but he was too tired to get up. He hollered for the visitor to come in, and he heard the door open. Heels clacked down his hallway, and Amelia Largay entered his living room and regarded him. He was in his chair, feet up, coffee in hand.

"Hey," she said, looking as exhausted as he felt. "Have you slept?"

"No, I didn't want to miss a thing," he said, gesturing at the television. "Over six hundred, from every state and province. A bunch in Europe, and more around the world."

She dragged her feet to his couch and slumped down. "My congregation wants answers. I don't have any."

"None of us do. We can preach about God's plan, but we're just guessing."

"Maybe guessing is all we ever do."

He raised his brow at her. "Sounds like *you're* having a crisis of faith."

"Not at all. Today's events considered, it seems almost impossible to do that now." She laughed lightly, as if suddenly getting the punchline to a joke she heard days ago. "But we're spin doctors, all of us. We tell them what they want to hear."

Jensen's neck warmed as instinctive defenses rose. "I've never faked my faith to my congregation."

"Me either. But we find ways to appeal to our congregants. Look at all our Protestant denominations; whenever someone disagrees with church doctrine, he runs out and starts his own branch. Each claims to be the right one. Meanwhile, every individual has a different idea of what his personal God is. Yet you and I stand in our pulpits and pretend we all believe in the same thing."

Jensen sighed, tipped back his coffee, and gulped the rest down. "Maybe you're right. And maybe God is tired of all of Christianity's splintered factions. Maybe the halos are about unification."

But the television suddenly caught her attention. "Breaking news," she said. He grabbed the remote and unmuted the sound.

" — they're being called angels by most," the Fox News anchor said, "and all over the world, and apparently not in contact with each other, they're announcing press conferences.

With no communication between them, each has claimed the voices they're hearing are instructing them to speak at exactly six o'clock Eastern Standard Time—and they admit they don't even know what they're speaking about."

Footage of various angels rolled. All of them had halos and they were all nervous, worried, confused, and afraid. They also looked exhausted.

The co-anchor picked up the report. "It appears that none of the angels have any connection at all except for this. Yet they all have halos which produce unearthly sounds in an unknown language, and now they're all interpreting those voices as directing them to hold these unilateral press conferences. We also understand that these conferences are to occur wherever these haloed angels were first discovered by others."

"I just don't get it," Amelia said. "I can understand why God would use *some* atheists; it's a good way to make His point to non-believers. But why *all* atheists?"

"I don't have to tell you about God working in mysterious ways."

"Well, amen to that," she conceded. "He's never been more mysterious."

It was cold that evening, although not quite as cold as it had been for Jensen's early-morning trip to City Hall. That didn't keep anyone away from Bass Park, which was a mass of people countless thousands deep. Main Street was impassable. The statue of Paul Bunyan, with green pants and red-and-black plaid jacket, an axe over his shoulder and a peavey in his other hand, towered above the masses like Goliath over the Philistine army. Across the street, the Hollywood Slots casino was dark, its windows shattered after vandalism by those who had decided the haloed angels meant it was time to bring Bangor back from the brink of becoming Sodom or Gomorrah. The crowds were exceptionally righteous, looking to ensure Bangor wouldn't become the target of God's wrath now that He was returning.

Jensen and Amelia, dressed for the cold this time, met with City Manager Stinson on Buck Street, between the park and the Bangor Daily News building, and police escorted them through the crowds to the white community-band gazebo behind Paul Bunyan.

"My God, look at them all," Amelia breathed, and Jensen did. The rippling blanket of people was an exciting mix of every faith, like a patchwork quilt of many colors that somehow blended harmoniously. Groups were singing, holding lit candles in the dark, swaying in unison to unheard rhythms by streetlights, their frigid breath creating a steady fog over their heads.

"Marvelous," Stinson said with a broad smile. "Just spectacular. And all around the world, there are gatherings like this."

"Will you be introducing Michael?" Jensen asked.

"No, he asked to speak alone. He's in the cruiser over there, waiting."

Jensen followed Stinson's gesture, toward a convoy of police cars parked on the grass near Buck Street. He found the one in question easily enough; it was the one with the soft, golden glow emanating from within. He checked his watch. "Well, any minute now."

As if on cue, the crowd suddenly launched into a unified cheer and arms went up as Michael exited the cruiser, looking more tired than Jensen felt. The halo hovered over his head as if locked in place by invisible bolts. The people watched as a half-dozen cops escorted him through the roaring crowd. The ocean of bodies parted for him like the Red Sea for Moses, and then closed behind him.

"That poor guy," Amelia said.

Jensen looked at her in surprise. *"Poor guy?* Michael and the other angels will go down in history as the greatest religious figures since the days of the Old Testament. How can you feel sorry for him?"

"Just look at him," Amelia said as Michael made his way up the steps to the podium, flanked by his law-enforcement entourage. "Soon, he'll accept the importance of all this, but until then, he's an unbeliever who's been thrust into it. It must be very difficult for him."

"This isn't difficulty," Jensen said. "Strange, certainly, but not difficult. Difficulty is what Christ endured on the cross."

"Maybe not. Jesus had total faith."

Michael was at the podium now, golden halo sparkling silver. Someone adjusted the microphone, and the sudden feedback acted like a magic spell that instantly quieted the crowd. Michael cleared his throat, and then he spoke.

"Thank you all for coming," he said in a weak, tired voice, checking his watch. "I know this sounds crazy, but the voices have told me what to say. Other people have listened to the voices I've heard, and they didn't make sense to anyone. But then they did to me, and they told me to speak to you at six o'clock. I guess it's happened to the others like me."

"Angels!" someone in the crowd yelled, and it was instantly echoed by others until the crowd was roaring the word as one, over and over again.

Michael raised his hand, shaking his head, the halo moving perfectly with him, and the crowd silenced again. "I'm no angel, no saint. I'm just a messenger." He checked his watch again and said, "It's time."

Notebooks were everywhere. Hundreds of video cameras were pointed at him. Citizens, reporters, and news crews all readied themselves.

Michael closed his eyes and tilted his face heavenward, the halo angling as he did so. His arms came out to his sides, half raised, palms opened and aimed skyward, and he spoke.

"The," he said.

Then he opened his eyes, lowered his hands, tilted his head and his halo back down. The entire crowd was silent, awaiting.

"That's it," he said. "T-h-e. The."

Murmuring went up through the crowd. Amelia and Jensen exchanged looks. From behind them, Stinson hissed in surprise, "What? Did he say 'the?'"

"He did," Amelia said.

"What kind of message is that?" Jensen said.

Excited discussions rippled around the crowd. Clearly, everyone was confused. Michael spoke again. "Please... don't ask me to explain it." His voice was cracking. "The voices spoke to me, told me to come here and say that word. I don't understand why. I don't understand any of it. But the voices told me to say it, and that it would soon make sense. I ask you... to please... be patient..."

"He's breaking down," Jensen said.

He was. Michael was trembling, his eyes glazed. Tears streamed down his cheeks. He swayed where he stood.

"Breaking down, nothing," Amelia said. "He's *falling* down."

Jensen rushed across the gazebo just as Michael's knees gave out. He collapsed into Jensen's arms, and the crowd erupted into chaos.

Jensen and Amelia were at Stinson's big Victorian home, where Michael was asleep in a guest room. The television was on in Stinson's hardwood-floored living room, as TVs had been, nonstop, just about everywhere in the world.

"But what does it all mean?" Stinson said, probably for the fiftieth time that night.

Jensen and Amelia had long since given up answering him. They focused on the newscast.

"The reports are in from all over the world," the Fox News anchor said. "There are seven hundred twenty-one of these angels, and at precisely six o'clock Eastern Standard Time, each one relayed a message consisting of exactly one seemingly random English word."

The co-anchor picked up the lead. "People everywhere are trying to decipher this. It's believed that the random words somehow form a complete message, but the seven hundred twenty-one words could conceivably form any number of combinations, so it's unclear when, if ever, the message will be understood. Many feel that the angels may yield more clues..."

"They may never figure it out," Amelia said. She had a notebook in her lap, along with an alphabetical printout of all the angels' words, and she'd been scribbling and crossing out possible combinations all night. "I've been interested in cryptography and puzzles since I was little, and I haven't the first notion what it could mean."

"There's a key somewhere," Jensen said. "They'll figure it out."

"And what if they don't?"

Jensen looked at her bemusedly. "Don't tell me I have to remind you to have faith in God."

"Don't start on me. You're starting to sound like Reverend Clark."

"We're presented with something miraculous; don't question it," he said. "God will reveal himself in time. There's no need to doubt."

"Doubts seem reasonable to me," Stinson said. "Are you saying you don't have any of those feelings, Pastor?"

"Of course I do. I think God intends it this way. He's given us a big mystery and he's testing our faith."

"That's what this is all about?" Amelia said. "The whole thing—the halos, the atheists receiving them, the cryptic messages—is all just a test of faith?"

"I can't imagine all of this just being any one thing, but I'm sure a test of faith is part of it."

"They'll fight this, you know," Stinson said. "Atheist organizations are already challenging the divinity of this— loudly. They're convinced it's some elaborate hoax and they're demanding scientists be allowed to test the angels."

"Let them," Jensen said. "We can endure it. That's what having faith is all about. They can try to disprove it, but they'll fail."

Just then, the Fox News anchor suddenly blurted out, "This just in—the message has been decoded!"

Jensen grinned and tossed up his hands. "Ask and ye shall receive."

The code key was almost blatantly obvious. Starting with the Atlantic Time Zone and working west around the world by longitudinal degrees, minutes, and seconds, the words were read in order. The news shows put up computerized maps with colored dots showing the angels' locations. Michael's word, "the," was second in the message, after a similarly confused angel in Halifax, Nova Scotia who had spoken the word "children."

Everyone called it, simply, "The Message." It was read on every newscast in the world, printed on every newspaper's page one, hyped on every magazine's cover. It inundated Web sites, blogs, and social-networking pages across the Internet. Instantaneously, it became one of the most available written works in the history of the world.

But the most sobering example of its divinity was the audio recording. Enterprising audiophiles everywhere had pieced together the words uttered by the seven hundred twenty-one angels. The result was a bizarre euphony of distinct voices, speaking together as if one person. It was played on television, radio, and the Internet—easily the most listened-to piece in history. It began like this:

> *Children, the time has come, finally arrived. The greatest day in God's Creation is here, is at hand. What lie have you been told by nullifidians, the evil nonbelievers? Lo, ever shall you celebrate in your virtue, your great righteousness! He told you through the writings, the*

holy books. But to you some would proclaim them lies, evil falsehoods. Now you shall see their impieties, terrible blasphemies. It is a test of faith to endure this pain, terrible agony? But that test decides who gains the wonders of Heaven and who suffers the scourges of Hell, the burning inferno. What of the nonbelievers, vicious disbelievers? Lo, religion has been shunned by these heretics, sly infidels!...

The Message talked of sinners and unbelievers. It spoke of the glory and power of God. But most importantly, it related that Judgment Day would happen one year from the date The Message was delivered.

Over the next three days, people quit their jobs, abandoned their homes, and made pilgrimages to the places where the angels had appeared. Jensen lived at his church for those three days, amazed at how many people were suddenly so repentant. As such, he hadn't seen or heard from Amelia until she called him on the third day, and they got together at his house. The TV was on in his living room as they enjoyed hot coffee together. They were barely comfortable when she noticed an asthma inhaler on the floor, and she picked it up and chastised him lightly.

"That's a pretty important piece of equipment to have kicking around the floor," she said with a wry smile as she offered it to him.

He took it, shook it. "Nearly empty. No worry—I must have a dozen of them. I've used them a lot in the past few days, you know."

She cocked her head. "Having trouble?"

"Everything sets my asthma off," he said. "The cold and the excitement do it, and there's been plenty of that recently. I'd love to have a cat, but I'd be unable to breathe inside of a half-hour."

"Got it—no asking you to house-sit my cats on my next

vacation," she said, and they were both laughing over it when the news broke on TV.

"An amazing turn of events today," the Fox News anchor said, his eyes wide. "Around the world, reports are coming in that the all the angels have lost their halos. It happened, in all cases, while they slept. We'll have some of the top religious scholars to discuss the significance of this, so stay tuned..."

"What do you think it means?" Amelia asked over her coffee.

Jensen shrugged. "They've served God's purpose. Their work is done. And ours is to save as many souls as we can in the next year, before Judgment Day."

"I wonder if it's that easy."

He couldn't believe what he was hearing. "You're always so quick to question. Do I need to save your soul, too?"

"I'm not questioning. But I wonder about our arrogance. It isn't our job to save souls—it's God's job, and people have to want to be saved. It's like your asthma inhaler; the pharmacist and the doctor don't chase you down to make sure you have it. You know you need it, so you take the responsibility to fill your prescription and take care of yourself. We have the same responsibility for our spiritual well-being."

He stared into his coffee. "Well, then, we help those who want to be saved. Even the doctor had to tell me I needed an inhaler in the first place. Even the pharmacist calls me to let me know my prescription's ready. We all need help."

She sighed. "It's going to be a long year."

"It will all be worth it," he said with a smile. "Finally, the world will see we were right. After all, even though the scholars have found references to virtually every religion and connections with every faith in The Message, there's no denying the strong Christian slant on it."

He felt her staring at him, and he met her eyes. Hers were big, her mouth agape. "I can't believe you just said that," she said. "Are you missing the point about all faiths coming together? We're supposed to be as one with this."

"We *are* as one."

"Not with statements like that."

He waved his hand, growing frustrated with her constant doubting. "Okay, forget it."

"I can't forget it." She stood up, sloshing her coffee on his rug. "I can't be that arrogant, Mitch. Arrogance won't get us into Heaven. And besides—" She looked around, almost as if she were nervous. "What if the world doesn't end? What if we've read this all wrong?"

His annoyance finally boiled over. "There's nothing to read wrong!" he cried. "It doesn't get any clearer than this. Now forget these questions, or find someone else to ask!"

They exchanged glares for several long moments, and then she grabbed her purse and coat and headed for the door. Somehow, his pride wouldn't let him call after her or chase her. Instead, he listened to her clack the door shut, shuffle down his walk, and get into her car.

As she drove away, the anchor said, "A fascinating turn of events indeed... but this entire story has been one fascinating turn after another since late Saturday night. What surprises are next? We have religious scholars from all faiths here to talk about that now..."

"What surprises indeed," Jensen mused, sipping his coffee.

On an impulse, he grabbed his Bible, set it in his lap, and tried not to spill coffee on it as he watched TV.

He didn't expect to see Amelia for several days, but she showed up at his church early the next morning and found him in his office. He looked at her from behind his desk for many long moments as she leaned against the door jamb, a big smile on her face.

He held up his hands in surrender. "I'm sorry. I was being arrogant, and there was no need for it."

"You're right," she said, still smiling. "Have you heard

that Michael is missing?"

He blinked in surprise. "What?"

"He's gone. So are all the other angels."

"Well, praise the Lord," he said, breathless, sinking back in his chair. "He's called them home."

She laughed. "I don't think so. I think it was for their protection from religious zealots like you and me." She stepped into the office, producing a red folder. "Care to see what I've been doing?"

He felt nervous about taking it from her, as if he were Adam considering the apple from Eve. "What is it?"

"It's the truth, Mitch."

"Meaning?"

"I'm a Unitarian Universalist minister. We cater to all faiths, and we use writings from various faiths—we look for what makes sense and we embrace it. I've made it my career to read religious texts and analyze them intensely, and I've been a fan of logic puzzles since I was a kid. It took me a while to figure this one out."

"You're starting to sound like the atheist detractors."

"Are you afraid to hear what I have to say?"

"No." He reached out and took the folder, laid it on his desk. He didn't think he'd be able to dispel the fear he had of opening it, but somehow he managed. There was a stack of loose pages inside, and he recognized the text on the first page.

"It's The Message," he said.

"Yes. Check out the sentence structure. Every line ends by repeating the last word or idea, usually synonymously. The first sentence says 'People, the time has come, finally arrived'—*come* and *finally arrived* repeat the same idea. The second line is 'The greatest day in God's Creation is here, is at hand.' *Is here* and *is at hand* say the same thing. The format is the same all the way through."

"This has all been noted by others."

"Yes, everyone assumes it was to ensure we knew where a

sentence ended, so the next word begins a new sentence. That way, potentially confusing sentences starting with, for example, "and," won't be accidentally appended to previous sentences as independent clauses—"

"What are you, an English major?" He was getting irritated again, and he didn't know why. Maybe it was because she usually ended up making sense in the end.

"Yes, actually, but that isn't what this is about. Turn to page two."

He felt as if he were reaching for electrified pages, and the sensation made him ill. He reached anyway and turned it. The second page had the first five sentences of The Message in a numbered list:

1. Children, the time has come, finally arrived.
2. The greatest day in God's Creation is here, is at hand.
3. What lie have you been told by nullifidians, evil non-believers?
4. Lo, ever shall you celebrate in your virtue, your great righteousness!
5. He told you through the writings, the holy books.

"This has also been done," he said. "People have treated The Message as a single-chapter holy book, and they've numbered the sentences as verses."

"Yes, they have, because we religious types are certainly creatures of habit," she said with a sarcastic tone and a grin to match. "It occurred to me that there's a pattern in The Message. I stared at the sentences for hours, trying numerical tricks, reading things backward, skipping words, and so on... but I was overanalyzing it. It might as well have been highlighted in orange. Turn to page three."

He felt his heart thundering in his chest, but he fought his irrational fears and turned the page. Page three was a duplicate of page two, except some words were boldfaced and capitalized.

He stared blankly.

"It's the second word in every line," she said excitedly. "It reads logically. Go ahead, read it."

1. Children, **THE** time has come, finally arrived.
2. The **GREATEST** day in God's Creation is here, is at hand.
3. What **LIE** have you been told by nullifidians, evil nonbelievers?
4. Lo, **EVER** shall you celebrate in your virtue, your great righteousness!
5. He **TOLD** you through the writings, the holy books.

"A hidden message, sent by God," he said, excitement spreading across his face. "'The greatest lie ever told' is surely a reference to the nonbelievers."

"I'm afraid not," she said softly, and she was still smiling. He met her eyes again, and fear crushed his heart like an icy fist. "Turn to page four, and read the entire message within The Message."

He couldn't. He couldn't bring himself to turn the page. He couldn't even tear his eyes from hers.

"Do it, Mitch," she said. "Get it over with."

He felt his chest tightening and his breath getting shorter, but he fought back every instinct he had, reached for the notebook, and bet it all on God.

The greatest lie ever told to you is that of religion. It now returns upon you a thousandfold. This staged event a service by those who are forever in search of logic, reason, intellect, and science: proudly wrought by United Atheists. Amen, brothers! One last thing: The truth is out here.

That was how United Atheists officially punctuated it, but the hidden message within The Message was discovered by many people pretty much simultaneously. Within a day, the hoax was exposed and United Atheists took full credit for its orchestration. The "angels" had fled for their own protection, just as Amelia had suspected. It took weeks of calming down before any of them agreed to speak publicly, and then they met secretly with reporters.

The most celebrated United Atheists member was John Fontaine, a brilliant scientist specializing in holography. He had developed tiny devices that were implanted in the angels' skulls; they were powered by the human body, generating the illusory halos. Coupled with a high-frequency sound generator to produce the cherubic voices nearly at the upper limit of human hearing, the entire divine façade fooled everyone.

United Atheists had made its point, but many religionists refused to accept the facts and proclaimed the hoax the work of the devil. They cried for legal action, and across the United States many of the angels were charged with fraud. The Supreme Court quickly ruled that a practical joke didn't constitute a crime; it was freedom of expression, and nobody had been defrauded of anything. "Religion has been putting one over on people for thousands of years," said the director of United Atheists after the Supreme Court decision. "It's only fair that we get treated with the same indifference when we perpetrate a hoax of our own."

That didn't stop the ultra-conservatives from claiming their religious freedom had been violated by atheists, and like so many things they disapproved of, they demanded a constitutional amendment to prevent such a travesty of justice from offending good Christians ever again.

The battle was still raging when Mitch Jensen sat in his living room, a trembling, red-eyed mass of a man. He'd show those atheists, who were making a mockery of everyone's beliefs, by having the last laugh with God up in Heaven. He'd already stopped by the local animal shelter on his way home, donated a pile of money to that good cause, and adopted a cat. It was a particularly lovable, cuddly one, and he felt its effects just on the drive home.

The animal was curled up in his lap as he sat in his chair. Mitch had already tossed his asthma inhaler on top of the TV, which was showing the latest reports on the furor of those who had been duped. He could see the inhaler across the room, even as he felt his lungs constricting as the asthma shut them down. He heard his own fighting, wheezing breaths, and it didn't hurt. It was okay. He'd sink into an oxygen-deprived sleep, and wake up with God, and prove everyone wrong.

As the life in his worldly body waned, he never saw a light at the end of a tunnel; his vision only darkened. The last thing he saw was the bright glow of the TV in the dark, the fuzzy image of the white asthma inhaler atop it, and then even that faded to black. He felt himself growing cold, until everything was as cold and dark as that January morning when he had gone to City Hall to meet Michael Barry. At the end, he laughed silently at the bitter irony of it all, and prepared to go laugh with God.

*   *   *

It was over a year later when Amelia Largay saw Michael again. She had just found a table in a downtown café when she saw him sitting two tables away, face buried in a Richard Dawkins book. Nobody had seen him in that time, and she wasn't letting him get away. She gathered up her purse and hurried to his table, abruptly sitting down across from him. He looked up in surprise.

"Hello, Michael," she said. "Or whatever your name is."

"Hi, Ms. Largay," he said. "It's actually Michael."

Amelia was certain she wouldn't have been angry with Michael if not for what had happened to Mitch. She took a deep breath, clasping her fingers before her on the table, before she looked him in the eye. He looked back, expectant.

"Why?" she said.

"Everyone knows why," he said.

"I'm not talking about the big reason," she snapped. "I mean *your* reason. It wasn't just about this atheist cause. You had to have a personal reason to embrace that cause, much less participate in the big charade."

He returned to his book. "I'd rather not have this conversation."

"Oh, you're going to have it," she said, and he met her seething eyes. "It may have been a big joke to you, but Mitch Jensen died because of it."

Michael lowered his eyes and pursed his lips. "I heard, and I'm sorry. But his poor choice isn't my responsibility. And I can assure you, Ms. Largay, what we did was not a big joke to any of us. If all you got out of what we did was that we were pulling a practical joke, then you missed the point."

He was frustrating her because she knew he was right. "I just need to know your personal story. If I can make sense of that, I can move past the anger and hatred. I don't like either of those feelings. So please help me."

Michael slumped back in his chair, tilting his head back and staring up at the vintage tin ceiling of the old shop. "We all have our own reasons," he said. "As for me, I spent my childhood with a father who beat me every day and justified it with his Bible, and still I held the same blind faith I was told I had to hold. When my mother caught my father with his hand down my sister's pants, she intervened, and he beat her nearly to death. And still I had faith. When the pastor of my church molested me, I told anyone who would listen, but nobody believed, and instead I was punished — but still I had faith.

"When I was eighteen, I found a new church and it was much better — until my psoriasis acted up. Nobody had ever seen such a thing, and I explained it to them, but they wouldn't listen to the science of my skin condition. Instead, six of them took me out behind the church and beat me. They believed the skin lesions were signs of possession by Satan, and they fractured my skull trying to get him out. And then they sent me away and told me not to return until Satan was gone. But I still had faith.

"I met the woman I'd marry at the next church, and everything seemed good for a while. She was quite devout, and preached biblical morals to me for the three years we were married—all while screwing various young men she met during weekly Bible study. By now, I can tell you, my faith was waning, and I questioned the possibility of a God who watched over all the things I had endured and let them all happen, usually in his name.

"My wife got the house in the divorce, and I was living in a rented room when I lost my job. I was starving, so I went to the church food cupboard for something to eat. But they'd heard I'd been questioning my faith, and they denied me food and threw me out."

He slumped back, exhaling with a trembling shudder. Amelia stared, wide-eyed, open-mouthed, as he composed himself, fighting back the tears.

"Those are my stories," he said. "I can't speak for everyone else."

"Those are bad things," Amelia said, "but it doesn't mean all religious people are evil."

"No, it doesn't. But I believe all religions are shams. People have their reasons to follow their religions, but that doesn't make them good people. They never seem to practice what they preach, and they usually seem to pretend they're being good in case their gods are watching. I'm not saying atheists are perfect, but the atheists I know don't do good things to earn heavenly rewards. They're good people because they choose to be."

He got up and grabbed his coat. "This wasn't a big joke for us, Ms. Largay," he said. "It was a statement. So please, when you're mourning Mitch, and when you're pissed about what we did... just think about that, will you? We're not monsters.

We're just sick of the hypocrisy and sick of all the lies. Now they have to live with falling for *our* ruse, which merely played on the fairy-tale mentalities of religion—and I'm never going to apologize for that."

He walked out of the café, leaving Amelia alone with her thoughts. She sat there for a while, oblivious to the bustling people and the noises out on the street, thinking about the things he'd told her. And her mind kept going back to places she'd long tried to forget.

She went to a place where, at age seven, she'd been made to stand in the corner for sixteen hours when she'd asked her mother if there really was a God, after her mother had told her to be open with her questions. She returned to a place where, at age thirteen, her father had whipped her with a belt for skipping Sunday school to be with a boy, the week after her father had skipped church to have sex with Mrs. Dixon next door. And she went to a place where the Teen Youth Group leader kept her late after a meeting one Saturday night in the church annex, and had made her promise not to tell what had happened there against her will.

She shook herself out of her reverie. Michael had been gone for some time, but she knew she had to find him. She snatched up her purse and hurried out the door.

If only his halo were visible.

*T*hirty-nine members of the Heaven's Gate cult believed that a spaceship following the comet Hale-Bopp would take their souls away. In a series of mass suicides in the 1990s, about 74 people from the Order of the Solar Temple died. And, of course, Jim Jones led 909 people, including 274 children, to their deaths at Jonestown in 1978. These events show the startling level of belief humans can have in the ridiculous, and their blind faith in the people they follow, but they don't compare to the countless millions who have died over the centuries in the name of religion. Vincent L. Scarsella takes this frightening motif a big step further in this powerful tale, and asks us to envision a world where the horrors of religion come to a terrifying pinnacle involving the entire human race. This is speculative fiction, so Vince has license to demand that we suspend disbelief, but in today's world, no imagined religious horror should be dismissed out of hand. All too often, the bad things come to pass.

Calling God's Bluff

Vincent L. Scarsella

*"For all life longs for the Last Day
And there's no man but cocks his ear
To know when Michael's trumpet cries
That flesh and bone may disappear,
And there be nothing but God left."*
— *William Butler Yeats*, The Hour Before Dawn

*"The central observation of those who study suicide
is that, in some places and under some circumstances,
the act of one person taking his or her life can be contagious."*
— *Malcolm Gladwell*, The Tipping Point

At two a.m. on the morning we left for the Calling God's Bluff Festival, Mike Hansen, my law partner and best friend in all the world, uncorked our last bottle of Dom Perignon.

"A toast!" he said, swaying a little. "To death!"

Two hookers we had picked up to take along for the ride were sleeping in front of the fireplace of Mike's lakeside bungalow under afghans Mike had retrieved from the back bedroom and tossed over their naked bodies. A dying flame cast long, malevolent shadows across the floor to the wall behind us. Every now and then a cinder popped off the charred hunks of smoldering logs onto the polished oak floor. One of the whores, Kayla—Mike's date, the one with the husky voice and short, ash-blond hair—cracked out a snore every now and then.

I was sprawled out on the floor, and after Mike took a swig of the champagne he offered me the bottle. I declined. Enough was enough. We had been partying all night, smoking joint after joint of expensive pot and snorting too many lines of the purest coke. In the middle of all that, Mike had popped open our last three bottles of the Dom Perignon left over from celebrating the $14.5 million Gleason verdict last year.

Last year... had it only been a year?

Around midnight, we had started kissing each other's whores, stripped off our clothes and found ourselves engaged in a wild, orgasmic free-for-all. Somehow, after all that, after all the booze and coke and pot and sex, I was completely sober. And my declination of another swig of champagne seemed to have sobered up Mike as well.

"Are we really going through with this?" Mike sighed and fell backwards onto the sofa.

Mike and I had been friends twenty years but we had never been closer than that night. We had made love to each other's whores. And, two days from now, we were going to face the end of our lives together.

"Yeah," I said. "We're really going through with it. By this time Sunday, we'll be dead."

He stared into the glow of dying embers in the fireplace.

"No, not dead," he corrected, with a slight burp. "Calling God's bluff."

Incredibly, right then, the prospect of that—of death—didn't frighten me. I was a true believer at that moment, certain that death for us and for all mankind was the right and proper thing to do. Dying would finally and forever deliver us from the folly and evil of life. Amen.

"Yeah," I said and smiled. "Calling God's bluff."

Calling God's bluff.
That had become our mantra, our battle cry.

It had started out as a whisper in some long-forgotten place. A letter to the editor, a comment in some chat room perhaps. A call to a radio talk show host. We presumed that the Teacher, or whatever he was being called back then, had started it all in a moment of epiphany, after the idea had incubated and evolved in his mind all his life. Someone reported he had practiced his routine years ago on some street corner. Or maybe he had just heard someone mention it off the cuff one day and had adopted it as a mission all his own.

Nobody was sure. And nobody cared anymore how the whole thing had started. All we knew was what the Teacher was saying made perfect, logical sense.

"What we'll be doing, my friends, is simply this: calling God's bluff!" he had proclaimed in his best wide-armed, white-robed, long-haired Jesus-Christ-Superstar style, exuding that supreme confidence and determination that we had come to know and love. He had first used that phrase, *calling God's bluff,* during one of his prime-time sermons, his grand infomercials that had become the highest-rated shows of all time, with more viewers worldwide than the original runs, reruns, and syndications of *I Love Lucy, Gilligan's Island,* and *Seinfeld* combined.

Calling God's bluff.
Day after day and night after night, on his radio talk shows, Internet sites, and television infomercials, and in his bestselling

book—entitled, of course, *Calling God's Bluff*—and on Oprah, the Preacher reminded us that our lives were absolutely and positively meaningless.

And that there was one, and only one, infallible Truth: No matter what we did, death came. And then, in an impassioned sermon just a few minutes past midnight this past New Year's Day, the Teacher gave us his stark solution, finally revealing what he had been irrevocably leading up to all that time:

We must kill ourselves.

All of us. The whole human race in one act of bravado and scorn, the ultimate act of calling God's bluff.

He even gave us the exact date and time when we must do it. When, at the Holy One's command, all of humanity over the entire planet—from Ho Chi Min City to Tehran to The Big Apple to the jungles of the Congo to Hollywood, Vegas, and Chicago—in one mass act of release, would snuff itself out in a universal act of self-extinction, coinciding (so it was later claimed by certain of his disciples) with some astral, cosmological alignment of the heavens.

He would lead the event in front of a live audience, at least a million strong, at something called The Calling God's Bluff Festival, on some wide-open farmland on the plains near Buffalo, Wyoming, USA.

Crazy, right? No way to sell that.

So how did he do it? How did the Preacher convince type-A guys like Mike and me that the lives we led were not worth keeping? That we should give up our law firms, our dental practices, our vice presidencies, mutual funds, 401(k) plans and stock options, IRAs, country-club memberships; our SUVs and Hummers and BMWs and Jaguars; and, most of all, our expensive, overpriced, overtaxed homes in safe, slumbering, sterile subdivisions? How was he able to convince us that, because of death, our lives literally meant nothing, and that, therefore, the only thing that mattered was calling God's bluff in a unified mass suicide of human consciousness?

Somewhere, some snappy reporter blamed it on *memes*. An idea that spreads like a virus, eventually infecting everyone no matter how ridiculous or specious the idea may later seem—spread in this case by the best propaganda masters of all time—the Teacher, whose charisma made Jesus Christ and Adolph Hitler seem like pikers, and his thousand and one disciples.

The Teacher had appeared out of nowhere in an era that some disc-jockey philosopher had termed "The Great Depression of the Soul," 2000's style—derivative and lost. Despite our prosperity, our riches, our longevity, we were empty. Capitalism could provide us with fancy cars, nice clothes, and expensive jewelry—for some, at least—but it could not end the ultimate fear which burned in the backs of our brains from the first time we could think.

The worm at the core: *death.*

And, so, there we were, heading west to The Mother of All Festivals in Mike's vintage aquamarine 1964 Mustang, complete with the gleaming silver bucking bronco on the front grill. Mike had bought the car a year ago, just before the Reverend's sudden and unexpected appearance on the scene of the modern global village. It had been the latest jewel in his growing collection of antique cars, accumulated in the past couple of years during his lapse into middle age. This craze had followed hot on the heels of his divorce from Gloria, his wife of twenty-five years, and the abandonment of his three teenage daughters.

Just before nine that morning, Mike had started banging things around. The hookers and I finally woke up groggy, with throbbing heads. Somehow, we got ourselves together, showered, dressed, and jammed into the Mustang, coffee cups in hand, and headed west.

Pamela, my whore, had to pee not ten minutes into the trip.

She was a rough-voiced city girl about half my age, a tan gypsy with gold rings on every finger and long golden earrings. She had even put a ring through her pierced left eyebrow.

Looking back at her and Kayla squeezed next to each other in the backseat, I suddenly regretted that I wasn't taking this drive with my wife, Carol. Instead, I was with this gypsy girl who didn't have the slightest clue what was going on. To her, this was some kind of mixed-up adventure which would end up okay like everything else in her messed-up life. I had followed Mike's lead with some middle-age craziness of my own and only three months ago, smack in the middle of the Holy Man's crusade, and perhaps because of it, abandoned a solid eighteen-year marriage.

We stopped at a rest area along the interstate to let Pamela pee. The place was jammed with cars and campers, truckers and motorcycle gangs. Hundreds of delirious people were rushing from their parked vehicles to restrooms and refreshment areas, and returning just as quickly to get back on the road and resume the last and greatest journey ever.

We were all going to the same place, the "The Mother of All Festivals," as it had come to be called, and there was definite camaraderie and excitement in the air. Positively giddy, people were giggling at the thought of what they were part of, giving each other nods of recognition, handshakes, high-fives. Mankind was united as it had never been, a virtual jamboree of peace and love and positive connection.

"Let's go!" Mike urged as we hurried back to the Mustang. I took the front seat, while the girls wearily stuffed themselves into the back again without much complaint. The Mustang was soon churning out of the rest area and blending into the traffic jam that was heading west down Interstate 90, America's Main Street.

No cops. No highway patrol. It was a breeze. The only "Authority" on the road that morning was the Preacher's green berets, His self-proclaimed Truth Squad Warriors, thousands of kids in olive revolutionary uniforms.

Every now and then, a patrol of them would storm past us on loud, souped-up Harleys. They were cocky pricks, if you asked me, with a holier-than-thou attitude that got under my skin whenever I had the displeasure of having to deal with one of them. That, fortunately, had been infrequent before this trip so there seemed no need to worry over their apparent over-zealousness. The message was the Preacher, not these hench-men with their delusions of grandeur.

But, just past Cleveland, one of them came speeding along-side us and gestured haughtily with his left thumb for Mike to pull over. Like some sour-pussed redneck highway trooper, the soldier swung off his Harley and swaggered over to the driver's side window with a sneer equal to his attitude.

"You late for something, partner?" he said to Mike, nod-ding and looking seriously pissed off. "You cut off a station wagon of kids back there. Almost drove them off the road. Gonna kill yourself and somebody else before it's really sup-posed to happen."

Mike kept his cool, nodding deferentially. It was noticea-bly unlike him. I had always known Mike to be somewhat bel-ligerent in the face of authority. I was expecting to hear him tell this self-proclaimed trooper to go fuck himself.

But all he said was, "No problem, comrade," and consider-ately added, "We're off to the festival. Just anxious to get there, I guess."

The kid still had that cocky smirk and spit onto the gravel next to the side of the car. I thought I saw some of the spittle mar the finish on the door of the Mustang.

"Yeah," he said. "Aren't we all. Just slow down." With a sarcastic snigger, he added: "Comrade."

Then the kid was gone, swaggering back to his cycle like a full-feathered peacock.

"Bastard," I muttered, when he was out of earshot.

Our mood was definitely sour. We were going to the biggest

bash of all time in a suddenly bummed-out state of mind.

"You've got to be kidding me," Pamela chimed in. "What the hell was that?"

"His army," I answered. "Scary, ain't it? Pricks like that. Meet the new boss, same as the old boss."

"Naw," Mike broke in, over it just like that and upbeat again. "Just one little prick. And, anyway, the Preacher's gotta have 'em. They're a necessary evil." He turned to me with his wide, blue eyes and confident, toothy grin.

If nothing else, the incident had the effect of slowing Mike down, which wasn't such a bad thing. He stabilized at 67 to 70, every now and then glancing up at the rearview mirror.

Late that afternoon, we stopped at a Bob Evans for a late lunch. A selection of restaurants and diners had been commandeered by units of the Preacher's warriors so that the mass of people on the road heading toward the Judgment Day Festival could eat. After all, until the mass suicide of mankind occurred, you still had to eat. Since there was no need for money anymore, the meal was free.

"That's what I'm gonna miss, if nothing else," I commented while twirling a toothpick through my teeth, waiting for the girls to return from the ladies' room.

"What's that?" Mike asked.

"Burgers."

He laughed. "Not sex?"

Then I laughed.

The radio didn't play a song, no matter what station I tried. Nothing but news about the festival, stuff we'd heard a thousand times. Old speeches of the Preacher being replayed over and over *ad nauseam*. On other stations there were round-table discussions of professor types assuring everyone about the righteousness of what we were doing. The All-Knowing One seemed to have brainwashed everyone, even the most hard-nosed, world-weary journalists, intellectual masturbators, and think-tankers.

Memes, I thought.

As Mike drove on, and the radio droned out all thought, our conversation stopped and silence overcame the car. Not long after, the girls and I were fast asleep.

Finally, just outside Sioux Falls, South Dakota, Mike pulled into another rest area. He gave me a shove, said he was beat. Would I mind taking the wheel? I yawned, glanced down at my watch. It read 10:30. I told him I'd be happy to.

We roused the girls and they squirmed out of the Mustang. For a few minutes, the four of us stood at the side of the car stretching our legs and backs. Finally, we ventured to the restrooms.

"Not so crowded now," I said to Mike, who was in the stall next to mine. "Not so happy either." The rest area was pretty much deserted, with only a few tired stragglers like us stumbling in.

"Lot of people probably already bedded down for the night," Mike said from his stall.

"Saps'll miss out on getting there first thing tomorrow and being close to the action."

Without much fanfare, we were on the road again, with me driving. Not long afterwards, Mike and the girls were fast asleep. Mike even accompanied Kayla's snoring.

With nothing better to do, I clicked on the radio and tuned it low so as not to disturb them.

The highway was not as jammed with traffic as before. I needed something to keep me alert, something to put me in the right frame of mind for the hours of night driving ahead, preferably some music. I fooled around with the dial, going from end to end several times. All I got was static or the continuous drivel of over-ebullient mini-preacher evangelists, shouting out things about the coming "rapture," "rhapsody," "soul-lifting," "god-bluffing," and a hundred other glorious-sounding names for what we, as a race and species, would be doing around noon the next day.

I continued jumping from station to station, hoping to get lucky and catch some good ole rock 'n roll. I'd listen for a time to the clatter, broken only by an occasion spasm of snoring from Mike or Kayla or Pamela, or the whimper of one of their private dreams.

Finally, I latched onto a station that wasn't spouting the party line. Somehow, a heretic, or group of heretics, had taken over some nearby, low-level FM station and were blaring their own brand of propaganda.

"Stop!" pleaded the announcer. "Don't do it! In the name of mankind, in the name of God, reject this insanity."

Despite myself, I kept tuned to the guy. He sounded so frantic, so genuine. In a stark, clear tone, he declared that the Reverend was a fake, part of the Devil's crusade. He had somehow duped us all, that his "mission" was false, the insane ravings of a madman. There would be no revelation from God or any Cosmic Entity if we all joined in and killed ourselves, only the end of civilization, the extinction of mankind.

"You will neither reach God by doing what this false prophet has asked you to do," the radio guy exhorted, "nor the Kingdom of Heaven. You will only attain the Kingdom ruled over by death and oblivion. The Kingdom of the Great Deceiver, Lucifer!"

Oblivion. Death. The way he said it frightened me, brought home the magnitude of what we were doing. The reality of it.

"You must cease and desist this madness. We implore you to join us against this folly. Despite our forced silence, there are many who have been able to quietly resist the wicked charm of the False One who preaches death as salvation.

"In small, hidden corners we exist. We will survive after he leads the rest of mankind into death. From that catastrophe, we shall rise up and rebuild the world. We have taken over this radio station tonight to preach this message of hope and resistance, so that more of you can be saved. Please listen and join us in rebuilding our world and avoid eternal damnation and oblivion."

He went on and on, assuring his listeners that the resistance was real and that the Preacher's mission was pure folly. Every now and then, his words were broken by a cackle of static, caused, perhaps, by a bolt of lightning from some distant Midwestern thunderstorm.

As I listened to his rant, a pang of doubt crept into my very soul. I began to long for my former life, despite its banality and aimlessness. What we faced instead was, perhaps, an even worse fate: oblivion.

I was roused from this gloomy introspection by commotion in the radio. The announcer was shouting incoherently, frantically. An instant later, there was the unmistakable snap and pop of automatic rifles. The radio fell silent. Dead.

Then, another voice came on. "This station has been liberated by the Army of the Prophet. Disregard the prior broadcast of falsehood you have heard. It was blasphemy."

There was no other sound after that.

How had He convinced six billion people to kill themselves at precisely the same moment? "Through death, we shall find God," He promised, assuring us that the mass suicide of the entire human race would be the ultimate display of our Faith in God's existence. "He will intervene," the Preacher guaranteed, nodding and smiling beneficently. "He will not let us truly die. Instead, he will recognize our suffering and end the misery of our lives always darkened by the prospect of death."

After a pause, looking up at heaven, he had proclaimed: "Death will thenceforth be banished from our dreams, from our vocabulary, and we will laugh in wonder with the angels."

The confidence of His voice, His words, gave us no doubt.

"Once and for all," He proclaimed, "We must spurn the

natural existence in which we are presently trapped.

"Forever.

"Amen."

"Amen!"

We all had cheered, believing.

"Amen," I whispered.

Michael had suggested that we put in a CD of one of the Reverend's sermons after the fiasco of the heretic radio show. It had visibly shaken me. I couldn't even drive anymore.

"You all right?" Mike asked.

The girls had fallen asleep, indifferent to the commotion. We were driving in blackness in little traffic. It was two a.m.

I sighed, nodded. "Wow!" I gasped. "That was mind-boggling. It was like I had never heard the Preacher."

"We're gonna be there in a few hours." Mike looked at me.

From the tape, the Preacher's determined, confident voice boomed out to the throng of converts jamming the seats and aisles of some municipal auditorium. Mike lowered the volume so he could talk to me, see if I was all right.

"I can't wait," I told him feebly, unconvincing.

We rode on in silence for a time. The Preacher's sermon played on the tape, a low nattering, too low to distinguish what he was saying. But we knew it by heart.

"Wasn't it so silly before?" Mike broke in. "When we used to believe in life, the lives we led, as if they meant something." He laughed to himself. "As if any of it mattered. As if, when we died, we had accomplished something—besides, perhaps, to perpetuate the race for some unknown reason."

I wondered why he was telling me this—rote stuff, axio-matic, understood by everyone, even little kids.

"Yeah," I agreed, with a sigh, wondering, *But what if he was wrong?*

I didn't say this to Michael, I only thought it. But thinking it seemed offensive, criminal. It was the first time since the day

I first watched the Preacher's Show-of-Shows last New Year's Day that I had experienced such apprehension, such doubt. Doing so now, on the eve of Judgment Day, frightened me. My face went pale. I was feeling dizzy, nauseous. To fend it off, I closed my eyes and tried to sleep.

Seeing this, Michael reached over and turned up the volume.

"God will not let his children die." The Preacher's voice was firm, confident. "We are calling Him to us."

Calling God's bluff.

But I kept thinking, what if he doesn't take it?

I finally did fall asleep. When I woke up, I saw that we were speeding down the straight, flat interstate. The sun had not yet risen sufficiently to give color to the bare, gray landscape which had been split in two by the black asphalt.

I looked over at Mike. He seemed okay. The radio was off.

"Where are we?" I asked, straightening.

"Almost there," he beamed. "Just crossed into Wyoming. About an hour more."

I looked back and saw that the girls, too, were stirring.

I was surprised by the lack of traffic along this stretch of highway. It was so near the festival. I thought maybe that Mike had taken a wrong turn, gotten us lost. But within minutes, we almost crashed into a clog of vans, RVs, trucks, cars, and motorcycles.

We stopped, and crawled for a time. Despite the traffic jam, no one was bitching or growling over the problem. We were almost there and everyone seemed mollified, relieved to be this close. Conversations exchanged across cars, people asking where you were from, hoots and hollering, even some joyful horn-blowing.

"When we gonna park?" Kayla asked from the backseat. "I gotta pee."

Next to her, my Pamela chimed in: "Me, too."

"Look," Mike said, "we can't just stop here, in the middle

of this traffic. You'll just hafta wait."

But after another couple minutes, we stopped for good. This became quite apparent when a throng of people in front of us exited their vehicles all at once and headed west, presumably toward the festival stage.

"I guess this is where we park," Mike shrugged.

With that news, the girls and I let out collective sighs and we joined the mass abandonment of the cars. It felt good to be outside, stretching in the warm, morning breeze. About twenty yards off the highway, there were some trees and brush where the girls scampered to squat and relieve themselves. Mike and I laughed as they rushed off. Unabashedly, we unzipped our pants and pissed along the side of the interstate next to the cars, copy-catting a handful of other guys likewise pissing into the soft summer wind.

With our bladders empty, we entered the mass migration heading toward the Festival. Men, women, and even kids, people of all shapes and sizes, colors, creeds, sexes, and persuasions, heading with uniform determination toward the main stage, like an inexorable river disgorging into some lake.

After about a mile of walking with this rush of humanity, Kayla started to whine. "My feet hurt," she complained. "Where are we going? Is this the right way?"

Trudging onward, we tried to ignore her. I was struck right then with an almost overwhelming realization that we were among a vast accumulation of humanity, a living ocean of people stretching out for miles. The center of gravity of this mass lay ahead of us, down a low, long slope of trodden grass and barley and wheat, ending at the festival stage. All at once, we just stopped, this entire mass of humanity, so abruptly that we almost ran into the backs of the people in front of us. Tallest among us, Mike tried to look over the top of the crowd. He guessed that we were still probably five or six miles from the stage.

"This is it," he informed us with a shrug. "Nowhere else to

go. We'll have to watch it from here." He laughed. "The cheap seats."

Everyone around us seemed to have come to the same conclusion and started looking around for a convenient place to plop down.

"We can't even see the stage from here," Kayla whined. Some of the folks around us were already sitting down, laying out blankets and coolers on the crushed grass.

"Looks like this is the best we can do," Mike said.

Kayla tsked, clearly displeased. "We coulda stayed home," she griped. "We coulda partied in front of the TV instead of coming all this way. From here, I don't even feel part of it."

"But we're here," I said, tired of her whining. "We *are* part of it."

Kayla frowned, unconvinced. Pamela bent over and whispered in my ear that she was always this way, a royal pain.

"Well," Mike sighed. "Let's find a spot."

With a shrug, he selected a patch of grass and unfurled the blanket he had carried from the car. We were distracted momentarily from smoothing it out by the sudden appearance, out of nowhere, of a passing patrol of sour-pussed truth soldiers.

Without apology, the patrol ate up a narrow swath of grass and dirt as they tramped through, rudely disbursing the settling crowd. Everyone stopped whatever they were doing to move aside and gawk at the Preacher's self-proclaimed army, his guardians of right, with their hard expressions and camouflage uniforms and brown berets. In that moment, I was reminded of storm troopers from Nazi war documentaries. That was my second inkling that maybe what we were doing wasn't quite right.

After the patrol passed, we arranged ourselves on the blanket.

"We are going to die today."

That statement, stark as a thunderclap, came from some guy on a blanket a few yards away. I wasn't sure of the exact location of the voice, but I could discern surprise and tension. An unanticipated mood of dread had descended upon us. We were stricken by second thoughts, misapprehension, a longing for things past. Our faith in the wisdom and truth of the Preacher's mission had ebbed.

"We are really going to die today." The voice was now incredulous.

It was as if we all had suddenly realized what we were about to throw away, the folly of the Reverend's theory. There were other comments, similarly edged. But no one went far enough to suggest that we should get up and leave, that we should abandon this foolishness. The four of us did little talking. Kayla complained about being hungry, regretting that we had left a bag of potato chips in the Mustang. She seemed to have no conception why we were here—to die. To her, it was as if we were part of a rock concert. And, perhaps, that's what it was like for most people: just another human happening.

"Is it too late to go back for it?" she asked Mike, who gave her a disgusted look as if to say, *You're going to be dead soon, so what does it matter, you dumb bitch?* At least, I felt like saying it for him.

"No, honey," he said to her softly, as if to a child. "It's going to start any minute."

I huddled Pamela into my arms while Kayla smoldered over the forgotten potato chips. Poor Mike tried to mollify her by stroking her blond hair.

I began thinking how useless and stupid our lives had become with nothing to live for except death itself. I imagined everyone at the festival felt that way that moment, all 1.5 million or so of us: sad, tired, alone, dreading and expecting death and, possibly, oblivion, like the heretic DJ had predicted. It became profoundly still, as if everyone had stopped moving and talking. Even the insects were silent. No birds flew. We were trapped, inert beings. There was nothing left to do but wait.

Incredibly, an hour passed like this. I checked my watch

every five minutes. And then, a few minutes before noon, people down toward the front of the stage started to rise.

"This is it," I heard Mike mumble to himself. I saw him squeeze Kayla's hand.

Finally, our section rose and stood with the others.

There was giggling, the nervous kind, some outright laughter, too, and yes, sobbing. It was not unlike when the featured band came out at the start of a rock concert. Somebody shouted something. Another person screamed and kept screaming. A baby cried. This unorganized, spontaneous noise evolved into a persistent roar which seemed as if it would never end.

From the distance, on the tip of my toes, I managed to see between the bobbing heads in front of me why we had stood and why everyone had started cheering. I checked my watch again. It was 11:57.

The Holy One, the Reverend, the Preacher, had come out onto the Festival stage. He stopped and bowed at center stage, stood up, and saluted his audience. Then, he blew kisses to the TV cameras lined up at every conceivable angle. The crowd was howling. Everyone seemed suddenly secure now that he was finally out there, with us. Our faith and confidence had been restored.

Finally, with his long, black hair flowing in the gentle breeze, wearing the simple ankle-length white robe that had become his trademark, the Holy One delicately gestured, like some kind of latter-day Pope, for us all to quiet down. It took a couple minutes, but finally we settled down and waited for the next move.

He looked up and stared for a time.

"Hey, God!" he shouted, still looking up into the clear blue sky. "It's the last day. Your Judgment Day has come at last for what you did to Adam and to Eve and to all of us. We are right now, right here" — and then he shouted viciously:

"Calling your bluff!"

A great wave and roar rolled out from the stage as the crowd rose up to the fringes. The ground shook under our feet as we got caught up in it, standing and howling into the deep blue sky. It took a long time for the Preacher to quiet us this time. As he smiled beneficently, he seemed in no great hurry. He waited patiently, scanning the immense assemblage streaming ten, fifteen miles out from the stage. Finally, when the cheering faded, he started again, his voice booming into the thick, hot August air from enormous black speaker boxes positioned in rows extending outward from the stage for a hundred yards.

"I am," he said, "the Wizard of Oz, the Second Coming of the Christ, the first coming of Mankind, and, maybe, the Anti-Christ." His laugh was long and low. "I am matter and anti-matter. And I am here to take you on a one-way trip to par-ra-dize."

Another spontaneous roar rose up and spread out from center stage, reaching, it seemed, into Heaven. It did not last as long as the previous storm, nor was it as vigorous. We were settling in, wondering, waiting, only now sensing that this was really happening and that we were really part of it.

At last, the crowd again quieted.

"Into God's embrace we shall ride headlong this day!" His voice quavered, resonated. "He shall have us at His table this night, as his eternal dinner guests. And, tonight, we shall eat from that table and the food shall be the answers to all our questions!"

Even from this distance, I could feel his overwhelming presence. My heart ached to be closer and yet I was giddy to be this close, close enough that I could see him in person. His arms rose up in a characteristic pattern we had all come to know. Squinting, I could even vaguely perceive his eyes glaring out at us all in fierce, unstoppable determination. My thoughts turned momentarily to that radio guy, the heretic who did not believe the wisdom and authority of the preacher's words. How could he, how could anyone, question such manifest preeminence?

"Now it is time." The preacher's voice suddenly lowered. Then, after a breath, he whispered hoarsely into the microphone: "To die."

All across the world, in countless millions of homes, everywhere, in the most isolated, primitive villages, even in caves where aborigines yet lived, the word had spread. Everyone was experiencing this moment. When the Reverend gave the order, I, we, and they were going to kill ourselves. We were all, all of humanity, going to call God's bluff and end the meaninglessness of our lives.

The great religious leaders, though they had tried desperately and incessantly to stop us, had failed. Their words, their sermons, their threats of excommunication, had fallen on deaf ears. Their message had been no antidote for the simplicity of the Preacher's call to ultimate action.

And, anyway, the Preacher had long ago debunked all religions. In simple, understandable terms, he had revealed them as phony myths, built on fantasy rather than truth.

"Just listen to what they have to say," he had cleverly implored, and after a small, derisive laugh, continued: "Hear how silly and hollow they sound. Jesus, for example, an immaculate birth (that is, without the benefit of sperm and egg)? Rising from the dead and walking around for a few weeks to prove that he is God's son and had been born and died for our sins, whatever they may be. That's about as believable as the one about Santa Claus living at the North Pole."

We had all laughed silently over that, nodded our heads. Wasn't it silly to have faith in such an absurd and somber religion? He likewise debunked Buddhism, Islam, Confucianism, Hinduism, Judaism, and any other religion you could name.

Having said all that, the Preacher then told us why only his way made sense, why only self-imposed extinction would solve the ultimate problem of the human condition: In a life where death was inevitable, what was the difference if we all went at once, now, instead of waiting to go one by one, as we had done throughout the ages and were destined to do for countless more, until the sun went nova or burned out or some other cosmic cataclysm liquidated all memory of the human species? Why not meet that fate together, all at once, unified, and offer up ourselves to the ultimate truth—right now?

In the face of these arguments, and the way The Holy One extolled them, not a church, not even the Pope or the Ayatollah or the Dalai Lama or the Reverend Billy Graham could come up with a compelling counter-argument, except some general admonition against suicide: "Don't give in to this ugly, vile despair." They beseeched. They pleaded. But nobody listened.

We were not committing suicide, the High One had responded. We were simply going to have a direct, face-to-face conclave with God, The God, on *our* terms, not his. Wow! Now that was profound, powerful stuff, and the Preacher's response, so confident and strong, had made it feel righteous and honorable.

Calling God's bluff.

The little pill was in the palm of my hand. I observed it for a long moment. Rock candy, I thought. It resembled rock candy. It had the crystalline shape, rough texture, and milky color of something I had eaten as a kid.

It had been passed out like candy at various distribution points just about everywhere on the planet the last several weeks. I had picked up mine in a McDonald's parking lot near my apartment only a couple days ago.

"One to a customer, if you please," the truth trooper had said as he reached into a small black pouch attached to his belt and handed me the pill.

And now the time had come to take it.

The Preacher lifted his arms and looked up into heaven. Suddenly, without further ado, He gave the order. "It is time!"

He bellowed. "Let us go meet God."

Wide-eyed, dumbstruck, we all watched as he actually took the pill. A hand went to his mouth and after an instant, he collapsed upon the stage. Then everyone else on stage around him, his closest disciples—Jessup, Rupert, Falinger, Kafelli, Noreham, Lancaster, D'Angelo—names and personalities who had become so familiar to us all, together with his inner circle of movie and rock stars—had fallen.

A collective gasp emitted from the crowd. This thing had irrevocably been put into motion. He had done it, and now we were expected to follow, to effectuate His plan, to deny our instinct for self-preservation. A moment later, I noticed that some people around us had calmly swallowed their pills and were falling into their lovers' arms or in lumps onto the ground. Pamela was squeezing my hand so tight it hurt. She was a whore, not a zealot. She hardly understand what was happening and why. I tried to wiggle out of her grip but she wouldn't let go.

"It's happening," she whispered to herself. "It's really happening." Suddenly, she didn't seem like just a ditsy whore.

People were shouting, yelping, exhorting each other to go through with it. Babies were crying. Mothers were moaning. Take it! Someone exhorted. Do it! Go for it! Call God's bluff!

My eyes were fixed on some guy maybe ten yards away standing like me with his hand tightly holding the hand of his woman. He had the pill pinched between the thumb and index finger of his other hand. He was staring at it, trying to reach that momentous decision to fling it into his mouth and die. Then, all at once, he did it. He just did it. In one swift fling. And in the next moment, his body twisted around and he fell to the ground. His wife or girlfriend screamed. Trembling, in the next instant, she too popped the pill and fell in a heap across his body.

Many couples and families around us were, like us, holding back, feeling the exuberance for this thing fading away like a dream. We all stood in stunned silence, unable to move. Around us, a lot of people had already dropped dead.

I wondered what Carol and the kids were doing right then, whether they had already taken their pills and lay sprawled across the living room floor, dead, in front of the big-screen television I had bought just weeks before I had abandoned them.

Suddenly, truth squads were upon us, dozens of brazen, arrogant bastards in brown camouflage, pointing rifles and ordering us to take our pills, shouting at us that we were cowards, that the Reverend and God were waiting for us.

Mike turned to me. "Let's just do it, man," he urged. "See what happens." Then, he smiled, just smiled, before ever so gently placing the pill on his tongue. I reached for him. Too late. A instant passed and Mike fell into his hooker's arms. She shuddered and screamed and passed him over to me.

"Mikey!" I shouted. "Mikey!"

The years of our friendship, all those memories, all those laughs, gone.

I lowered him onto the blanket and pried open his mouth with a finger, trying to get the pill out. But it was too late. He was dead. Dead. I wondered what he was seeing. God?

His hooker was clearly losing it. She was mumbling something. Pamela was desperately trying to console her, but she too was having difficulty holding on. Some other people around us were taking the pill, killing themselves. It seemed for the moment the only thing left to do.

My attention was distracted momentarily by a thirty-something guy with a goatee sitting on the blanket next to ours. A woman, maybe his wife, was dead in a lump next to him. Another guy was lying motionless, dead, next to her.

"What's in it?" asked the guy with the goatee. It took me a moment to realize he was asking me.

"Huh?" In the background, I could hear Kayla's senseless muttering.

"In the pill," he asked. "What's it made of?"

"Cyanide," I told him. "Kill ya instantly."

The guy nodded, looked away from me, then put the pill in his mouth. In the next moment, he slumped to the ground. I knew he was dead.

"Shit," I whispered to myself. It felt as if I had killed him.

At that moment I realized that I couldn't go through with it. I didn't want to die. I no longer wanted any part of the Holy Man's crusade. The heretic DJs exhortations were blaring in my brain.

In the distance, back toward the cars, I noticed a commotion. People running. Then there was the pop and spit of gunfire. Truth squads were shooting nonbelievers, the people who had given up the faith and were running away. Men, women, and children. In the midst of the running, I heard screams. Then I saw a whole wave of people fall. Murdered.

I turned to the women. They wore shocked, scared expressions, incapable of defending themselves. Kayla surprised me by moving a trembling hand to her lips. She tasted the pill by licking it. That was enough. She was dead in an instant, and collapsed at our feet. Why the impulse struck her to do it, I'll never know. Perhaps she couldn't have explained it either.

For her part, Pamela looked at the pill in the palm of her hand. Suddenly, she threw it onto the grass. "Fuck it," I heard her say.

Then a bullet ripped a hole in her forehead. I jumped and turned. From about twenty yards, I saw a truth soldier's M-16. He had wasted her for throwing the pill away. He started randomly picking off other people who hadn't yet taken their pills and were standing around mulling over what to do. I counted four, five people shot and killed—splat, just like that. Seeing him whirl around looking for more, I dropped to the ground and rested my head on Mike's left thigh.

More soldiers came over and helped pick off people standing around in shock, unable to move or act. Then they started poking through the bodies with the barrels of their M-16s, making sure, I guess, that there were no fakers like me. I started to panic. They were no more than twenty yards away. After an excruciating minute or so, I got lucky. I heard one of the soldiers shout, "There's more of them! Down there!" The entire small platoon headed that way with their rifles pop-popping, picking off the scattering, panic-stricken men, women, even babies in their mothers' arms.

For an indeterminable time, I stayed right where I was, lying on my dead friend and beside the poor hookers, desperately trying to look dead. After awhile, there was only the buzz of flies. Even the soldiers appeared to have abandoned the place. Maybe they had killed themselves, shot themselves in a kind of feverish rapture as they joined their Master in Heaven.

How had we been so stupid? How had we been duped? I started crying thinking of the billions—*billions!*—of children that had died for this, never to have lived.

But maybe I was wrong. Maybe the Teacher and my dead friends, and the thousands who had died in these fields, and the billions (billions!) around the world who had likewise followed the Teacher's example and killed themselves, maybe they were with God at this very moment, shaking their heads at my folly for not joining them. But I still had the Pill. It was in my hand. I stared at it for a long time while the late afternoon sun boiled down upon me.

Finally, with a shudder, I flicked it into the grass and rubbed my hands across my jeans.

For a long time, I laid there. All around me, it was strangely and inexplicably silent. Had everyone died except me? Somehow, after the long bright day had faded to dusk, then black, chilly darkness, with the blazing diamonds of stars blaring above me, I actually managed to fall asleep. Only once did I stir at the sound of gunfire popping from a distance.

* * *

I woke up just as the first light of day was rolling over some low hills to the east. Everything was bathed in gray and mist and stillness. There was a distinct, uncomfortable chill in the air, and in low places, fog hugged the ground.

It took a few moments for my head to clear, for the awful events of yesterday to focus into reality. Next to me were the already-bloated bodies of Michael, Pam, and Kayla. As I cautiously lifted my head, I saw a whole mass of death, thousands upon thousands of silent bodies. And the gentle buzzing of flies, like a demented voice in the wind.

I wondered suddenly how many had survived. The one thing I was sure of, God wasn't around. But what that meant, I didn't know. One school of thought was that God wouldn't intervene unless every last man, woman and child was dead. Nothing short of the extinction of the whole human race would mean anything to the universal God.

The theory—or Truth, I should say, espoused by the Holy Man himself—was that as long as a great majority of humans killed themselves, God would be forced into Revelation. Some scientists predicted that if too many of us died, the survivors would be as good as dead and follow not long after.

When there seemed to be no one around, not another living soul or a truth soldier lurking in the shadows for a faker like me, I started crawling along the wet grass, heading for a thicket of brush and trees.

Hoping for the safety in numbers.

C one Zero, Sphere Zero" first appeared in 2008 in the anthology Cone Zero published by Nemonymous. This story is, for me, a puckish, yet serious, experience in the blindness harshly imposed by a form of religion disguised as physics. In an incredibly believable way, the protagonists — with sudden brave independence — scale beyond restrictive human gang-packing emotions via mathematical formations of environment towards heights (or depths?) that show there is a hierarchy of beliefs. It is a "Science Fiction" of the spirit to provide the brave freedom to ignite the parthenogenesis of truth from "Story."

— D.F. Lewis, Editor, Cone Zero

Cone Zero, Sphere Zero

David M. Fitzpatrick

The sinister Enforcers, bedecked in the bright-red body-suits and head cones all citizens feared, came to Jellin's living cone shortly after the Light once again illuminated the World. An Avatar came with them, hovering nearby, observing everything as one of the eyes of the Immortals. Jellin hated those soft-looking balls of pink-orange flesh as much as he hated the Enforcers. It was because of what had happened with an Avatar near the end of the last Light that the Enforcers had come, Jellin knew.

"You are Jellin, son of Lumbis, son of Riksen?" the lead Enforcer said, more an imperative than a question. They knew who he was.

"I am," Jellin said, feeling his mouth parch. Agonizing memories of the pain cages he'd endured in his youth flooded through his mind, and he tried not to tremble.

"You are to appear before the Oligarchy."

It sounded like a statement, but Jellin knew it was a command of absolute authority. He knew he was in serious trouble; there would be no warning for what he'd done to that Avatar. In fact, Jellin couldn't recall anyone ever having the courage — or stupidity — to kill one of them before.

"May I get my coat and my head cone?" he asked. He knew they couldn't refuse him, since being in public without one's head cone was a serious violation — for him, and for the Enforcers who denied him getting it.

"Quickly."

He retreated into his living cone. The Light streamed through the triangular windows as he went to his dressing room and pulled his white coat on over his white bodysuit and found his matching white head cone. He fitted it into place over his bare head, and he realized he was trembling.

He turned to head back to the door and gave a start, stifling a yelp of surprise. The Avatar that had come with the Enforcers was there, hovering half a man's height away, studying him. They were always unsettling to behold: slightly squished ovoids with textured surfaces, barely glowing a light pink-orange hue, as if illuminated from within. Each had a subtle indentation that was slightly darker in color, more a light red shade, which was what people called the eye. An Avatar's eye always faced whatever it studied.

He regarded it in silence, and his thoughts went astray as usual: How did the Avatars fly as they did? Was there intelligence inside their roundish forms? Or were the supposed Immortals watching through them, as everyone was foolishly told to believe?

He banished the thoughts. He had to keep his mind clear. He didn't believe the supposed Immortals or their Avatars could read his thoughts, but it was best not to take chances. He stalked past the intrusive Avatar and felt it move in behind him as he left his living cone. Outside, he followed the lead Enforcer down his walkway, and heard the other two marching in step behind him. He was suddenly very scared.

They walked the trodden dirt paths that weaved in graceful

curves in and about the living cones of the community. Nearly naked children playing in their white loincloths stopped to stare from beneath their white head cones in gape-mouthed awe as they passed, and soon adults were peering out doorways at the spectacle. Avatars dotted the air here and there, some intently watching the children's games, others following adults around. They did that often, randomly appearing to study citizens for as little as ten breaths to as long as several complete Lights.

As they marched, Jellin could see the Light in the middle of the World, mounted atop the massive metal pole that shot skyward from the Master Cone towards which they headed. He couldn't see the Master Cone yet, as it was only about thirty men high; but the pole that spiked skyward from its peak was easily a thousand men tall. The Light, burning fiercely atop the pole, was a massive orb that illuminated the World.

Jellin glanced up as he marched stolidly behind the Enforcer, and beheld the ceiling of the World. The Cone they lived inside was massive, its apex so high above that it could not be seen. He knew from the scholars that it was as high as the World was wide—about ten thousand men high. In every direction, Jellin could see the smooth wall of the Cone, angling down from the zenith far above.

He lived a thousand men away from the center of the World, so it wasn't too long before the living cones became crowded together in the high-population area. Soon, he could see the Master Cone towering above the smaller living cones. The living cones grew larger and grander the closer one got to the center of the World, housing citizens of higher social levels. Eventually, the largest of them housed the Oligarchs themselves.

Eventually, they made it to the Master Cone in the center of the World. The massive metal pole shot out of the top of Master Cone, but Jellin couldn't look up at it without being blinded by the burning Light high above. They led him up the hundred-step stairway and through the towering, triangular door, then through the gargantuan cone and into its expansive central hall. He'd only been in once, as a child, when a Scholar had taken Jellin's class there, and it was as cold and empty as he remembered. It was ten men across; on the very far side of the hall was the protruding curve of the thick metal pole that ultimately held up the Light. In leveled rows of seats before the pole, he realized the Oligarchy was gathered.

They were all seated, wearing flowing blue robes and blue head cones. Twenty-two Oligarchs were on the lowest level, then eleven, five, and three; above them sat the Oligarch of the Fifth Level, the Master Oligarch, presiding over them all. It was a hierarchy of power, but even those on the lowest level were as far above Jellin socially as the Light was above the World. He went very suddenly from scared to terrified.

"Jellin, son of Lumbis, son of Riksen," the amplified voice of the Master Oligarch boomed. Jellin could see him speaking into a tube, which was linked to many cone-shaped outlet horns which somehow made it all louder.

Jellin felt his heart pounding madly in his chest as he dropped to one knee and bowed his head. "Yes, Master," he called out as strongly as he could manage.

"Do you know why you're here?" the Master bellowed.

"Yes, Master," Jellin said to the floor.

"Indeed," the Master said. "Look at us, and tell us why."

Jellin raised his head, beholding the forty-two grim faces that regarded him as the criminal they believed him to be. "It was an accident, Master. The Avatar was behind me, and I didn't know. I spun about so quickly —"

"Silence!" the Master roared. "We're not interested in your tales of fright regarding an Avatar. We've all been startled by the eyes of the Immortals before. Enough of your whinings, and tell us if you know why you're *really* here."

Jellin was stunned. He was certain the Enforcers had come

for him because of what he'd done to the Avatar, but apparently that wasn't the case. Destroying an Avatar was certainly punishable with a pain cage until death, but...

"I am commanding you to tell us why you're here, citizen," the Master said, his dark voice cleaving through Jellin's muddled brain.

"I'm... sorry, Master," Jellin managed. "I do not know."

"I see," said the Master. "Oligarch, read the charge."

An Oligarch of the First Level stood and unraveled a scroll, leaning in to speak into his own tube. "The citizen is charged with violating the Code of Life in questioning the nature of the World."

Jellin's mind tumbled. What was this all about? He knew better than to talk about his secret beliefs to anyone. He hadn't said a word to a single soul.

"During last Light, did you not tell one Bendik of your belief that there is a larger World outside the Cone?" the Oligarch on the First Level asked.

Jellin blinked in surprise. Was that was this was about? Did Bendik run his mouth again, as he had when they'd been children, and tell someone something he shouldn't? But Jellin had been careful for thousands of Lights to not say anything in Bendik's presence that could remotely be construed as—

"Answer the question!" the Oligarch of the First Level hollered, and Jellin shook himself out of his reverie. "Did you tell Bendik there is a larger World outside the Cone?"

"I did not, sir," Jellin said, choosing his words carefully. "I merely was considering the Cone's zenith, far above us. I wondered aloud if it is constructed like the Cone's wall, down at the base."

"But there is nothing to consider about the zenith," the Master boomed from above. "The zenith is like the wall—like the entire Cone. There is nothing but the Cone. This is the World."

Why?! Jellin screamed inside. *Why do you think that? Why can there be nothing else?*

But he retained control, and nodded dutifully. "I understand, Master. It was just a random musing; I was merely curious about how the Immortals wrought this marvelous Cone."

It was the kind of answer scholars burned into the heads of children and everyone expected to hear, but he wondered if it would be enough. Yet the ensuing silence stretched on for far too long, surpassing discomfort and becoming almost painful. In fact, Jellin realized that, after a fashion, the rest of the Oligarchs seemed to be faltering a bit, their hard gazes softening, their eyes darting to and fro—as if they, too, were wondering why the Master hadn't responded for so long. Jellin was feeling quite helpless when the Master suddenly said, "Oligarchy, this meeting is convened. Enforcers, leave the accused here."

They looked surprised, but the Oligarchs rose without argument and left their levels, filing out in their blue robes. They all fired dark glares at Jellin as they passed; he watched, confused, as they went, followed by the three red-clad Enforcers. The last Oligarchs to leave were the three of the Fourth Level, and one of them stopped next to him, awaiting the Master Oligarch to arrive.

"As ordered, you may leave," the Master said to the Fourth.

"This is highly irregular, Master," the Oligarch said, regarding his superior with slitted eyes.

"But within the confines of the Code," the Master said. "I'll not order you again, Jaupal. Leave us."

Jaupal nodded, glared viciously at Jellin, and then turned on his heel and left. The Master waited until Jaupal was gone before turning to face his prisoner. Jellin had rarely been this close to an Oligarch before, and certainly never this close to the Master. Now, but half a man apart, the man towered a head taller than Jellin and, in his billowing robes, seemed so much huger. His face was old and worn, angular as if sculpted from stone, and his eyes were a brighter blue than his robes.

He regarded Jellin sternly.

"You're afraid of me," the Master said.

"Yes, sir," Jellin said, hearing his voice quaver.

"You have nothing to fear," the Master replied, and his voice was lower and softer. "I have read your history, Jellin. When you were young, you flirted with sacrilege quite often."

"All children stray," Jellin recited automatically. "When I was punished, I learned the errors of my ways."

The Master actually chuckled then, a light smile etching itself into his chiseled face. "I don't think so. Children tend to transgress three or four times, because the punishment for questioning the nature of the World is quite severe—as you well know. You spent far more time in pain cages than most children. Twelve times, was it?"

Memories raced through Jellin's mind like a thousand sharp rocks. He remembered his incarcerations in the pain cages: strapped tightly within the form-fitting bars, arms and legs spread wide, naked and enduring the pain of an Enforcer who repeatedly stabbed him with needles. Emotion over-whelmed him, and he closed his eyes to fight the threatening tears. He nodded in silent answer.

"Twelve times," the Master repeated, moving slowly to walk around Jellin. He moved out of sight, footfalls muffled beneath the robes as he orbited his captive. "The first time is brief—a few needles, in for just ten breaths. Every subsequent time in the pain cage means more needles and many more breaths."

Jellin could feel the phantom memories of the long nee-dles, like elongated cones, sliding through his skin and rip-ping their way through fat and muscle as they spiked deep inside him. They were fatter towards the ends, and they hurt even more as they went deeper. And they had tiny, sharp nubs on them, and the Enforcer would twist them as they slid them in...

"And you went twelve times," the Master said, shaking his

head as if in awe as he finished his circular pacing and stopped to once again face Jellin. "No child ever had, as far back as anyone can remember, or heard told in stories. By that twelfth time, the Enforcers were inserting thirty-six needles, and letting you scream for one hundred twenty breaths. And those needles burn, don't they?"

They did, like fire, after his sixth trip to the pain cage. And they got hotter every time after that. Jellin tried not to remember, but the Master was making him.

"You never transgressed again after that twelfth trip, but somehow I suspect you merely learned to keep your mouth shut. You had ideas that there was more to the World than what we see here in the Cone, and ideas like that which remain through twelve pain cages don't ever go away. Do they?"

Jellin didn't answer. He didn't dare to.

"Tell me what the World is," the Master said.

"The World is the Cone, ten thousand men high and ten thousand men across," Jellin recited. It was rote, as given him by the scholars. "The Cone is the center of everything. Outside the Cone is Oblivion, and the Immortals who created us and provide for us." He felt like an idiot for even acting like he believed it, even if it was exactly what the Master expected.

"How do the Immortals provide for us?"

"The Immortals provide food and water, wood and stone, cloth and tools, and cause our waste to be removed," Jellin said. "We cannot see them, but we see their miracles every day. They are ever-vigilant, constantly watching us through their Avatars."

The Master stepped suddenly closer, leaning in until his nose almost touched Jellin's. "Do you really believe all that dung, young man?"

Jellin froze. He didn't believe in *any* of that dung, not one stinking lump of it, but he never told anyone — not since he'd learned to shut his mouth after his twelfth pain cage. But it sounded like the Master didn't believe in any of that dung, either. He snapped his head leftward, at the Avatar which floated just out of reach, its reddish eye silently watching them. How could the Master dare to say such things in the presence of an Avatar?

But certainly, the Master was only trying to trick him into admitting his blasphemous beliefs. And as an adult, he knew time in pain cages wasn't measured in breaths, but in Lights. They'd insert countless needles that twisted in burning agony, and leave them there until the violator finally stopped screaming and crying and begging. Most died; those that didn't usually went mad, and were later given over to the Immortals during the sacrifice that was held every thousand Lights. The few survivors were never quite the same—but never violated the Code of Life again.

"I asked you a question!" the Master barked, but his face wasn't as foreboding as it had been. "Do you really believe in all that dung?"

And in that moment, sheer illogic and senselessness overtook Jellin, and he realized he just didn't care if they locked him in a body-contoured pain cage for a hundred Lights and drove him insane. He'd spent his life faking stupidity in order to escape torture, and now he realized being insane or dead would be a much better existence. So he took in a shaky breath and said, "No, Master. I don't believe a word of it."

"Is that so?" the Master said, his brow furrowing, his blue eyes darkening. "Then what is the true nature of the World ?"

He was in too deep now to stop. "There are things outside the Cone, and they aren't Immortals," he said, almost fiercely. "This isn't a World—it's a prison. And we're made to believe this ridiculous garbage to keep us all in line."

"I see," the Master said, stroking his chin thoughtfully. "And what do you think we should do to heretics like you?"

"Nothing," Jellin said. "All citizens should be free to think and feel how they wish, and free to speak their minds."

The Avatar floated silently nearby, watching. Jellin glared

at its eye, as if challenging it. The pain cage awaited him; what more could they do?

"Tell me about this accident you began speaking of earlier," the Master said. "You turned around, and were surprised by an Avatar. What were you going to say?"

He'd already sealed his fate; there was no point in mincing words now. "I was going to say I accidentally hit it with a rock," he said, stoic and square-shouldered. "I was going to say I turned to throw it, and the Avatar was there. But it was no accident." Energy surged through his body like the Light illuminating the World, and Jellin liked the feeling.

"Ah, killed one, did you?" the Master said, almost bemusedly. "Hit it right in its eye, and it floated straight up into the sky, didn't it?"

It had, popping skyward like a rock sinking in water, only in reverse. He'd stood there, mystified, as it tumbled up until it became a speck, and finally vanished. "Yes, Master," he finally said. Why was the man so calm about this? Why was he not calling for Enforcers?

The Master stepped in closer until Jellin could feel the man's hot breath on his face. "That took a lot of courage," the Master said. "That, or you're truly that sure of your convictions. But no worry; I happen to know the Immortals don't punish us for destroying Avatars. Come to think of it, has anyone ever seen the Immortals strike anyone down for anything? Of course not. Only *we* strike our fellow citizens down."

Jellin blinked in surprise. It wasn't the response he'd even remotely expected, and he had no idea what to say.

The Master stepped back, surveying Jellin, and then he smiled. "Do you know where my country home is, son?"

"It's... near the Cone's wall," Jellin said, confusion spinning around in his mind like a tangled ball of string. "I'm not sure where."

"It is located precisely on Trajectory 572," the Master said. "I am hereby commanding you to meet me there, alone, at the end of this Light. I also command you to tell no one of this conversation. Your very life depends on it. Do you understand?"

Jellin felt himself nodding dumbly, and let himself bask in the confusion as the Master called to the Enforcers to allow Jellin to leave. The Avatar followed.

The Master Oligarch watched Jellin vanish through the hall's door. He breathed deeply, the fires of excitement scorching through his body. This could be it, he knew. But first he'd have to deal with Jaupal. He knew he had only to wait a short time, and presently Jaupal entered the hall and moved toward him, blue robes flowing. He stopped challengingly close to the Master Oligarch.

"A strange occurrence here today, Zindel," Jaupal said.

"Nothing strange at all," Zindel said. "But mind your place, Jaupal. In these chambers, you'll not refer to me by my name."

"Ah, excuse me, *Master Oligarch,*" Jaupal said with a mock bow of the head. "Silly of me to forget my place — but surely you can understand, given your aberrant behavior today."

Jaupal always was a daring sort, and it annoyed Zindel. He stepped closer to his underling, face to face and eye to eye with the man. "Careful, Jaupal. The codices of the Divine Compendium make the penalty for questioning the Master Oligarch quite clear."

"They do indeed," Jaupal said evenly. "Just as they make clear the penalties for all forms of blasphemy — no matter who is guilty of it, regardless of his station."

They traded dark stares for several long moments, and then Zindel smiled. "That's what I've always liked about you, Jaupal — you're never afraid to take a stand for what you believe is right. Now, I am leaving shortly for a few Lights of rest. I'll see you back here for the next session."

Without another word, he stepped around the Oligarch of the Fourth Level and strode out of the hall. He could feel the other's eyes boring into his back as he went, but even Jaupal couldn't sway him from his mood.

Because he'd finally found the one he'd waited for all his life.

The World had one thousand trajectories spiking out from the Master Cone. The thousand numbers encircled the Master Cone's base, with marks to help citizens orient themselves. Jellin found Trajectory 572 and set off when the Light had faded to about half-brightness. It would be dark soon, and it was already dim enough that he could barely see the distant, sloping wall. By the time he was almost to the edge of the World, he could barely see anything but the illuminations inside the living cones—which grew sparser as he went, until they were but rare beacons in the dark. All the while, the lone Avatar flew along beside and behind him, like some physical manifestation of a programmed conscience that he had no interest in heeding.

The Master's country home was exactly in line with Trajectory 572, and the structure sat barely twenty men from the Cone's wall. He trudged through the grass to the living cone's door and raised his hand to knock.

And then he hesitated. This was insane. What was he doing here, after Light, at the Master Oligarch's country home? Had he lost his mind?

He was trying to decide whether to turn around and flee when the door opened. The Master smiled out at him, and it was very strange. One wasn't required to wear a head cone at home, but it was still bizarre to see the Master Oligarch without one. He was as bald as all citizens, and he wore a white bodysuit.

"You're... you're wearing white, Master Oligarch," Jellin stammered.

"Yes, the color of the lowest class of citizen," the Master said with a chuckle. "I tire of the blue robes, really. Now, do come in, and don't call me Master Oligarch. My name is Zindel; please use it." He gestured over Jellin's left shoulder. "I see you brought your friend with you."

Jellin looked back at the Avatar hovering there, studying him. He nodded. "This one came with the Enforcers, and hasn't left me."

"No matter; bring it in with you."

Dazed, Jellin followed Zindel in. The place was larger than Jellin's living cone, but not terribly extravagant. Zindel offered him a seat on one of the three sofas arranged around a triangular table in the sitting area, and then brought him a bottle of purple water. Jellin was immediately impressed; only Oligarchs got purple water. He'd never tasted anything like the sweet liquid before.

Zindel sat on another sofa, drinking his own bottle of purple water. On the triangular table were food cones of colors Jellin had never tasted, and Zindel offered them freely. Jellin ate hungrily, popping cone after cone in his mouth, savoring the alien flavors and enjoying every moment of it. Zindel regarded him in silence as he ate and drank for a short while, as if Zindel understood what a unique pleasure it was for him.

"I dream of something more than the sustenance provided us," Zindel finally said. "I dream of a world beyond this Cone. Like you, I believe there is more. We agree there are no Immortals, but everything we need appears to us every one hundred Lights, without fail. Citizens have seen it come into existence, right out of nowhere—a flash of light, and there is all we need. If not Immortals, then who?"

"I don't know," Jellin said. "But I believe there is some reasonable explanation that doesn't require Immortals."

"Excellent answer. I, for one, reject the very idea that any one being is superior to any other. Our society is entirely based on such a hierarchy; I don't like it, but I've lived it because my forefathers have been Oligarchs for tens of generations. But my grandfather had his doubts, and he secretly told them to my father and me when I was very young. But my father violated his trust, and immediately reported my grandfather's blasphemy to the Oligarchy." His face grew dark and sad. "He sent his own father to his death in a pain cage, and took his place as Master Oligarch. I was just a boy, but the logic of my grandfather's words — and the terrible, mindless behavior of my father — has stayed with me ever since.

"It's simple logic, really — which is something that is sorely missing in the Divine Compendium. When children ask why the World is shaped like a cone, we open to the Codex of Creation and explain that the Immortals made it that way to emulate their own Grand Cone. When they ask what's outside the Cone, we open to the Codex of the Immortals and explain the vast nothingness called Oblivion. When they question something in the Divine Compendium, we open to the Codex of Commandments, which instructs us to never question anything, and to the Codex of Punishments to show them what awaits them if they do. And just for good measure, we always throw in a bit from the Codex of Destruction, telling them the fate that awaits us all should the Immortals be sufficiently angered. You know the story."

"Yes — the Immortals will destroy the shell of the Cone, and expose us to Oblivion," Jellin said. "I know it well. The twelfth time I was sent to the pain cage was because I pointed out a contradiction that I was sure even the Scholars would have to see, but of course that didn't happen."

"You're talking about the contradiction with the Codex of Creation, I presume."

"You know it?"

"Quite well. Creation states that the Immortals set the open-bottomed Cone down, embedding it a great rock floating in Oblivion. But Destruction clearly says the shell has a closed bottom, and the Immortals filled it with stone and dirt."

Jellin brightened excitedly. "Yes! It's so dreadful a contradiction — yet the Divine Compendium was allegedly written by perfect, inerrant Immortals."

"Exactly. That's to say nothing of the Codex of Prophecies, where no two Immortals have the same view of the future, and often the same Immortal tells us two different things."

Excitement welled within Jellin. "Then change will come to the Cone at last! You're the Master Oligarch—all you have to do is decree changes, and they'll happen. Our people's eyes will finally be opened!"

"Now wait a breath," Zindel said, holding up a wrinkled hand. "If I start talking about these things, they'll have me in a pain cage as fast as any other citizen. I'm already under suspicion for earlier today, when I dismissed the Oligarchy to speak with you alone."

"You mean... you put yourself at risk?" Jellin said.

"Quite. But for a good reason, son—you! I've never heard of a child who endured twelve pain cages. A few go five, maybe even six... but twelve! I've followed you quite closely, Jellin, and I knew there was more to you than a stupid child. You're the first person I've ever been able to discuss this with, and that's very refreshing. But more importantly, you've shown you're not afraid to think differently, no matter the consequences. You have the rare gift of rational thought—which will help lead our people to the truth of what is outside the Cone. But the first step to that is for us to leave the Cone."

Jellin's mouth sagged open. "But how can we possibly do that?"

Zindel gestured beyond him. "With help from our ever-vigilant friends."

Jellin turned to the forgotten Avatar which floated silently at the edge of his vision. "The Avatars? How can they help?"

Without a word, Zindel rose, bottle of purple water in his hand, and stepped toward the Avatar. The pink-orange thing pivoted in the air, skittering back and surveying him, but never saw it coming. Zindel suddenly cocked his arm back and threw the bottle at the Avatar. He was only half a man away, and the Avatar had no time to react. The bottle smashed squarely in its eye and there was flash of bright light. The Avatar tumbled through the air and into the wall as the glass shattered on the floor. Black smoke puffed out where its eye had been, and it rocked forward until the burned-out eye faced the floor. Then it shot straight up and into the ceiling, bouncing a few times until it came to a stop, unmoving.

"That's what happened when I threw the rock at it!" Jellin cried, coming to his feet.

Zindel chuckled. "I discovered that five thousand Lights ago. That particular Light, I was in an exceptionally bad mood when one wandered into this very country home, when I was trying to enjoy solitude. I reacted without thinking, striking it with my fist. I was astonished when it flew up to the ceiling, but once I thought about it, I realized what it meant. Since then, I've worked diligently to bring my invention to life."

"What invention?" Jellin asked.

"Come with me."

Zindel led him to the rear of the spacious living cone, then up the stairs to the apex level. Jellin expected it to be just like any living cone's apex level—a open-spaced second floor, the ceiling of which was cone's pinnacle. But when Zindel opened the door at the top of the stairs and gestured proudly within, Jellin looked in and stared, mouth agape.

The ceiling was packed with hundreds of floating Avatars. They were all clearly dead, with only the ceiling keeping them from shooting ten thousand men high into the sky.

"How did you kill them all?" Jellin said, astounded. "How have you not gotten caught?"

"After the first one, I was admittedly afraid of the supposed Immortals," Zindel said. "But no retribution came, and I realized the Avatars were merely creatures of some sort, not the vehicles of divine eyesight. So whenever one came to me, I'd wait until I was indoors and alone, and I'd kill and capture them. After I had ten or so, I began experimenting. Ten

Avatars contained in a net will hoist a large jug of water without a problem."

Jellin's mind opened with understanding like the Light in the morning. "You're saying we use them to hoist a man into the sky — to see what is at the zenith?"

"Yes!" Zindel said, excited, his eyes sparkling. "I believe the way out of the Cone must be at the zenith, and we must go there. I weigh just the same as thirteen jugs of water, so one hundred thirty Avatars can lift me. I have four hundred Avatars in here — *four hundred,* Jellin — enough to lift three times my weight!" He turned to Jellin and placed his hands paternally on the younger's shoulders. "I've constructed a lightweight basket in the back yard, and I've made a net from strips of cloth. The net will hold all four hundred Avatars. They will lift us into the sky, Jellin, and take us to the Cone's zenith, where we will discover the secrets beyond this World!"

The sky basket, as Zindel called it, was a man-and-a-half long and nearly a man wide. In its center was a hole wide enough to climb up through. They spent the next morning tying the sky basket to the ground with several ropes, so it wouldn't float away without them, and securing the cobbled-together netting. The netting was made of strips of cloth, tightly spun and knotted with others, its small openings not nearly large enough for an Avatar to slip through. After a brief lunch of orange water and an assortment of food cones, they made many trips in and out of the house, using a smaller net to move the Avatars outside and stuff them into the big netting.

By the time all four hundred Avatars were jammed inside, the netting had expanded quite admirably. The basket was off the ground, pulling taut the ropes that anchored it. Jellin was amazed: Zindel had done it. This was actually going to work. They were actually going to the zenith of the World.

The netting was ring-shaped, surrounding the sky basket's outer walls and piling high above. But the inner ring was open, which Zindel said would afford them access to the zenith when they got there. To clear the tops of the Avatars, Zindel had built a ladder that laid neatly on the basket's floor.

The last thing they did was secure what Zindel called the "main line" — a rope that was tied to a metal anchor point just inside the central hole in the middle of the sky basket. It snaked down to a metal loop in the ground, then shot across the lawn to a bigger loop that was embedded in the wall of Zindel's living cone. It then doubled back to the first metal loop and back up through the middle of the sky basket, where it was again tied.

"When we're ready to leave, we cut all the ropes — except this one," Zindel said. "It's ultimately attached to the living cone, which I assume will be well more than enough to keep the sky basket secure. Once this is the only rope anchoring the sky basket, we'll know for certain that my guess is correct: that our flight will indeed be level. When we're absolutely certain, then we'll untie the main line."

And then it was done and ready, even as the Light began to dim and darkness began to creep through the World. They stood together in the dimness, sipping cold red water and regarding their achievement, and Jellin didn't feel any bit of the vast social separation that had always been a given between a lowly citizen and a member of the Oligarchy.

The mesh-formed torus of dead Avatars floated magically in their cloth-ribbed prison, lifting the basket just six or seven hands off the ground, straining against the many ropes securing it firmly to the ground. To Jellin, the construct seemed much like him and Zindel — like it, too, was straining to leave the ground and explore the zenith of the Cone.

"Why do you need me?" Jellin said softly as the Light grew ever darker. "You did everything yourself. You could go alone."

Zindel sighed, sipped his red water, and smiled. "On the one hand, I suppose I want a comrade in this — one who believes as I do. But for more practical reasons, I need you as a witness. I intend to return and tell others what is outside the Cone." He broke off and furrowed his brow. "I suppose it's a bit late to ask this, but are you willing to return with me, risking death in a pain cage, to tell the people the truth?"

Without hesitation, Jellin said, "Yes. I'm afraid, but I'll not back down now."

The remaining faint Light snuffed itself out, and the World was cloaked in utter darkness. Zindel patted Jellin on the shoulder and said, "Let us get some sleep. At first Light, we embark on this grand adventure."

Jellin came awake suddenly. Zindel was shaking him frantically. "Wake up!" he cried. "The Oligarchs have arrived with Enforcers!"

Jellin leaped from bed, fully awake, yanking on his shoes as Zindel said, "They're almost here—the entire Oligarchy, and tens of Enforcers. Get to the sky basket while I stall them!"

"But you're coming with me!" Jellin cried as they bolted for the cone's rear door.

"Right now, they can't see the sky basket behind the cone," Zindel said as he threw open the back door. The sky basket and its netting full of dead Avatars floated above the grass, pulling the many ropes taut. "It will take you several minutes to untie the ropes while I stall them. Undo all but the main line, and I'll make a run for it. Go!"

Jellin ran across the yard, crawled under the bulge of Avatars, and squeezed up into the basket. He began deftly untying the rope anchors. One by one they fell away; with each one, the sky basket jerked roughly, angling differently, threatening to rip the remaining anchors free. Finally, only the main line remained, keeping the sky basket level. As Zindel predicted, it balanced perfectly.

Jellin stood and looked over the Avatars. He could hear muffled sounds from the front of the home, but he couldn't tell what was going on. Surely Zindel must have realized the ropes were untied by now!

He waited, terrified and uncertain, at the ready.

"On whose authority do you bring the Oligarchy to my home?" Zindel demanded of Jaupal, putting on his best show of absolute authority.

"As Oligarchs of the Fourth Level," Jaupal said, gesturing to his two peers flanking him, "we have the authority to make all decisions when the Master Oligarch is not present."

"You seek to move against me?" Zindel said, face hard and eyes dark. "You'd better be sure of your allegations, Jaupal—whatever they may be."

"You chose to speak to the citizen named Jellin alone, which was very irregular," Jaupal said. "Then you released him, unpunished and unquestioned."

"That is my prerogative as Master Oligarch," Zindel said. "Don't forget that."

"Nevertheless, your behavior has necessitated this," Jaupal said. "Citizen Jellin has been missing since the Light before last—strangely, when you decided to retreat to your home for rest. With a unanimous vote of the Oligarchy, we have come here to search your home. If we find that you are colluding with a citizen in matters of blasphemy, your punishment will be swift and severe."

"And if you're wrong," Zindel growled, "I shall replace the entire Fourth Level of the Oligarchy and send you all to the pain cages."

Jaupal seemed nervous for a moment, but then he smiled. "We shall see." He turned to the horde of Enforcers standing at the ready. "Spread out. Search the cone, and the land around."

"Belay that order, Enforcers," Zindel barked, and the red-clad men stopped in their tracks. "I am the Master Oligarch, and you shall obey me." He knew it wouldn't buy much time, but he had to be sure Jellin had the sky basket untied.

"Enforcers, you will do as ordered," Jaupal said evenly. "The Master Oligarch is under investigation. The Code prohibits him from punishing you for following our orders. But defy us, and you will all go to the pain cages."

The Enforcers began moving again, and Zindel knew there was no stopping them. He said, "Wait—there is one more thing to consider."

The Enforcers paused, looking to Jaupal for guidance. Jaupal said, "What is that?"

"You must untie the rope," Zindel said with a smile, and then he hollered it: "You must untie the rope!"

"What?" Jaupal said.

"You must untie the rope!" Zindel screamed wildly, waving his arms and wailing in Jaupal's face. *"Untie the rope! Untie the rope!"*

And for good measure, he hauled off and punched the confused Jaupal in the face.

"Untie the rope!"

There was no mistaking it. Zindel wanted him to untie the rope. But if he did, he'd fly away and leave Zindel behind.

There was sudden furor from around the living cone— noises of many men.

"Untie the rope!"

He dropped to his knees and frantically untied Zindel's complex knot as quickly as he could. *Come on, Zindel!* he cried out in his mind.

And then he heard the thundering footsteps of many men as he released the knot, and the sky basket was free. He felt it shoot straight up as the rope snaked through its loop and out the bottom of the basket. He peered over the edge as the sky basket rose, and he saw the long rope bouncing across the ground, feeding back through the far metal loop as he rose.

And then he saw Zindel, careening into the back yard, as ten Enforcers pursued. Zindel went out of his sight below, and then Jellin felt the basket jerk violently. It kept rising, albeit a bit more slowly, and when Jellin scrambled to the hole to look down, he saw Zindel dangling from the rope. He hung just at its tail end, and he was already two or three men off the ground. Below, Enforcers leaped up at him, to no avail. More Enforcers, followed by Oligarchs, rounded the living cone even as the basket sailed high above them.

"Climb!" Jellin hollered to the spinning Zindel.

Zindel was, hand over hand, and even as the Avatar-stuffed netting bumped into the sloping wall and jolted violently. Zindel swung wide, bashing into the wall as the sky basket skittered at an angle up the wall, heading for the zenith.

As soon as Zindel was close enough, Jellin reached precariously down through the hole and helped haul him in. They balanced their weight by sitting at opposite ends of the basket, and Jellin cried, "What happened?"

"I punched Jaupal in the face," Zindel said with a smile. "I can't tell you how good that felt. I broke and ran in the confusion, and just barely caught the rope before it would have been out of my reach."

He struggled to stand and looked up. The Cone's sloping wall was barely above their heads, and the sky basket continued heading up at its steep angle, the netting of Avatars sliding up the wall. The whole thing spun slightly as it bumped along.

"We're rising a bit faster than I thought," Zindel said. "We should make the zenith very quickly."

Jellin glanced out the hole, at the ground far below. "I suppose this is a bad time to ask about how we get back down."

"We remove Avatars, one at a time. Eventually, we should begin descending."

They rode skyward in silence for a long while before Zindel peered out over the Avatars, shielding his eyes, and announced, "We're rising above the Light."

Jellin stood and looked out over the mass of Avatars that was lifting them above everything. Sure enough, they were rising above where the Light glowed brilliantly atop its pole in the center of the Cone.

"We've already traveled beyond where any dreamed," Zindel said. "Soon, we'll know the truths that are hidden from us."

Every time Jellin peered down through the hole in the basket at the World far below, he was terrified. But every time he looked up at the zenith far above, he was excited. It seemed to take forever, but he guessed it was nearly time for the midday meal when he could see the curving, sloping walls narrowing and coming together.

"We're almost there," Jellin said. "I see the zenith. I can actually *see* it, Zindel!"

They closed on it, and suddenly they were there. The Avatar cushion bounced into place, rocked side to side, and then moved no more. Above them was the zenith, just half a man above their heads, and the ring of Avatars surrounded them on all sides. It was eerily dark, save for the Light shining up through the hole in the basket's floor and lighting their enclosure. It was like a new World, all their own. He glanced down through the floor hole, and far below was the brilliant sphere of the Light.

"There's a seam of some sort there," Zindel said. "Let's get the ladder set up."

Jellin could see it, just above the Avatars. It was like the very zenith of the Cone, about a man across, was set atop the whole thing.

They juggled their feet in order to get the ladder off the narrow basket floor, and managed to prop it up against the wall of the Cone, just above the Avatars. The ladder's feet fitted into steadying braces Zindel had built into the basket's floor.

"There are no dead Avatars trapped up here," Jellin observed. "Somehow, the dead ones are let out."

But Zindel was already climbing the ladder, getting up as far as he could and feeling the seam. "There's space in here," he called down. "I can just fit my fingers in. Maybe there's a — wait, I feel something."

And suddenly, there was a groaning sound, and the zenith of the Cone began to yawn open like a giant mouth. On some unseen hinge, it tipped up and away, humming as it did, and Zindel and Jellin stared up in wonder. Above, there was blackness. Jellin held his breath as the zenith tipped out of sight, and as Zindel slowly rose to poke his head out of the top of the World. Jellin heard the man suck in his breath.

"What is it?" Jellin said. "What's out there?"

"The Divine Compendium is wrong," Zindel called down. "I didn't know what to expect — but I didn't want this."

He descended the ladder and collapsed heavily into the basket, looking like a beaten man. "They'll never believe us," Zindel said, crestfallen. "They'll put us to death in pain cages no matter what. They'll just say that's what Oblivion looks like, and blame us for incurring the wrath of the Immortals. But even if we did convince them, we're still trapped in this World forever. Go ahead... see for yourself."

Jellin did, scaling the ladder carefully, his hands and legs shaking. He made it to the top, slowly poked his head out, and beheld the World outside the World.

The Cone was inside an impossibly huge sphere, a hundred thousand men across, but there were other Cones. And there were Cubes, Spheres, Pyramids, Cylinders, Domes. Geometric shapes everywhere on the inner surface of the sphere, next to the Cone and upside-down above it and everywhere else in between. The shapes were separated by the space of a hundred men; directly adjacent to the Cone was a smaller sphere, a towering rectangle, a squat cylinder, a dodecahedron, a pyramid, and another cone — that latter narrower and taller than Jellin's own.

And throughout the inside of the megasphere, millions of Avatars flew. They zipped this way and that, moving from one shape to another. Jellin watched in utter shock as tens of them, in a tightly-grouped cloud, swarmed silently to the top of the adjacent rectangular structure. A door in the top of the structure flipped open, and several dead Avatars popped out, floating toward the center of the gargantuan sphere. The new Avatars zipped into the tower, and the small door closed.

Jellin could see the wall of the Cone was barely two hands thick, and when he peered over the edge at the bottom of the sphere far below, he saw what were clearly steps formed into the side of the outer wall. His eyes searched the other shapes around him, and he spied a few other formations like it—one going down the side of a pyramid, another circling around the outside of a dome, yet another zigzagging back and forth across the face of a cube.

Jellin clambered back down the ladder and collapsed in the basket across from Zindel. The two sat in stunned silence.

"What does it mean?" Jellin finally asked.

"It means we haven't escaped our prison," Zindel said, his voice flat. "We've only realized that our Cone is but one cell in a prison more vast than we could ever imagine."

"So all those shapes are worlds, full of people like ours— unsuspecting people?"

Zindel sighed and nodded. "I think so."

"Then we have to find a way out of the sphere," Jellin said.

Zindel laughed weakly. "And what do you think is outside the sphere? Maybe a larger sphere, or a cube, or something, with more giant shapes containing other cones and spheres and pyramids."

"It can't go on forever," Jellin said. "Eventually, there must be an outside to all this."

"Maybe. Maybe not. But no matter what, we're stuck here. Returning home means death. We can't go out there, for we don't know where to go to find the sphere's exit. Even if we wanted to, we have no food and water."

There was a humming sound, and the zenith of the Cone slowly flipped back into place. They watched until they were again sealed in.

"There is one way to perhaps convince them," Zindel finally said. "Listen to me: I'm going to give my life for our cause, Jellin."

"What?" Jellin cried.

"Yes—I'll jump from here, straight down at the Light. The impact may well destroy it. Think of it—one of us destroying the work of the Immortals!" His eyes were wide, and he looked a bit crazed. "When you return there, you tell them what happened—tell them that I jumped to destroy what their Immortals have wrought!"

He came to his feet with a holler, and Jellin came to his, and Jellin was faster. He leaped across the open hole, terrified he'd fall, and collided with Zindel, bringing him back down. The offset weight caused the sky basket to pitch suddenly over, and Zindel hollered in surprise.

"You can't jump!" Jellin cried. "You can't leave me to do this alone!"

"You fool!" Zindel yelled. "It's the only way!"

"You're the fool!" Jellin yelled back. "They'll kill me no matter what happens! We have no choice but to leave the Cone. We may die out there, but better to take that chance than return to this cursed Cone where a painful death is certain!"

Zindel's wide eyes softened, and he finally remembered to breathe again. "Either way, it's death—senseless death in a senseless prison."

"The only hope of making any sense of it is to go out there," Jellin said. "Did you not see the steps? Whoever put our people in the Cone must have assumed that one day we would emerge on our own. There are steps on the other shapes—they must have always known we'd one day leave these prisons. It's our responsibility to climb down there, Zindel—maybe our responsibility to free people from other shapes, too. We need to let them know what it's like outside their worlds."

Zindel nodded slowly, a weak smile working its way across his face. "And this is why I needed you on this adventure, Jellin. Without you, I'd be falling for the Light now, and nothing would have changed—not in our World, not in anyone's World."

Jellin reached out and squeezed his hand. "Then let's explore these many Worlds. We free all those we can, and find a way out of this sphere—and out of whatever contains it, and on and on until we finally unlock the secrets kept from us."

Zindel smiled and came to his feet. "All right," he said. "We'll do it. For reference, we're leaving Cone Zero, inside Sphere Zero. I say we start with Cone One, which I believe is adjacent to us."

"I vote for Cube One," Jellin said with a grin. "A lifetime inside one cone is enough for me right now."

Zindel chuckled. "Point taken. Cube One it is."

They reopened the Cone's zenith, and abandoned their sky basket and Cone Zero. They began the long descent down the outer stairs and into the future.

About the Authors

Dan Barker became a teenage evangelist at age 15. He received a degree in Religion from Azusa Pacific University and was ordained to the ministry by the Standard Community Church, California, in 1975. He preached for a total of 19 years, while becoming heavily involved in writing and producing Christian music. But Dan outgrew his religious beliefs, publicly announcing his atheism in January 1984. He attributes his change to reading beyond Christian writings. He is the author of several books including the fascinating *Losing Faith in Faith* (1992) and *Godless* (2008), from which his story in *Atheist Tales* is excerpted. With his wife, Annie Laurie Gaylor, Dan currently serves as co-president of the Freedom from Religion Foundation. His latest book is *The Good Atheist: Living A Purpose-Filled Life Without God*.

Gary J. Beharry's work has been featured in *Sybil's Garage*, *AlienSkin Magazine*, and *Tabloid Purposes IV: Something Macabre This Way Comes*. During his existence in the realm of the Mundane, he works in the adult-education field, volunteer tutors, and rents a room owned by two cats. In his free time he travels to other worlds, or is welcomed into the known but hidden magical realm of Earth, where he documents his journeys and happenstances, hoping to share his adventures with the Mundanes.

David M. Fitzpatrick's 50 short stories have been published in magazines and anthologies in the United States, the United Kingdom, and Canada. He has co-edited two anthologies and edited five more. By day, he is a Special Sections writer for the Bangor Daily News in Bangor, Maine, and freelances as well. He lives in Brewer, across the river from Bangor. He keeps hoping Stephen King's errant Muse will accidentally land on his house on the way to King's. No luck yet.

Jane Gallagher was terrified of letting anyone know she didn't believe in the silly stories she was being fed in church and Sunday school, because she was sure she was the only one in the whole world who had such an obvious mental-health problem. She eventually came to terms with her lack of belief, embraced logic and reason, and came out of the closet. She finds amusement in the bemusement of those who can't understand how she could be so immoral and set on losing her soul to everlasting torment. She'd just rather keep writing.

James Hickey says: "I've done all sorts of writing — fiction, journalism, essays, drama, screenplays. The overall focus has remained the intersection of nature, society, and individual that shows up in this yarn, however. Whether the context has been academia or tall tales, the important issues have revolved around basic matters that many people ignore. From Texas to Massachusetts to Southern Appalachia, the same sorts of stories have always appealed to me, whether true or invented out of whole cloth. I don't pretend to know all the answers, but years of study have grounded me in basic issues, and I love asking questions."

John Lance lives in New England with his beautiful wife and daughters. His picture book *Priscilla Holmes, Ace Detective* and his middle-reader novel *Charlotte Cauldron and the Prince of Nevermore* were both published in 2009. He has also authored a collection of short stories, *Bobby's Troll and Other Stories*, and has appeared in a number of anthologies, most recently *All About Eve* in 2010.

Earl Lee is a freethinker, librarian, and writer living in Pittsburg, Kansas, and has written for *The Humanist* and *Truth Seeker*, including an article in the best-selling anthology *You Are Still Being Lied To*. His books include *Libraries in the Age of Mediocrity* and a parody of the fundamentalist *Left Behind* series called *Raptured: The Final Daze of the Late, Great Planet Earth*. He is listed in the reference book *Who's Who in Hell*.

Marianna Manns is a young Canadian author being published for the first time in this book. She grew up in Toronto and is now an English major at University of Waterloo. An avid reader of speculative fiction, she enjoys writing both fantasy and science fiction, and feels that both of these genres are useful for commenting on the effect of religion on society. Brought up in an atheist household, her father has been a great influence on her, encouraging critical and independent thought.

Her main belief is that a society can function morally without reliance on a supreme being dictating what is right and wrong, and that religious governance is oppressive and unnecessary.

Corwin Merrill is an unabashedly vocal militant atheist who believes the world may well become a pile of theocratic dystopias like the one he depicts in his story in this anthology. He believes it's the job of anyone concerned about religion continuing to regain a foothold in our personal lives to fight to ensure that doesn't happen. He loves speculative fiction—except for the Bible, which he says is a collection of weak mythology originally done better by other religions long before the Jews and Christians regurgitated them. He likens that to crappy movie studios today remaking previous masterpieces and ruining them.

Bill R. Moore published about a dozen short stories and poems before he and his wife were killed in a car accident in October 2010. Bill was a solid crusader for what he called the "noble cause of atheism." To learn more about Bill, read the dedication at the beginning of this anthology.

Vincent L. Scarsella has published his work in print magazines *The Leading Edge, Aethlon: The Journal of Sport Literature,* and *Fictitious Force.* In September 2007, "Vice Cop" was included in the anthology *New Writings in the Fantastic.* In March 2008 "Practical Time Travel" found publication in *Bound For Evil: Curious Tales of Books Gone Bad.* "Homeless Zombies" appeared in the April 2009 anthology *Dead Science.* "Killers" appeared in the June 2010 release *War of the Worlds: Frontlines,* while "The Time Traveler" appeared in the September 2010 companion anthology *Timelines.* Vince also has numerous short stories published on online zines. Coming attractions include his novella "The Dream Within," scheduled as an e-book by Blue Wood Publishing.

Dan Thompson lives in Huntsville, Alabama. He spent eleven years in the Army before leaving to work on a degree. Since then he has worked for private industry, NASA, and the Department of Defense, applying new technologies like lasers and digital electronics to such diverse areas as weapons systems development, manufacturing processes, and meteorology. He is now a civilian with the U.S. Army. The earliest thing Dan remembers reading was science fiction. Besides SF, he enjoys scale modeling, writing, reading, and movies. He also supports space exploration and likes to keep up with the latest developments in related fields of science.

Sarah Trachtenberg is a freelance writer and amateur stand-up comedian in Massachusetts. She credits her angst to being from a very neurotic Jewish family. In addition to writing about atheism, she writes social and political commentary and about consumer issues. Please find her online at Not My God at www.sarahtrachtenberg.com and on Facebook.

www.ingramcontent.com/pod-product-compliance
Lightning Source LLC
Chambersburg PA
CBHW051245260626
47162CB00002B/622